I0764508

Speed Dialing the Dead

Boyd Russell

iUniverse, Inc.
New York Bloomington

Speed Dialing the Dead

iUniverse books may be ordered through booksellers or by contacting:

iUniverse
1663 Liberty Drive
Bloomington, IN 47403
www.iuniverse.com
1-800-Authors (1-800-288-4677)

ISBN: 978-0-595-49742-3 (pbk)
ISBN: 978-0-595-49608-2 (cloth)
ISBN: 978-0-595-61230-7 (ebk)

Printed in the United States of America

Other Books By Author

"Brushes with Life - A Checkered Journey"

ACKNOWLEDGMENTS

Jacket design and illustration by Tabitha McGarvey – Moon Township, Pennsylvania. Her skill and creativity made a concept come alive.

To Donna, Lynne and Susan. Their input and patient prodding made this novel and the author better.

To the staff at iUniverse. Without their help and guidance this novel would not have been published.

DEDICATION

To Molly and Brett.

CHAPTER ONE

It had been three months since her death. Or was it two . . . ? Time had become an elusive notion, sidestepping his half-hearted attempts at capture. He didn't want to know, it would only focus his grief. She was gone . . . left to him as a daily barrage of disconnected memories - confronting him from somewhere . . . everywhere! Scenes from their lives together waiting, with stealth, to ambush him - a waft of perfume from a passing woman - a passage of music he was too slow to change - his *unintentional* opening of her lingerie drawer - her coffee cup staring back from a kitchen cabinet - and the hundreds of other intimate encounters that screamed, "I'm dead! You'll have to pick up the dry-cleaning, and you'll have to remember the kids' birthdays this year, and you'll have to fight with the plumber, and you'll have to search for your favorite sweatshirt, and you'll have to . . . ." He slammed both fists down on the bathroom counter!

She was unrelenting in her dialogue. Sometimes whispering softly to him, sometimes laughing with him, sometimes scolding him, but always with finality, "I'm never coming home again . . . ever!"

~~~~~~~~~~~~~~~~~~~~~~~~~~~~
~~~~~~~~~~~~~~~~~~~~~~~~~~~~

It sprang at them, without warning. An annual checkup - a minor complaint to her doctor - a soreness just below her shoulder blade, "and, oh yes, food hasn't tasted the same lately, but that's good, I'm into clothes I haven't worn in a year."

"Fourteen pounds you say?"

"If you really think the tests are called for."

"It's nothing to worry about, is it?"

"Good, I get concerned when you doctors start doing tests."

Ten days later . . . .

"More tests?"

"They've already taken gallons of my body fluids."

"You must have some idea what you're looking for?"

"Well, all right, what choice do I have?"

Another week . . . .

"Marci, Bill, I'm glad you could come in on such short notice."

Marci smiled through the knot in her stomach. "Sounds pretty ominous Jeff."

"I'm afraid the news isn't good."

Marci clutched for Bill's hand and inhaled sharply.

He interceded, asking the question they were afraid to have answered, "What is it Jeff?"

Bill looked to Marci and offered her a squeezed palm for support as Jeff spoke, "its cancer." His eyes drooped from the weight of the "C" word!

Marci's rebuttal rattled with fear and denial, "There must be a mistake. I feel fine - I'm not sick."

"I understand Marci, that's why I had the tests redone. I didn't believe it either."

When the word "cancer" collided with Bill's life he tuned out. He could only nod when the what's, whys and wherefores were explained. His brain floundered with the whirlpool of scenarios now facing Marci and him.

She sat, stone still, hardening further with each new detail of her condition.

Bill's consciousness reclaimed itself as Jeff began the prognosis, "The good news is, we caught it early, and with the advancements in medicine and an aggressive treatment regime there's an excellent chance for a total remission.

Jeff paused for questions. The rebounding numbed expressions were his cue to continue. With an upbeat tone he plowed on, "I want to get you in the hospital right away. The sooner we attack this the sooner we can get you well."

She asked cautiously, "When?"

"Tomorrow."

"But, I -"

"I know this is sudden, and a little overwhelming. Let me take care of all the details. In the meantime, why don't you and Bill go out for drinks and dinner at your favorite restaurant?"

"But Jeff -"

"I know, what about the kids? I've already called Donna. She'll pick them up and care for them while you're out. It's no big deal, she can feed them with ours, and when you come by to get them I'll have the hospital schedule waiting for you."

Marci tugged at Bill's coat sleeve. Signal received he started to decline, "We appreciate the offer Jeff but -"

"No buts. I've thrown a lot at you and you need some time to yourselves to sort through it. Besides, you'll owe us one, and when Marci's back home we intend on taking a long weekend and leaving our hellions with you. Trust me; we're not doing you any favor."

Bill looked to Marci. She blinked approval. He conceded, "All right Jeff, but we'll hold you to that long weekend."

"Fair enough. Now the two of you get out of here and enjoy yourselves."
They all rose in unison.

With the concern reserved for close friends Jeff said, "I'm sorry I didn't have better news."

Throughout his explanation Marci had moved from rejection to stark terror and finally, acceptance. She'd heard his genuine concern throughout - and now, with feigned strength, she tendered her heartfelt gratitude, "Thanks Jeff. It may not seem like it, but I *do* appreciate your honesty and it means more than I can say to have you helping me through this."

They turned to leave. Jeff's request stopped them, "Bill, may I have a few words with you?"

Bill's face broadcast annoyance.

Marci intervened, "It's all right Bill I'll be in the waiting room."

Bill watched Marci pull the door closed behind her. Then he barked, "Okay Jeff, what's so damned important?"

Jeff rotated away, trying to avoid the words that followed. "It's worse than I told the two of you. Much worse."

"Wha.. . .what?!!! I thought you said we got it early and her chances of recovery are excellent?"

"I know what I said Bill, but the cancer has metastasized."

Bill crawled out from underneath the car that had just fallen on him. "You mean . . . ?"

Jeff pivoted back, "Yes. The cancer has spread. With the exception of her brain it's in all her vital organs."

Bill's eyes slammed shut. "No! Please God, no."

Jeff stepped forward, placed his hand on Bill's arm. "I'm so sorry Bill."

Bill's eyelids, heavy with the moment, rose slowly, desperately, "What now?"

"That's why I asked to speak to you alone."

Jeff paused, making certain Bill was grounded.

Bill wiggled his fingers impatiently in a, *Well, get on with it*, gesture.

Jeff ignored the prodding, then spoke resolutely, "Do you want me to tell Marci?"

Futility mingled with frustration as Bill fired, "Damn it Jeff, she has a right to the truth."

"I agree but I'm not sure I have the right to tell her."

"Christ Jeff! I don't have enough to deal with, now you're giving me riddles."

"What I'm saying Bill . . . this is your decision. I can't ethically, or morally, make the choice when there's a spouse or close family member involved. Even if I could, because of our relationship, I wouldn't."

"Will you at least offer an opinion?"

Jeff nodded purposefully. "My heart prays we beat this thing, but my head says we can't. We need a miracle, and, right now, Marci's hope is all we've got. My opinion . . . there's nothing to be gained by her knowing.

That said, if you feel differently, I'll bring her back in here and explain everything."

The dam burst. "That's just great Jeff! No pressure here. You'll be glad to deliver the bullet; you just want me to pull the trigger."

Jeff hesitated, torn between caring and a kick in the ass. He chose the latter!

"We've been friends for a long time. Hell, you and Marci are godparents to Amy. No one said this was easy, but feeling sorry for yourself and taking it out on me isn't going to solve the immediate problem. She needs you to carry your share of the load, God knows, hers is heavy enough. You can either stop bitching and face up to this or get yourself another doctor."

Wake up calls come in many forms. But a "kick in the ass" by your best friend is not the gentlest way to receive one!

Bill's features staggered from rage to recognition as he quipped, "Some bedside manner. Where'd you learn it? The Genghis Khan School of Medicine?"

Jeff relented with a smile, "I apologize. I shouldn't have been so blunt."

"No apology necessary, you're absolutely right. I'm acting like a jerk. It's just . . . ." Bill suddenly cringed. Shook his head and balled his hands to fists.

"What is it Bill?"

Torment tainted his answer, "I can't deal with this. I'm scared."

"You think I can? I'm scared too. You do the best you can, and pray to God you haven't done the wrong thing."

Bill rubbed his face with his hands, breathing deeply between his fingers. Seconds passed before he pulled them free. "We can't tell her. Without a thread to cling to she'll give up and die."

"All right then, that's settled."

"Is there anything else I should be doing?"

"Just keep her positive."

"Anything else?"

"Not for now. I've referred her case to the best oncologist in the city - Dr. Lee. She'll take over Marci's medical treatment from here. I -"

"Wait a second. We need you involved. I don't want some robot treating her, no matter how good she is."

"You didn't let me finish. I'm not going anywhere. I'll be available day or night for anything you or Marci need. I've just put her immediate care in the hands of someone more qualified."

"But -"

"Trust me on this Bill. This gives Marci the best chance."

Bill's shoulders slumped. "We can't get through this without you."

"I'll be right beside you every step of the way. Now you two go out and have that intimate dinner. You've got a lot to talk about. I'll see you when you pick up the kids."

"Feels like you're pushing us toward 'The Last Supper'."

"I didn't mean it that way."

"I know Jeff, I'm sorry . . . I . . . ."

Jeff stepped forward and placed his hands on each side of Bill's neck. "I would have done anything not to be the one -"

"No Jeff. Better you than a stranger. This sucks, but if it's got to be, we're damn lucky to have you."

In the car, several blocks from Jeff's office, Marci finally broke the silence. "What did Jeff want?"

Head frozen forward, fingers curled tightly around the steering wheel, he sidestepped her highly evolved sense of smell! "He just wanted to cushion the helplessness and frustration that are sure to come. He also wanted us to know that he'll be available for us anytime."

She mapped the side of his face with her eyes, searching for a crack in his response.

Several more blocks drifted by before she probed, "Well?"

He countered cautiously, "Well what?"

"Do you feel helpless and frustrated?"

"Do you?"

Attempting to redirect her growing anxiety she teased, "I asked you first."

"Yes . . . and no . . . hell I'm not sure what I feel. What about you?"

"It knocked the wind out of me - and I suppose when it settles in," her voice broke as she finished, "I'm going to be terrified."

Bill pulled their mini-van to the curb, turned to her, and with more conviction than he felt, gave Marci the bridge she needed, "We'll beat this baby . . . I promise."

His guilt was heavy enough, but when she leaned across and brushed a trusting kiss against his cheek it drove a stake through his heart!

CHAPTER TWO

Jeff had been right. They did indeed do everything they could . . . and more! It seemed to Bill they had stopped just short of waving a dead chicken over her lifeless form. Between chemotherapy, radiation treatments, nuclear medicine, and God knows what else, it had finally arrived at torture. Care had been replaced by research. Marci had become the Guinea pig in an elaborate trial of *any* experimental means of therapy. It was, of course, being done for that noblest of causes - "her welfare".

Worse, Bill was made an unwitting accomplice. He was battered repeatedly with, "To deny us a free hand could result in your wife's death." With his neck stretched dutifully under that guillotine, he acceded reluctantly to any and all requests.

On those rare occasions when Bill could displace Marci's daily inquisition he mused about a mythical doctor approaching him with a *magic bullet*. "I've got good news and I've got bad news. The good news is we can eliminate all traces of the disease."

Excitedly Bill would ask, "And the bad?"

"The bad news is the cure will kill her!"

~~~~~~~~~~~~~~~~~~~~~~~~~~~~~
~~~~~~~~~~~~~~~~~~~~~~~~~~~~~

Bill sat staring into his coffee. Jeff slid into the cafeteria chair beside him and announced, "The staff has a new procedure they'd like to try."

Without looking up from the designs the cream had made in his coffee he returned snidely, "And that would be what? Inject her with aardvark piss?"

Jeff fired back, "That's uncalled for."

"All right, I'll play. Has it ever been tried before?"

"Not on humans."

"What the hell does that mean?"

"It means that computer profiling indicates a marginal probability of success. Admittedly low, but still a shot."

Bill chuckled sarcastically. "You mean this hasn't even been tried on animals?"

"Well no, but -"

Bill was calm, but his tone froze Jeff mid sentence, "Then we've come to the end."

"Pardon me?"

Bill's frame shook with surrender. "There will be no more miracle potions, no more mystery rays, no more anything. It's over. The mutilation will stop . . . now!"

"You're sure this is what you want?"

Here it was again . . . if she dies it's your fault! He never expected this from Jeff, but then, it's hard for physicians to change their spots.

It was time someone jumped into the quicksand with him. "If this was your wife Jeff, what would you do?"

"That's not the issue."

"Oh, but it is. It's very simple - knowing what you know, what would you do?"

"You can't put -"

Bill's glare amputated the finish.

Jeff put his elbows on the table and leaned his forehead against his palms. After a few seconds of self-analysis he raised his head and dropped his hands. "I'll make her as comfortable as possible."

"Thank you Jeff. Will you see that the appropriate medical staff gets the news?"

"Yes."

"I mean it Jeff. If one more of these butchers touches her there'll be hell to pay."

"I'll take care of it."

Jeff raised slowly, instructions in hand, but was stopped by Bill's conciliatory closing, "It may not seem like it at this moment, but I couldn't get through this without you."

Empathy balanced Jeff's nod as he answered, "I know Bill, but it still means a lot to hear you say it."

~~~~~~~~~~~~~~~~~~~~~~~~~~~~

Resolution noticeably changed Bill's disposition. Able now to focus his full attention on Marci his mood changed from *deep* depression to *everyday* depression.
~~~~~~~~~~~~~~~~~~~~~~~~~~~~

He strode into Room 429 two days later to find a nurse and an orderly preparing to wheel Marci, bed and all, from her cubicle.

"Excuse me," he fired, "where are you taking her?"

They stopped. The nurse eyed him with mild contempt before saying, "And who are you?"

"I'm her husband."

She seemed to straighten slightly, permitting him the license to inquire. Still noticeably perturbed at the interruption she said, "We're taking her for treatment."

With considerable effort he restrained himself, "What treatment?"

"The treatment ordered by Dr. Findley."

"And who is Dr. Findley?"

Well now, he really *was* showing his ignorance. "He's only The Chief of Oncology for the hospital."

"I thought Dr. Lee was supervising her case?"

"Dr. Findley took over her care yesterday."

"Under whose authority?"

"I'm not privy to that information."

Bill's outrage was red lining, and Florence Nightingale's smug attitude was only throwing gasoline on the fire. Just short of explosion he stopped.

For once in your life be smart.

How often had he leapt without looking? Acting from impulse had, more often than not, left him feeling stupid and embarrassed.

Not this time. There are bigger fish to fry.

Anger is best served when sharpened with planning and purpose, and then surgically inserted in the target.

Through clenched teeth he said, "She's not going anywhere."

"But I have my orders."

He read her nametag purposefully, "Maybe I didn't make myself clear . . . MARY. Read my lips - she's staying right here."

Her response was severed by the blaze in his eyes. She sighed, and then shrugged. She only worked here, if the powers that be wanted to disagree, it was no skin off her nose. She couldn't however, resist a parting shot. "Dr. Findley won't be pleased with this interruption in the regimen."

This solar flare almost escaped Bill. It wasn't until Marci had been repositioned and all her monitors and drips had been reconnected that its subtlety struck home!

Mary and the orderly were walking into the hall when Bill asked, "I'm sorry nurse, did you say the regimen had been interrupted?"

She turned back, "Yes."

"Would you please explain?"

Exasperated with his unintelligible nagging she fumed, "The course was started yesterday. This was to be the second in the series."

"You're telling me she's already undergone Number One?"

This tore it! Not only was he uninformed, he was rude *and* hard of hearing. Hands on hips she scolded, "Well, yes. *Two* has a way of following *one*."

She spun to leave again. Bill tossed a volley over her shoulder, "Would you mind asking Dr. Findley to come and see me?"

Without looking back she delivered, with relish, her own parting volley, "Oh, I won't have to ask, when the good doctor finds out what you've done he'll find you."

Christ, he thought, *where do these people get their training!*

He took the few steps to Marci's bed and seated himself at her side. *At least Baby, you're so drugged you slept through this shit.*

He watched her labored breathing, occasionally reaching over to wipe the spittle from her chin as it leaked from the corner of her mouth. She looked so helpless. Hell, that made them even - he'd never felt more helpless in his life!

A tear pressed the corner of each eye as he tried to reconcile their "dance with death".

Some time later a figure swept into the room, Bill looked up, ready to launch, but it was Jeff.

"Jeff, I didn't expect you till later?"

"I was making my rounds. I -"

"You won't believe what's been going on here."

"Other than you disrupting hospital procedure? What hap -"

"Me disrupting hospital procedure?!! Why those arrogant bastards. Do you know -"

"All right Bill, calm down. You didn't let me finish. I was about to ask you what happened here when you cut me off."

Bill loosened, took a deep breath, and recounted his confrontation with Nurse Mary.

He was closing, "And that's about -," when a man in a white smock and stethoscope strolled in.

Jeff started to speak, but the new arrival ignored him and proceeded to Marci. He checked her pulse and quickly scanned the monitors before acknowledging anyone else's presence. He focused on Jeff as though Bill were invisible. "Dr. Blake, does Mr. Allen realize what he's done?"

"Dr. Findley, I wonder if we might discuss this outside?"

"Of course."

They moved to the corridor. Bill tagged along, the afterthought that he was!

Jeff spoke first, "Now Dr. Findley, please continue."

"As I was saying, does Mr. Allen realize what he's done?"

Compelled, Bill opened his mouth to respond. Jeff's hand on his arm intervened and Jeff spoke instead, "Dr. Findley, before we get to that - I thought Dr. Lee was in charge of Mrs. Allen's case?"

"She is."

"I'm afraid I don't understand. Are you saying she authorized this change?"

"Well, no . . . but -"

"Dr. Findley, I was quite specific with Dr. Lee, there was to be no further treatment of Mrs. Allen. The family and I wished only to make her as comfortable as possible. Did Dr. Lee not forward these instructions to you?"

"Yes, but this new alternative offers some hope."

"And what did Dr. Lee say about it?"

"She said she neither would, nor could, overrule the wishes of the family."

With the ease of a practiced surgeon Jeff inserted the scalpel, "And what about Dr. Lee's statement seems to have confused you?"

Life is full of surprises. Once in a while they're even pleasant! Bill smiled. *All right Jeff!*

Findley's expression soured as he backpedaled. "I believe this to be a viable option - with minimal downside and a legitimate chance of success."

"For whom - you, or her?"

"What's that supposed to mean?"

"If you could save her with an experimental procedure your grant funding would probably quadruple. If you failed, nothing lost, she was terminal anyway."

The tips of Findley's ears reddened as he blustered a defense,"How dare you! My only concern is for Mrs. Allen's recovery."

Jeff smirked at Findley's hollow rebuttal. "Lofty motives aside, the next time you disregard patient instructions I will have you before the board of this hospital. I will then join with the family in suit against you and this institution."

Findley's face now matched the color of his ears. He puffed up to defend himself, but Jeff canceled his opportunity. "You could at least have the courtesy to thank me."

Findley pulled back, sideswiped by Jeff's change of direction. "Thank you . . . for what?"

Jeff's veiled wink at Bill said, *play along*. "I've known Mr. Allen most of my life. He responds to situations with no regard for consequences. I suspect if I hadn't intervened he would have broken both your arms. It would make it difficult to perform surgery with casts on . . . don't you think?"

Jeff paused to enhance the snapshot.

Findley's eyes darted between Bill and Jeff as he shaped the image.

Picture complete, Jeff buried the nail, "Now, before he decides to disregard the M.D. after both our names, I'd advise you to leave."

"You're going to regret this. When I -"

Jeff's slowly shaking head said, "*Leave it alone.*"

Findley cracked his mouth to resume, paused to pondered Jeff's silent threat, squeezed his lips shut, then turned on his heal and marched down the passageway.

With disbelief Bill asked, "Do you really think I would have hurt him?"

With another wink Jeff answered, "Of course not, but can you honestly say what you would have done if I weren't here?"

"Yes."

"What?"

With his own coy wink Bill said, "I'd have broken both his arms."

The tension bled from Jeff as he countered with a broad grin.

Ice broken, or at least melted temporarily, Jeff resumed concerned friend mode. "I'm sorry Bill; I should have been more vigilant."

"How could anyone know that asshole would pull a stunt like this?"

"In all fairness, he *is* a brilliant physician, even if he does suffer from a God complex. You're welcome to pursue legal remedies, heaven knows he deserves it, but I'm asking you to let it go. Any action against Findley will only eat you up and serve as a wasteful, debilitating distraction. Marci needs your full attention - now more than ever."

Bill measured him before responding, "I suppose you're right. I wish I had the heart for it though. I would love to cripple that son of a bitch!"

After a quick trip to the coffee machine, they sat on a bench outside Marci's room. Each leaned forward, elbows on knees, cradling their cups between all ten fingers and staring into the imitation motor oil.

Without looking up Jeff said, almost casually, "Marci has a month, maybe two on the outside."

Looking straight ahead, Bill blew steam from the surface of the noxious brew. He tried casual too - as though, the more disinterested and distant the attitude the less damaging the news. "What happens now?"

For the next ten minutes Jeff explained in graphic, and sometimes brutal, detail the course of Marci's final days. The deliberate sigh that closed his recital imploded with sadness.

~~~~~~~~~~~~~~~~~~~~~~~~~~~~~

For the next two weeks everyone followed the script.

Marci deteriorated rapidly. She languished in and out of coherency - mostly out. The pain that had started as an intermittent annoyance was now constant - the only relief surfacing when her drug-laden system left on comatose vacations. Her body shrunk noticeably from day to day as the cancer, unchallenged, took control.

Bill stood daily vigilance. His only truancy being quick side trips to the children. Shortly after making her peace with them Marci had discontinued their visits. Choosing to be remembered as a whole mother rather than a rotting, incoherent stranger.

Along with Marci's downturn, and his forced lies and deceptions to the kids, Bill began his own deterioration. These ongoing concurrent events had their own cancerous effect on his spirit. For a spirit without hope must, by its nature, implode.

And Jeff, overseeing the dope brigade, offered an invitingly empty ear, waiting to be filled by family and friend's mounting anxiety.

~~~~~~~~~~~~~~~~~~~~~~~~~~~~~

Bill stood silent sentinel beside Marci's bed, gazing down on another place . . . another time. A picnic, a beautiful spring day, and they were single. They ate, drank, and flirted. They were negotiating a life together. Their ballet was underscored by a collage of things to come, and when their terms coincided they sealed the agreement with a kiss . . . .

Just above a whisper, a voice pushed its way toward his reverie, "Bill."
Again - an octave higher and strained by the effort, "Bill."
His eyelids fluttered open as he searched for the present.
She offered again, "Bill."
He shook off the past and reached to engulf her hand. He hesitated; her bones had become so fragile, might he snap these porcelain fingers? Instead, he cradled the appendage as if holding a fledgling.

"Marci, you're awake. Can I get you anything? A drink of water?" And then with hope, "Something to eat?"

She squeaked back, "No. Nothing, thank you."

Her face suddenly contorted as jagged bands of pains coursed through her.

He helplessly pleaded, "Should I get the nurse?"

"No, it's passing."

"They're supposed to be giving you something."

"They are, but it doesn't help much."

"There must be -"

"Bill, we need to talk."

No! Not yet. I can't. He tried deflection, "When you're feeling better."

"Please Bill, when are you going to stop this charade? There won't be *any* better. As it is, I'm only a person about twenty minutes a day."

"Don't talk like this, you're going to -"

"Stop it Bill! I'm dying. If you don't know that, then you're the only one in this hospital that doesn't."

Her anger riveted him - but more than that, her energy and resolve.

He hung his head and kissed the palm of her hand.

They both recognized this for the surrender that it was.

"All right Marci."

"Thank you. Now listen carefully."

His nod was patronizing. He didn't want this conversation, but if it gave her closure, well . . . he'd have to be ready. Wrong!

"What ever happens, don't let my father, or my sisters, have the children. You must protect them. And if something happens to you, make certain your brother or Jeff and Donna get them."

What the hell?!!!

He pressed for clarity, "I don't understand? You know I'd never let anything happen to them. But what's that got to do with your father and sisters?"

"I mean it Bill. As soon as I'm gone they'll move for custody and under no circumstances can that be allowed to happen."

"But Marci -"

Urgency ringed her plea, "Promise me, please, promise me . . . on your Mother's grave."

Jeff had warned him about the cumulative affects of the medications, but, this disturbing outburst aside, she seemed more rational now than she'd been in days. First things first - relieve her agitation and then he could address this strange revelation.

"All right Marci. Your father and sisters will have nothing to do with our children. I swear it . . . on my Mother's grave."

She relaxed immediately, as though his assent was the switch that cured her dementia.

With calm restored he could begin confronting this extraordinary turn, but unraveling *her* reality would require a diplomat's touch. Bill played with the words and their delivery. Satisfied with the composition he began, "Marci, why are you so concerned -"

Her ragged breathing stifled his inquiry. Driven by the cancer, and the opiates, she had lapsed into a charitable oblivion. He moved to rouse her - stopped his hand mid air. The prerequisite effort might cause irreparable damage. He resigned his quest, yielding to her frailty.

~~~~~~~~~~~~~~~~~~~~~~~~~~~~

With the need to conceal her *real* condition gone, a large and ponderous weight lifted itself from his shoulders. Along with its levitation, a dull ache that had nagged the base of his skull mysteriously vanished too.

Refreshed, after his best night's sleep in weeks, Bill sauntered down the hospital corridor toward her room. There was still this business of Marci's father and sisters, but his clearing head had convinced him that this was no more than a drug induced aberration.

Jeff was exiting as Bill entered. They nearly collided.

Jeff blurted out, "Before you see Marci there's something I need to explain."

"Nice to see you too, Jeff."

"I'm sorry, good morning Bill. I was preoccupied, afraid I wouldn't get to talk to you before you saw her."
~~~~~~~~~~~~~~~~~~~~~~~~~~~~

Bill's breath caught in his throat, "Why, what's wrong?"

Jeff's reply was guarded, "Nothing. It's just that when you see her . . . well, she'll be different - alert, vital, almost vigorous."

Puzzled by this turn Bill pressed hopefully, "I don't understand?"

Jeff tread lightly, "For no apparent reason some patient's condition suddenly reverses itself. This turnaround typically lasts a day, sometimes two, and then just as suddenly reverts back. Almost always they're worse than before. As though burning the candle that brightly, extracts twice their reserves. It's not unusual for this to happen two, maybe, three times before the end. Each person is different however."

Bill resisted Jeff's "wet blanket" approach, "Why can't she be turning the corner on this thing?"

"She can, and I pray to God she is, but her abrupt turn around is a classic pattern and I don't want to create false hope. I'm merely advising caution."

Damn doctors were beginning to sound like lawyers. Why must every piece of information have an "out" clause? Bill started to argue the issue, and then stopped, *This is not the time.* He conceded instead, "All right Jeff, I'll be cautious. Should I be alert for anything in particular?"

"No. Enjoy her while she's back, but don't be too let down if she leaves again."

"Advice noted. Now when can I see her?"

Jeff motioned him forward.

Cancer 101 complete, Bill inched curiously into Marci's room with Jeff following behind.

Jeff had been right. He wasn't prepared for the woman that had taken over his wife's body! She was propped up in bed. Her cheeks were full of color, her hair had been washed and combed, and she was wearing lipstick. The sledgehammer between the eyes however, was the warm smile she sported between the bites of steak she was devouring!

He coughed to conceal a gasp.

Marci looked up from the feast, "There you are sweetheart. I was beginning to think you forgot me. Thought you might have given up on me and decided to run away with that sexy redhead down the street."

Her teasing accusation combined with her anomalous appearance stifled any form of structured response. His muddled defense was a repeated throat clearing exercise that lasted for several seconds.

She chuckled, "Relax dear, I was only kidding. I know you'll wait until I'm gone before testing those waters."

He stared in stunned silence.

With obvious glee Marci continued to exploit her exalted position, "What's wrong with him Jeff? Have you been giving him some of my drugs?"

Jeff smiled. "I think he's surprised to see you so . . . well, so energetic." Mouth ajar, Bill continued to study her.

"I don't know Jeff. Surprise is one thing, but paralysis is something else again."

Bill closed to Marci's side, bent and kissed her tenderly on the mouth. Moved, she covered the impact of his gesture with more banter, "Now that's more like it."

He whispered to her, "You've never been more beautiful."

A tear welled to the corner of her eye as she reached, pulled him to her, and returned the kiss . . . with passion . . . .

Jeff chimed in, "I can tell when I'm not wanted. I'm going to make some rounds."

He turned and left the room - not that anyone noticed!!!

For the next two hours they talked shop . . . or, at least Marci did.

Had he made the house and car payments?

Were the kids getting enough to eat?

What about that mole on his back? He really should have Jeff remove it.

Had he gotten the fence repaired yet?

Her questions came so fast they collided with the backs of each other. As though accumulation of current events represented her reinstatement in the living world.

He dutifully spaced her inquiries with a, "Yes dear," or, "No dear," or, "I will dear."

The time raced from them.

Then, without warning, mid-sentence, she sighed, yawned, and drifted off to sleep.

Bill's bladder nudged the wall of his stomach. Relieve himself? No way! No minor annoyance could take him from her. Not even for an instant. He sat warm and comfortable, his content driven by her return to normalcy. The safety of their temporary haven settled around him and he too drifted slowly off to sleep.

Jeff peeked around the corner. The intrusion jerked Bill awake.

He whispered, "I'm sorry Bill, I didn't mean to rouse you."

Matching Jeff's decibel rating he answered, "It's all right; I was only on the edge."

Jeff murmured back, "Does Marci need anything?"

Before Bill could answer, his groin issued a sharp call for attention. An ignored bodily function becomes an angry bodily function!

Bill almost tripped as he shot out of the chair. As he passed Jeff's puzzled expression, he offered a frantic rasp, "Nature calls."

Several minutes later the bathroom door opened and a *less pressured* Bill emerged.

They stepped to the hallway.

Jeff spoke first, "Are you okay?"

Bill clipped his reply, "I'm fine. I wouldn't leave her and -"

Jeff's confused look cut him off.

Some things aren't worth explaining. When in doubt . . . punt! "You had to be there Jeff."

Non-explanation accepted Jeff moved on, "Does she need anything?"

"Are you kidding? She's great. It's amazing how she -"

Jeff's glare reprimanded him.

Bill countered quickly, "I know. You told me to take it slow, but you can't blame me for being hopeful."

"Of course not. As long as you don't get ahead of her condition."

In his first show of jest in weeks Bill snapped to attention and flashed a hand salute. "Yes, Sir. I'll be more careful in the future, Sir. Rest assured, Sir I'll -"

"You can stop now Bill. You've made your point. I'm -"

Marci clearing her throat interrupted them.

They moved expectantly back to her room and her bedside.

As she inhaled her eyelids raised. She blinked twice for focus and said, "Jeff, you're back. I must have dozed off. I'm sorry Bill."

"Not to worry. I got twenty winks myself."

Jeff took Marci's wrist and checked her pulse, while laying the back of his other hand against her forehead. "How are you feeling?"

"Better than I have in some time."

He checked her eyes. "Your signs and color are good. Let's keep it that way."

"Is that an order?"

He smiled and answered, "It is if it'll make you well."

She returned a grin and said, "You're the doctor."

"And don't you forget it. Now, I've got to look in on some *sick* people. I'll check back with you later."

He turned to leave. Marci's somber tone turned him around. "Jeff."

"Yes?"

"Bill and I want to thank you and Donna for watching the kids during this bout. Your personal attention aside, I'm not sure what we would've done without the two of you."

Uncomfortable with her declaration of sentiment Jeff tried lifting the mood, "When you're on your feet again you'll owe us big time." Then with a smile, "Payback is hell."

The trio laughed.

An about-face later and Jeff was gone.

Alone again, the silence pressed in on them. They rushed to fill it, blurting in unison, "Bill -" - "Marci -"

They chuckled at their verbal collision.

He offered her the lead, "You go."

Her voice took on a strength and formality that frightened him. "I need you to do something for me."

"Anything."

"Don't be so quick to agree. You might regret it."

He'd wanted so much to contribute during her illness. Be of help, somehow. But there wasn't anything *he* could do. Adding to his growing feeling of inadequacy had been her conspicuous courage, her stoic approach to the disease and all that surrounded it. Given this opportunity to shed guilt, he leaped, "Whatever you want, it'll be done."

She took a deep breath then said, "When I get bad again I want you to end it."

Sure, she'd set the trap - but he'd so graciously walked into it!
"What?"

"You heard me."

Oh, he'd heard all right, but when you're hit between the eyes by flying debris, no matter how small, it still feels like an avalanche.
He needed time. He opted for a diversion, "Why are you so concerned about keeping the children away from your father and sisters?"
Her eyes narrowed and she visibly tensed before asking, "Where did you get that idea?"

"From you."

"From me? When?"

"The other day."

"The other day?"

"Now who's being coy?"

"I honestly don't remember. What did I say?"

"Under no circumstances is your father or your sisters to have custody of the kids. You made me swear on my Mother's grave."

"Sounds like I meant it. Now that you've taken an oath I guess it's settled."

Anxious to pursue this line he probed, "You're going to be here so it was an easy contract to sign, but I still don't understand you're concern. Why -"

A smirk slowly walked across her face as she interrupted, "Nice try Bill."

Startled, he asked, "Wha-what are you talking about?"

"You know damn well what I'm talking about."

"No I don't."

"Your trick almost worked."

"Trick?"

"Divert the discussion on the drugged sick person. Do it fast enough and they'll forget the original subject."

"I was trying to get the issue of your family resolved."

"You said I made a believer out of you, where's the issue?"

"But Marci -"

"Later Bill, right now I need an answer to *my* question. Are you going to help me or not?"

He should have known better. She could always see through him. Truth be known, she had always been much quicker on the uptake. Just how quick he would come to know. He would look back on this moment and realize she had subtly affirmed his position on the children while never responding to his query.

He paused to consider an end run . . . she cut him off!
"Well?!!!"

"This is out of the blue. At least give me some time to get my bearings?"

"It's a straightforward request that deserves a simple yes or no answer."

"I would hardly characterize it so matter of casually. Helping someone kill herself is a very serious matter. Besides, I won't let you give up."

She sneered, "It's not your choice."

"But -"

"And I'm not giving up, I'm just giving in."

He broke down, "What are the kids and I going to do without you?"

"You'll -" her reply was severed by a shutter of pain. She doubled at the waist and wretched the remains of her steak lunch across the bed clothing.

Bill recoiled in horror. Shock over, he took her by the shoulders and eased her back on the pillows. "Can I get you something?"

With obvious effort she shook her head, "No."

He found the call button, depressed it, and then rose for the bathroom. Moments later he returned with two cold compresses. He carefully laid one across her forehead and with the other he gently wiped her mouth.

She looked weakly through her tears and said, "I'm sorry Bill. I -"

He quieted her with a, "Shhh . . . it's all right. You rest."

The nurse arrived and began the clean up. Bill could only gaze as she worked quietly and expeditiously through the emergency. Wasn't she aware of what had just occurred? How could she be so casual . . . so efficient? Before he could lecture her on showing the proper emotional attachment with patients and family she bundled the array of soiled articles and departed.

Bill sat, holding Marci's hand, and watched through watery eyes as she slept fitfully. When her suffering became too much to bear he hung his head and prayed to an estranged God for help.

Sometime later he was nudged from his negotiations by her labored request, "Bill."

Mired from his trading with the Almighty he straightened, "Yes dear?"

Her voice became something raw, deep and rasping - but worse, it penetrated like fingernails across a blackboard. "Do you love me?"

Under the best of circumstances this was a question laden with peril, but now, even the right answer could explode in his face.

He replied guardedly, "Of course I love you."

"Then how can you stand watching me suffer like this?"

He turned on the knife, "That's not fair, I -"

"It's only going to get worse."

"Marci, please."

"I'm sorry Bill, but you can't begin to imagine what this is like. If you truly love me you won't allow it to continue."

When all avenues of retreat are cut off . . . stall! Time had become his only ally. She might forget this conversation, or . . . God forbid, the cancer might resolve the issue for him.

"All right, I'll make you a deal. If you still feel this way tomorrow we'll figure out how to get it done."

"I won't change my mind."

"That's my deal."

Anger, then resignation creased her brow. "What choice do I have? If I could do it myself it would already be done."

This minefield averted, he moved to smoother ground, "The kids send their love."

~~~~~~~~~~~~~~~~~~~~~~~~~~~~

It had been two days since her relapse. She had become vegetative. She was rarely awake. When she was, her eyes were vacant, and what communication there was sounded very much like mangled gibberish.

Bill was left to deal with "a rock and a hard place!" Devastated by her setback one moment and relieved by her inability to plead the assisted suicide case the next.

Upon entering her room on the morning of the third day she greeted him with an upbeat, "Well, good morning."

His response was excited, but guarded, "You must be feeling better?"

"Some."

"Has Jeff seen you?"

"He was in earlier."

"What did he say?"

"He gave me a quick once over and seemed pleased with this turn."

"That's good news."
~~~~~~~~~~~~~~~~~~~~~~~~~~~~

For several moments the silence weighed between them. It was finally pierced by Marci calling in Bill's marker, "All right Bill, you got a two day reprieve. Are you going to help me end this . . . or not?"

"But you just said Jeff was pleased."

"It's the eyes Bill. Always the eyes."

"What?"

"Jeff can say anything he wants, but his eyes keeping saying, 'I'm so sorry Marci. I wish there was something I could do.'"

"I don't think -"

"Bill, please! Are you're going to help me or not?"

This time it was his eyes.

She pleaded, "I'm begging you Bill."

"Marci, you can't give up. You've got to keep fighting."

"With what? There's nothing left but pain."

"I understand, but -"

"No you don't. You can't begin to imagine."

"There must be something they can give you?"

"They're giving me everything they've got. It's not helping."

"But -"

She turned cold, matter of fact, as she riveted him to his chair, "You never were a strong person. You've always been flash, little substance. I've known it, but I loved you and until now it didn't matter. In your own way you've cared for the children and me – fed us, housed us and kept us secure. I suppose I shouldn't blame you, you're simply incapable of being direct and decisive." She stopped, glared, and then skewered him with venom, "But I do!"

He slumped, noticeably, from the burden of his reply, "Marci, I can't."

"But you said –"

"I know I did, but I can't."

She began to cry. Between the tears she choked out, "God damn you!"

He raced for a haven. "How could I face the children if I did this?" He didn't wait for an answer. After all, this debate was more for him than her! "I'm sorry kids, your mother died today . . . I killed her! But, I did it because I loved her. I'm sure you'll understand when you're older."

Once started, the need to defend himself overcame any rational order. His justifications flowed like an opened tap. It became a simple case of quantity versus quality. Throw enough shit at the wall and something was bound to stick!

"They're sure to figure out what I've done. I could be prosecuted. Then, who's going to care for Bill Jr. and Molly?"

Or, "How could I face your family if the truth came out?"

And on . . . and on . . . .

Marci lay, quietly, scornfully, throughout Bill's adagio of rationalization. As he moved from one pirouette to the next her expression grew deeper, but strangely curious. After all, how many excuses could dance on the head of a pin?!!!

Finally, stretched to the breaking, he opened his mouth to play the *sin* card. It was *immoral* to kill someone. Someone as devout as Marci; would surely buy into the "mortal sin" defense.

The words wouldn't come. They lay lodged in his throat. He hadn't been near a church since he'd been a boy - and then, only the threats of hell and brimstone from his Mother had coerced his attendance. He was about as religious as Adolph Hitler. He'd been praying desperately to that long forgotten God to save her. Now he was prepared to use that *same* forgotten God to legitimize this pretense.

He cringed inside as he measured the depth of the bullshit! *How far are you prepared to go Bill? Does your deceit have a limit?* Before he could begin the debate Marci leveled him!

"You bastard! You'd rather watch me vomit my guts out, or shit myself, or become a shriveled, wrinkled mummy than do what's needed. When did you ever ..."

Marci's berating came at him like claps of thunder, but it fell on deaf ears. Bill could no longer hear. Instead, he was left staring at his own hypocrisy, his own deficiencies – and finally, magnified by his own guilt, they collapsed on him like a giant tsunami!

She had become the poster child of his cowardice, and he hated her for it! When he could no longer face himself he turned, without a word, and exited her room. Her contempt followed him down the hall. Each hurled expletive driving another spike in his back.

~~~~~~~~~~~~~~~~~~~~~~~~~~~~~~

For the next three days Bill avoided Marci. He planned his trips around her medication, making certain she would be asleep or unconscious when he arrived. After a few moments by her side he would leave under the guise of seeing to the children or whatever excuse justified his departure. These deluded footsteps were an effort to erase his guilt and deflect him from the truth. Knowing he couldn't confront her without confronting himself he rushed home to hide. Once there he searched every avenue of diversion. Every one however led back to his mainstay – "Scotches of the Modern World." After two days of drinking every style he could lay his mouth on he determined in one of his few coherent moments that there was no such thing as a bad Scotch! Drowning one's self in alcohol however has one major drawback. It ultimately chases you back to the very thing from which you are running. So finally, with no side doors remaining, Bill was forced to face himself. A most painful process
~~~~~~~~~~~~~~~~~~~~~~~~~~~~~~

for anyone, but for someone already riddled with guilt and self doubt, a gauntlet of emotional boogie men!

The truth slowly bubbled through his denial. He was a coward. Had been all his life. When he was a boy he walked blocks out of his way to avoid a confrontation with anyone he *thought* was a bully. All the while telling himself how he'd relish the opportunity to end that slug's "tough guy shit." In high school he'd gone out for the football team because the girls loved strong athletic types . . . didn't they? When the coach made him a linebacker based on his ferocious attitude he made certain to avoid any head on tackles. Oh, he got lot's of credit for his bruising play, had even made all conference, but inside he knew he always got to the pile-up a fraction of an instant after someone else had done the work. And now, in business, he took credit for his peers' ideas and concepts. He never went out on a limb – that would require a core belief, fortitude, taking a chance . . . no way. Yes, he was a coward, and worse he was a lazy coward. Always leaving someone else to foot the bill!

Bottom line – Marci was absolutely right about him. The truth spread through him like a chain reaction - he *now* realized that *she* had been the strength of the family, the underpinning of their peace and prosperity. She handled the finances, saw to the children, and saw to him. He was only a figurehead, the mouthpiece of their domain while she directed its path and made the necessary course corrections. She had artfully allowed him to believe his own public relations and skillfully reined him in when his pomp and bluster threatened their general welfare. Marci had permitted him the "flash" while inconspicuously backing him with "substance".

Well, here it was. He wasn't a man. Hell, he wasn't even a person. He had no redeeming value. There wasn't one reason for his existence . . . except one. As he reached for the nearest bottle of single malt he thought, *I can drink with the best of 'em.*

Four hours and two liters of Scotch later Bill sat on the floor, back against the living room sofa. His head had become a giant paperweight for the misery that was drowning him. Unable to move and barely alive he pissed his pants. Could he sink any lower from despair and self-contempt? Apparently so – he then vomited all over himself.

Lying on the carpet, *the* poster child for human waste, he wanted to kill himself, or at least he thought so until the irony of the situation seeped through the debris.

I'd kill myself if I could, but I can't. That would require guts and we all know I don't have any . . . I just threw them up!

He tried to chuckle, but could only drool instead. Just before he passed out a novel thought tickled the edge of his fog. *With regurgitation comes catharsis.*

~~~~~~~~~~~~~~~~~~~~~~~~~~~~

Fighting demons, particularly your own, builds a voracious appetite. Somewhere after a gallon of coffee and the biggest breakfast he'd had in weeks he had decided to end her suffering. Bill came down the hall to Marci's room his shoulders square and purpose in his step.

Jeff met him at the door and announced, "I tried to call your house."

A red flag unfurled as Bill shot back, "What's wrong? What is it?"

"Sit down over here."

Jeff took Bill's arm and led him to a bench. Reluctantly seated, Bill's eyes begged the question.

Jeff stared back compassionately and said calmly, "Marci is gone."

Expecting the worst offers no protection against it. Bill slumped.

Jeff continued, "About fifteen minutes ago. That's why I tried you at home and then your cell phone."

Bill reached into his windbreaker and withdrew the instrument. He'd forgotten to turn it on. He shook his head before offering, "Did she suffer?"
~~~~~~~~~~~~~~~~~~~~~~~~~~~~

"No. She went peacefully."

"Thank God for that. But I should have been here. I -"

"Don't Bill. You can't win that one. We had no way of knowing. Just be glad her suffering is over and that she's in a better place."

"Damn it Jeff. She shouldn't have been alone. If I hadn't been home feeling sorry for myself I –"

Jeff took Bill's shoulders and squeezed, "Stop it Bill! It's over. You couldn't have changed a thing. You need to look forward now, not backward."

Bill started to protest, but Jeff's forceful expression ended the discussion. Instead, he inhaled slowly and asked hopefully, "Can I see her?"

"Of course. Take as much time as you need. I'll see that you're not disturbed."

"Thank you, Jeff."

Jeff nodded, "I'll be right here when you're done."

Bill entered Marci's room and closed the door carefully. As though closing the door loudly would disturb her final peace. Marci lay there with the blanket pulled over her chest and her arms exposed at her sides. Her head was propped on a pillow. Her eyes and mouth were closed. If Bill hadn't known he would have thought she was resting. Then again . . . she finally was. He pulled a chair to the bed and sat down. He took her hand, leaned forward and kissed her gently on the lips. Holding her hand ever so gently he spoke mournfully to her angelic form, "God damn you Marci! I came here to do what you asked. I did care. I would've done it, but you wouldn't let me be the man we both needed me to be. And now . . . we'll never know."

He dropped his forehead to her hand and began to sob. Between the tears and the heaving he pleaded, "I'm no coward. I did love you, more than even I knew. Now you're gone. What am I going to do without you?"\

Self realization is a wonderful phenomenon, a life altering gift, but when it comes after the fact, when its patron and true benefactor is gone, unavailable to share its reward, it shrivels to a wisp of smoke.

For the next twenty minutes Bill retched with grief. For her . . . and himself . . . .

~~~~~~~~~~~~~~~~~~~~~~~~~~~~~~

The days that followed were a slow motion dream in shades of gray. Mercifully Marci had chosen cremation, sparing the children from a paper mache version of their mother. Remembering loved ones from the chest up in an ornamental box is a barbaric throw back to our Neanderthal ancestors. Neither he nor Marci could have inflicted that lasting cruelty on Bill Jr. and Molly. At the end of the memorial service Bill was presented with an urn housing Marci's ashes, as though this trophy of her life would bring closure and consolation to those remaining. On more than one occasion he nearly threw this morbid obelisk through the living room window. He had finally stored it away, choosing instead to fill the house with photos of the laughing, happy, counseling mother he and the kids cherished.
~~~~~~~~~~~~~~~~~~~~~~~~~~~~~~

CHAPTER THREE

He traveled an endless minefield of emotions. His time alone ricocheted from moment to moment with her. Each remembrance of her became a study of him. Each and every deficiency in him became magnified by the strengths in her. Missed opportunity upon missed opportunity to prove to her what she meant to him. His broken record was always in slow motion and always with the same outcome. His warped sense of reality pleaded for a different ending – one that left him, Marci and their family intact....

A chiming in the distance brought Bill back. There in the corner of the attic announcing his return was their retired grandfather clock. He sat cross-legged on the unfinished flooring surrounded by artifacts of her. Throughout his communion with death he had unconsciously pulled one after another toward him – and just as unconsciously had pushed them away. As he shook off Marci's fatal journey he looked down at the single object that remained – their portable phone and cradle. Dazed by the trip and the mysterious appearance of this forgotten relic he slowly extracted the hand set from its holder and scanned the numerical listing. Every corresponding name belonged to her – her friends, her sisters and finally her mother. Her mother, of course, no longer mattered since she had died eight months before Marci. Actually, no one really mattered since this instrument had been replaced a year before by a different make and model. Hell, he never liked it anyway; he never could connect the buttons with the complex matrix that controlled their functions. His preferences aside, the most damaging information reflected in the roster was the absence of anyone remotely related to him. After all, it had been *their* telephone . . . hadn't it?!!! He must know at least one person deserving a spot on the top ten? Surely he knew somebody?

His mind stretched . . . then slowly limped around the barn and back to where it started. He suddenly brightened. Of course, how could he have forgotten Jeff? Jeff was surely worth a repeat call. As he lingered on that thought the truth slowly leaked out of that balloon.

The truth hurts, even more when delivered with the weight of realty to a spot directly between the eyes. There was *no* friendship with Jeff, there *never* had been . . . . Every contact with Jeff and Donna, no matter how incidental, had been arranged in one way or another by Marci.

But I trusted him with Marci's care, her welfare, and her life . . . .

And that was all true, but had Jeff ever called to talk, to trade golf stories, or just say hello?

He paused to search his memory banks. The return silence came with a deafening thud!

Damn it, there must be someone?!!!

Another pause, another search, and then leeching through the clutter, *Of course, my parents.*

But ever so quickly, *No that won't fly.*

They had been estranged in his early twenties. And five years ago when they had been killed in a head on collision with a tractor-trailer he had refused to attend their funeral. His excuses had been senseless, but no matter, he hadn't cared then and he didn't care now.

His quest was now over. There was nowhere else to look. He'd become a man staring into a mirror – and the only person there was himself!

His head, pushed down by mounting depression, slowly drooped to his chest and then, just as slowly, raised itself and he bellowed, "You are alone you dumb piece of shit . . . and your only friend, your only ally and the only person that ever really cared is dead!"

The tears cascaded down his cheeks as he mourned her . . . and then . . . himself . . . .

Despair must have a bottom? *You would think . . . .*

My guilt must have an end? *Not while there is unwhipped flesh on my back . . . .*

Self-contempt must stop sometime? *When they create a word that fully describes my hatred for myself . . . .*

He roared again, "God damn you Marci! I can't do this alone. I'll never make it without you."

Bill glared at the handset. In this single moment it had become the messenger of his isolation. He snatched it from its base and with the vengeance it deserved he launched the receiver across the attic. It collided with the brick casing of their chimney and rebounded undamaged back to him.

As it wobbled to a stop before him, he exploded, "Christ! I can't even break the fucking phone!"

He reached to launch it again. Suddenly a light on the base blinked on, quickly followed by a dial tone, and just as quickly followed by the ratcheting sound of speed dialing.

He stared at the base, riveted with disbelief as the sequence continued until terminated by the unmistakable tone of connection. With each ring that followed a piece of reality fell away. Just when the weight on his chest threatened to crush him a voice forced its way through the static, "Hello?"

Ripped from his hand by a collection of colliding emotions the phone fell to the floor. Logic told him that an appliance without batteries and disconnected from a source of power for more than a year could not function. Add to that an intelligible word marching through a screen of disassembled noise, well . . . ? But then, he had clearly passed logic sometime back. He was now in another place. A place where . . . *I must be going insane.*

Somewhere in the universe a certain "Mr. Murphy" interrupted a meeting he was having with a group of aligned planets to announce gleefully, "Well, Bill, if you think reality has just made a u-turn then I suggest you grab both cheeks of your ass and hold on tight, because it's just about to get interesting!"

Bill fought to regain control of his ragged breathing. And then, just as his air intake began to level, Mr. Murphy announced with a wink and an impish grin, "Get ready Bill, here comes the fun part!"

As if punctuating Mr. Murphy's pronouncement a second, "Hello?" issued from that distant and muffled source.

Bill eyed the origin of interruption. The receiver wasn't dancing, it wasn't shimmering with some alien light, and it wasn't rocking from side to side. Instead, it just lay there looking back. He reached, but stopped halfway as fear and curiosity wrestled for dominance. His hand, nearly shaking, slowly broke free. As though drawn irresistibly to the flame it closed clammily on this synthetic harbinger.

Bill tried desperately to make a sound . . . any sound, but when your world is crashing around you it's impossible to be heard over the wreckage!

He gaped. More crashing and wreckage!

Forcing its way through the debris came a frustrated inquiry, "Is anybody there?"

Barely audible, Bill asked, "Wh-who is this?"

With a level of annoyance that shattered the static, "What? You'll have to speak up. You might try taking the shit out of your mouth."

The barb focused his reply, "I'm sorry. We have a poor connection."
"Of course we have a poor connection. You're not calling around the block. Are you on a Messenger XD 500?"

"A what?"

With receding patience, "The telephone you imbecile. What kind of telephone are you on?"

Numb and confused Bill searched the receiver for a name. Nothing. He scrambled to retrieve the cradle. There, on the side, "Messenger XD 500 – For those really important calls."

"Yes. But, how did you know?"

"I must be psychic", followed by a satisfied laugh. "I like that, I must be psychic," followed by more laughter. And then, with reconciliation, "I apologize. I just know that's all. For now we'll leave it at that."

"But why did you ask?"

"Why did I ask what? Oh, yeah. Because there's a 'filter' button on the base that should clear some of the static."

Bill searched. There it was, as advertised. He depressed it.

Continuing to shout, he inquired, "Can you hear me now?"

"You can stop shouting, I can hear you fine. Now, who are you?"
With a slight stammer, he asked back, "Wh-who are you?"

"Who is this you say? That's just great! How about, you called me. So, who the hell are you?"

He paused. Something in the tone . . . the attitude . . . but what . . . who? When in doubt, "My name is Bill. No, actually it's William. William Allen. Now, who are you?"

At this juncture our Master of Ceremonies, Mr. Murphy, poked his head from around a distant planet and said, "I thought it was good before, but it just keeps getting better." He grabbed his sides to keep the laughter from giving him a hernia. Then jumping up and down like a mischievous child he announced, "Try to grab something stationary Bill. This train is about to go over the edge!"

The reply from the other end of the connection was filled with agitation, "No. This can't be happening to me."

Bill jolted with recognition. Was this possible? He asked the question, not really wanting the answer, "Edith, is that you?"

A brief pause and then formally, "Yes, Bill. It is indeed your favorite mother-in-law. I thought dying was bad enough. Now, I'm really being punished."

It wasn't the best day in Bill's life when Edith died, but it was certainly one of his favorites. To characterize their relationship as stormy would have been an understatement. For their relationship to have improved to stormy they would have needed to fall in love with each other! Edith disapproved of Bill, no . . . more like, tolerated him! And, she had never missed an opportunity to let him know it.

The best defense is a good offense. Bill launched back, "This must be one of those cosmic jokes that science talks about. Or, maybe *you,* are the cosmic joke that science talks about."

Talk about throwing gasoline on the fire! Edith needed no more prompting, "Bill, you never were a match for me, are you sure you want to start this?!!!"

Bill chuckled as he fired back, "You're right Edith, but now I can hang up on you. I never had that opportunity before. I'm kind of liking it."

The King Cobra would run a distant second to Edith in a spitting contest. She struck, "You degenerate piece of – "

Between 'degenerate' and the multiple choice options that were about to follow, Bill realized a very salient point. What was happening here was waaaaay beyond his ability to comprehend. That said; he had still tripped over a path to the "other side". In his haste to gaff Edith he was jeopardizing the infinite possibilities that lay before him. With that in mind he interrupted, "I apologize Edith. Whatever we think of each other I should be honoring yours and Marci's memories and not picking a fight with you."

Silence. Then, "Rather you mean it or not, Bill, it's nice of you to say. I accept your apology."

They both paused to assay the terms of the peace.

Satisfied they had sealed an unspoken treaty Edith spoke, "All right Bill, why did you call?"

"I didn't call you. This was just some sort of weird mistake. Besides, why would I call, I thought you were . . . ." He stopped before completing the thought. Considering the current circumstances the word he was going to use had no application.

Before he could ponder the alternatives Edith finish his statement for him, "Dead, Bill. Go ahead, you say it. The facts are the facts."

She waited.

He struggled, and then relented, "All right Edith, I give up . . . dead. You died. You're supposed to be dead!"

Condescension laced her rebuke, "That's a brilliant deduction from a self absorbed drunk! Of course I'm dead, we were all at the funeral. I was the block of wax staring up from the casket."

"But I can't be talking to you."

"Right, Bill. What do you think this is . . . a recording?"

"No, but -"

"That's enough. Let's just agree, I'm dead and you *are* talking to me. Okay?"

"But, Edith – "

"I don't know why this is happening any more than you do. That's it! My time is valuable, apparently yours is not. What do you want?"

"I don't want anything. At least I don't think I do. I didn't intentionally call you. I was fooling around with our old portable phone and I guess it somehow dialed you. I'm - "

"You mean the Messenger XD 500?"

"Yes."

"That explains it."

"Explains what?"

"They thought all of those devices had been destroyed. I wasn't thinking earlier when you told me it was a Messenger XD 500. There's your cosmic joke Bill."

"You mean this won't work on any phone?"

"I guess not, no one else is calling me – and if they are they're not leaving messages."

Annoyed by her continual sidestepping he groused, "Is that supposed to be funny?"

She continued digging, "Not if you don't get it."

"Come on Edith, I'm totally confused."

"Join the rest of us non-entities. All I know is there's something about that particular phone that defies the normal space/time continuum. Whatever the hell that means."

"Can you -"

"Don't ask Bill. I hardly passed high school Algebra. How would I know what all of this means? I do know, I'm not supposed to be communicating with anyone from your side. And the longer I'm on here with you the more likely we are to be discovered."

"But I have a lot of questions."

"Does, I don't give a shit mean anything to you?"

"Please, Edith. I -"

"Bill, this call is over. You can try again some other time. There's a lot you need to know. Maybe I'll get a chance to tell you and maybe I won't. Goodbye."

He pleaded, "Edith, don't hang up."

It was no use. The line had dissolved to a hum.

CHAPTER FOUR

Their Ferris wheel bench had stopped one position from the top. Marci loved everything about Ferris wheels, the motion, the tranquility, the openness, the gentle movement of the air, but mostly the ownership of this special space that overlooked *her* piece of the world. Bill sat drinking in every aspect of her, and the moment, as she twisted and turned with childlike glee. Her smiling laughter slowly burned a hole in his heart, overwhelming him with her warmth and love. Jerking abruptly the giant wheel moved them to the summit.

Pointing her finger she excitedly announced,"Oh, Bill. Look, you can see our car down there. And down there you can see the shooting gallery where you won me that Panda Bear. And there, the sunset, the colors are magnificent from this vantage? Oh look, out past the –"

Her litany of observations was interrupted by the violent lurch of their carriage.

Concern filled her question,"What was that Bill?"

"I don't know dear, but I'm sure it's nothing."

Hoping that any action, no matter how ineffectual, would calm Marci he leaned forward and peered down at the structure. His body stiffened with the search, as though doing so would add credence to the endeavor. Then an even more violent lurch shook them. He felt the retaining bar come loose. As he reached to secure her, another jolt catapulted Marci forward. She grabbed the foot rail with one hand and hung in space swinging to and fro with the car. Bill clutched the armrest with one fist and grasped her wrist with the other. He tried desperately to pull her back, but with her weight tilting the car down and forward any attempt at leverage was fruitless.

Her eyes pleaded as she whispered, "Bill, save me."

He began to reach with his other hand, but stopped, they would both go if he lost that anchor.

"Hang on baby. They'll get us down."

"I don't think I can hold on much longer."

"Sure you can. Try for me," he begged, "please."

Slowly, one by one, each of her fingers came free, until she hung by his hand. Bill tightened his grip and began yelling for help, "Help us. Someone, please help us!"

The response came from a very dark place inside his brain, *No matter what you do Bill, you can't save her. You're not strong enough . . . you never have been!*

With that, his fingers began to uncurl from Marci's wrist.

She looked up at him and calmly said, "It's alright Bill, I understand . . . I still love you. Goodbye."

As she fell away he clawed at her image . . . and screamed, "Marci, don't go. Please don't leave me. I can't make it without you!"

He jerked upright, awake, in bed and in the dark, tearing at the vacant space beside him. He continued screaming her name and pleading for her return. The surroundings and consciousness slowly subsided his search. The involuntary opening and closing of his hand became a slow and methodical pounding on the mattress. She wasn't there. She wasn't anywhere he could touch her, hold her . . . love her. Drenched by the pool of his own sweat he was suddenly, and completely, aware of the concept of "shadow pain". He now knew its magnitude, its insanity . . . its excruciating throbbing. He had heard amputees speak about the torment of reaching to scratch or rub a missing part. Where were the words to describe the anguish, the agony, of reaching to embrace an *entire* person that wasn't there! He crashed back on the bed and began to sob. He did so until the sobbing turned to uncontrollable coughing. Sides aching, he finally rose and squelched the fit with a glass of Scotch and a very cold shower.

~~~~~~~~~~~~~~~~~~~~~~~~~~~~

He sat, legs crossed dutifully, on the attic floor staring at the Messenger XD 500. He had done so every day for the two weeks since his conversation with Edith. Each day he had jabbed the speed dial button for her. And, each day, the only return had been the deafening drone of silence. He was becoming convinced - the thought of being convinced caused him to pause with amusement. After his emotional gauntlet with Marci's death and his visit to "The Twilight Zone" with Edith, he was convinced of nothing. *Actually,* he thought, *I am convinced of one thing. And what is that?* he asked, *That I shouldn't be convinced of anything.* This convoluted piece of logic caused him to laugh out loud. *And I thought I'd never laugh again. Isn't it wonderful what a little psychosis can do for the disposition?* He rephrased the image to read, *I think I'm becoming convinced that my conversation with Edith was no more than a combination of too much Scotch and a desperate need for absolution.* He paused to reflect and then continued, *My God, a rational thought, maybe there's hope yet.*

He closed his eyes as his mind gently massaged the meaning of this notion. After several minutes he slowly lifted his eyelids and smiled to himself. As if decibels of sound would add credence he announced to the room with satisfaction, "I believe, Bill, you have just turned a corner. And to continue hoping there's someone at the other end of that phone is exactly that, just hope. It was simply a delusion and to cling to the idea that it was something else will only defer your need to move forward." He was finally free of the emotional straightjacket. With added decibels he continued to exorcise his demons, "You're going to put that phone back in the corner and leave it there. Let it be one of the loving reminders of Marci. Stored, as they all should be, in their appropriate order of importance."
~~~~~~~~~~~~~~~~~~~~~~~~~~~~

He hadn't felt this good in months. Hell, maybe never. He rose with purpose. His legs however, weren't sure they approved of Bill's abrupt change in position. Their indecision caused him to stumble, lose his balance, and kick the Messenger XD 500. The receiver bounced from the cradle and stared back from the floor. Perturbed by his loss of balance Bill reached for the device. As his fingers closed around it, the dial tone came on and it began the sequence of speed dialing!

His breath caught as he froze, *Please, don't do this to me. Not again. I'm not sure I can take it.*

That certain Mr. Murphy stuck his head out from behind the retired grandfather clock and mischievously proclaimed to the throngs following Bill's progress, "Come on Bill. Let's have a little fun. Besides, too much reality is not a good thing."

Had Bill been privy to Mr. Murphy's little joke he would surely have heaped bodily harm on him. Assuming, of course, Mr. Murphy had something akin to a body, which, he did not. The image of a disoriented Bill stumbling around the universe in search of his body caused Mr. Murphy considerable pleasure. As he disappeared he capped the picture with a self- satisfied grin and wink.

The interval between ringing tones felt like minutes. As each one passed without incident the weight on Bill's chest lightened. His vital signs slowly returned to normal. And then, somewhere in the agonizing space between eight and nine a voice bounced back with annoyance, "What do you want Bill?"

He choked out, "Edith, is that you?"

With contempt she replied, "Whom were you expecting? Let me guess, Santa Claus?"

Edith had always been able to fluster and frustrate him to the point of irritation. It was this irritation that displaced his panic. It was this irritation that displaced his pounding heart and ragged breathing. It was this irritation that cursed his dead mother-in-law and allowed him the ease to confront her, "Why are you doing this to me?"

"As usual Bill you manage to skate right passed the facts. If I'm not mistaken, you called me."

"I didn't really call you. I knocked the phone off its cradle and it dialed."

"Now I'm responsible for your clumsiness."

"Of course not, but . . . the hell with it. I did try and call for the past two weeks, but this was a mistake?"

Contrition softened her response, "I know."

He pressed, "You knew I was calling, and you did nothing. Do you understand what I'm going through?"

"No, Bill, how could I possibly understand what you're going through. You really are a self-centered ass. I'm DEAD Bill! Other than the fact that I don't know where I am, or even what I am, I've got nothing to worry about, but you. So, you'll have to forgive me, you dumb shit, for forgetting how important you are."

Leave it to Edith to go from point A to point B by the most direct route. He really did hate her! She never cared what kind of collateral damage she produced. She reveled in her ability to be snide and hurtful. To be condescending, to be . . . . A thought worming its way to the surface suspended his mental castigation of her. A deep breath fueled its completion. Was it possible that he really didn't hate her, but, in fact, hated himself for not having the balls to stand for his own beliefs? Did he, in fact, respect Edith for that very quality he professed to detest? And, thinking now, despite her rhetoric, had he ever heard her say anything that wasn't factual?

No, I haven't. If you can't take it, it's the truth that hurts, you dummy. He smiled; *here I am, having an epiphany. And it's coming from an argument with a dead person. How screwed up am I?*

With understanding comes civility. He bounced back, "You don't have to sugar coat it Edith, just tell it like it is."

Her reply was a slow and building laugh filled with warmth and recognition, "Touché, Bill."

"It's alright Edith, I deserved it."

"Probably, but not shot from a cannon."

It was his turn to laugh, "Maybe a BB gun in the future. Assuming we have a future?"

"I can't answer that. I'm not sure what's going on here. Oh, I knew about the Messenger XD 500, but I was led to believe that our ability to communicate with your side had been terminated."

"If we can declare a truce I'd like to keep talking to you."

"Alright, we have a truce, but that's the easy part. I'm not sure when we'll be able to talk, if at all. We'll talk when I can, and until we get discovered. How's that?"

"That's fair. But you make it sound rather ominous. What happens if we are discovered?"

"Nothing to you, but I'm not certain about me. This link is clearly some sort of strange anomaly, and though I've never been informed that I can't do this, I'm reasonably sure I'm not supposed to do this."

"I don't want you in trouble because of me. Maybe we should stop now?"

"Bill, I don't need any help from you. I've been in trouble most of my life. I need to rephrase that. I was in trouble most of my life. It's my decision. Unless you prefer to stop now?"

"*Heavens* no." He paused slightly in recognition of his miscue and then said, "Sorry, a Freudian slip."

"I appreciate the good wishes, but that has yet to be determined."

He weighed the words before asking, "You raised some issues earlier; may I ask a few questions?"

"As long as you don't expect answers."

He paused, but let it go, then continued, "Where are you, Edith?"

"I don't know for sure. I think I'm in some sort of holding area."

"Purgatory?"

"I suppose from your frame of reference that would be a reasonable definition, but the rules in your world don't apply here."

"Indulge me."

"Okay."

"Are you in pain?"

"Pain as you know it doesn't exist here . . . punishment does."

"In what sense?"

"Remorse."

His response was painted with speculation, "Remorse?"

"Remorse is the closest word I can think of. Words aren't used here, concepts are."

"Meaning?"

"The American Indians."

Confusion surrounded his simple reply, "What?"

"A single word in most of their languages can express an entire concept. It can express the beauty of a sunset, a sunrise, or the magnificence of a snow covered mountain. It's not the same, but it will have to do."

"I suppose I understand, but how does this relate to you? Is someone punishing you?"

"Yes."

"Who?"

"Me."

"I'm sorry Edith, but you've lost me again."

He could feel her searching in the brief silence that followed. Slowly, with purpose, she spoke, "If you broke your leg, would that hurt?"

"Of course."

"Well, remorse hurts a place deep in your spirit, and it's a pain more excruciating than a broken arm, a broken leg, even a broken back. Confronting yourself and all you've done in your life can be agonizing – and I have nothing to do but confront myself every moment. And no one can hurt you more than yourself."

Finally, something he could relate too. After all he'd done to himself, after all the nightmares, after the daily beatings offered by his subconscious, and after . . . and after . . . and after. He acknowledged, "I think I understand Edith."

Their shared silence was an announcement of their shared understanding.

Bill broke their unique moment, "Are you alone Edith?"

"More alone than you can possibly imagine."

"Will you always be alone?"

"I don't know; I hope not."

"Will you move someplace else?"

"I don't know, but I have this sense that when I've done everything I'm supposed to do here then I'll be permitted to leave."

"You've been there over a year already."

She chuckled before answering, "Time has no meaning here Bill. It's a notion for you and the late Mr. Einstein. To you it's a year. To me it feels like the blink of an eye."

His patience wearing Bill pressed, "Time is more than a notion. How can you measure your existence without it?"

Edith replied in kind, "Bill, you need to accept certain ground rules. If you won't then our conversations are going to be very short. Didn't I just say to you, 'As long as you don't expect answers'?" Her tone changed as though she were speaking to an infant, "If I don't understand, then I can't very well tell you. This is all new to me. It feels like the first step of a very long journey. The problem is, I have no idea where I'm going and what will be there when I arrive."

He relented, "I'm sorry Edith. It's difficult for me to get my mind around what's happening."

"For me too."

He tried again, "You don't know what you are?"

"No."

"What does that mean?"

"I don't have a physical form."

"You don't have a body?"

"No."

"What do you look like?"

"Nothing either one of us would recognize.

"That's double talk."

"You think so? Let's try it this way. If you discovered a brand new color, what would it look like?"

He smiled. He had her now . . . or did he? How could you describe something "brand new" in any terms other than those that currently exist – and how could existing descriptions shape a totally new hue. There in lies the rub. He reached with his imagination. It simply wouldn't stretch far enough. He lost as much imaginary ground as he gained. Just short of putting a knot in his brain he stopped, shook his head and surrendered to Edith's assertion.

"You win. It seems an impossible task at best."

"Shazam! I wish I'd thought of that." She changed gears, "Our time is getting short, is there anything else for now?"

"When I told you that I had tried calling for two weeks with no success and that this time I knocked the phone off the cradle you said you knew. I assume you knew that I'd called because of an alert system?"

"That's correct."

"But when you said you knew did that also mean that you knew I had kicked the receiver off the cradle?"

"Yes."

"Can you see into this world?"

"Not seeing as you know it, but more of an awareness of action."

"And that's permitted?"

"Yes."

"I would think that intrusion would be out of bounds."

"It's not."

"Why not?"

"Part of my remorse gauntlet is the ability to review those people and events that shaped my life."

Bill pondered the ramifications of her statement and then skated out onto the ice, "You can watch anything?"

"Not watch Bill. I told you; aware is the closest I can come to describing the ability."

"Watch, aware, whatever you call it; you are still able to view whatever you want?"

"Alright have it your way. Yes, I can watch whatever I want."

He had arrived at the thin ice. He wasn't sure he could ask his next question, but then, he wasn't sure he could not. With considerable discomfort he inched forward, "Did you watch Marci and I making love?"

She responded snidely, "If that's what you'd call it?"

He launched back, "What does that mean?"

"Simply, you weren't very good at it. So, in my opinion it's a stretch to call it lovemaking."

"That's not fair to Marci, Edith."

"I didn't say Marci, Bill"

With his ego crashing through the ice he fired back, "What the hell are you implying Edith?"

"Marci must have really loved you to put up with your brand of 'lovemaking.'"

"She never had any complaints."

"Try reading between the lines. I just said, 'she must have really loved you.'"

He stammered to defend himself, "I don't think that's fair. Besides, -"

Edith cut him off, "Relax, Bill. You don't need to defend your wounded manhood to me. I wouldn't have put up with your lack of ability, but I'm not the issue, she was. She must have been satisfied, and I use that term loosely, but it was what she felt that counted. And, I only watched one time. It was less than exciting, and not worth watching again."

The next question begged to be asked. With his ego crumbling around him he crawled forward, "Are you still watching me?"

"Occasionally."

"Have you watched me when I'm alone?"

She chuckled, "Yes, Bill. I'll save you the effort. I've watched you masturbating."

"Damn you, Edith. Is that how you get your kicks, spying on people?"

"No. I only watched that once too. You're not very good at that either. Although, you are better at that than you were with Marci."

His anger red lined, "You antiquated voyeur. What gives you the right to look over my shoulder?"

With a hint of contrition, but just a hint, Edith said, "I wasn't exactly looking over your shoulder, but I apologize. I meant nothing by it. There's nothing to do here but examine myself. Hell, I'd watch grass grow to have something to do . . . anything to do. It won't happen again . . . I promise."

He relented, "Alright, Edith. Thank you."

Given an opening, Edith felt compelled to keep turning the screws. She impishly countered, "Of course, you're going to have to trust me when I say I'll stop peeking."

"Damn you, Edith."

"Relax, Bill. I'm just pulling your leg, or some other appendage you would like pulled."

She punctuated her comment with a giggle.

With his embarrassment about to stop his breathing he replied meekly, "Please, Edith. I feel bad enough."

"All right, I'll quit. What's next?"

He stopped to shape his next question. Everything until now had only diverted them both from the only question that was worth asking. His jaws tightened as he pushed the words past his lips, "Where's Marci?"

"Bill, I have to go."

He now demanded, "Damn it, Edith. Where is Marci?"

"Sorry, Bill. Next time."

"Please, Edith. I need -"

His plea was amputated by a muffled click followed by a distinct hum.

He stared at the mouthpiece momentarily before replacing it. He'd been so close to answers about Marci. Edith knew what he needed, why was she toying with him? His helplessness overtook him as he dropped his face into the palms of his hands and began to cry.

CHAPTER FIVE

His car drifted to a stop in the garage. He poked the door closer on the visor. As it began unwinding its way to the floor he attempted to rub the fatigue from his face and neck. It had been a week since his go-round with Edith. He had tried every day to open that channel, but she wasn't answering. The way she broke off the call just as he asked about Marci had left him confused, frustrated, and angry. Either way, the dull ache that circled his head had gone from an occasional visitor to a chronic companion. He wasn't sure if it was stress associated with Edith or the continued price of too much Scotch. He had toyed, hopefully, with the notion that a serious medical condition was generating his discomfort. After discovering Edith the thought of another place, any place, other than here, intrigued him. He had finally decided that his misery deserved more time for cultivation, and a welcome illness offering a reasonably quick end would leave too much flesh on his psyche.

Oh well, the immediate solution to this dilemma was waiting in his liquor cabinet. He dragged himself from the car and fumbled the key into the lock. With more effort than it should have required he negotiated the door and entered. The darkened interior that greeted him suspended his movement.

He straightened, *where are the kids?* He strained, then, *they're at Jeff and Donna's where you took them yesterday. Remember dumb ass, everyone decided you needed a couple of days to yourself. Time to clear your head and all that stuff.* He smiled, *I guess everyone was right.*

But wait, when no one was going to be home he always left two lamps on a timer. One might have gone out, but what are the odds of two going out at the same time? Pretty high he'd bet. His breath caught. He reached to engage the mudroom wall switch, someone yelled from inside his head, "Stop! There may be someone on the other side of the light. If there is, you know the house in the dark . . . they won't."

The conference with himself over, he prepared for stealth. He opened and closed his eyes several times to adjust to the low light level.

Satisfied with that decision, he whispered to himself, "That's better."

His brain was prepared to play Ninja Warrior but he wasn't sure his body was. He made the first step; actually it was more of a slide than a step. Secure with this attempt he began moving through the mudroom and into the kitchen. Halfway across the kitchen he paused. Could someone else hear his heart? He could not only hear it, he could feel it trying to escape through his rib cage. And his breathing matched the intensity of his pulse.

All right, calm down. Maybe you should back out of the house and call the police.

This alternative made perfect sense, and the old Bill would have retreated instantly, but this Bill was trying to be someone new . . . someone different . . . someone better!

Two deep breaths later and his heart stopped pounding and his air intake became normal.

Smugly he thought; *that's better. I can do this.*

He inched successfully through the kitchen and into the family room. With each advancing move his fear of the unknown lost ground to the thrill of the hunt. He began to search all the spy novels he had read for his next "smart" option. Amidst the brilliance of all those "novel" ideas came a very simple, but effective alternative. He would move to a corner of the room, sit down on the floor, and wait. From that inconspicuous vantage he could hear and, or see anyone moving through the house. He dropped to his hands and knees and crawled to the nearest corner giving him a protected view of his surroundings. Pride filled his lungs as he pulled himself to a sitting position, crossed his legs and began to watch. How long had it been since he had formulated a viable thought and then put it to work. He couldn't remember, but it sure felt good. It had been some time since the blood coursed through his veins with purpose.

He waited. His internal clock sounded like Big Ben and tolled just as slowly. Suddenly the lamps in the family room flashed their arrival. The burst of light overpowered Bill's eyes. He blinked several times before he could focus.

"Hello Bill. Why are you on the floor in the corner? And why have you been skulking around your own house?"

His eyes followed the voice to one end of the sofa. They shot just as quickly to the other end, where another, "Hello Bill", resided.

Sitting comfortably, legs crossed, were two beautiful women dressed in gun-metal trench coats. They would have been bookends except for the fact that one was blond and the other had coal black hair. Under other circumstances his libido would already have been in overdrive. Under these circumstances however he was less than aroused and more cautious. These two stunning creatures were Marci's younger half sisters - Pamela and Patricia! They were Edith's daughters from her second marriage. They were separated in age by two years and nearly ten years younger than Marci. He had not seen them since Marci's memorial service. He couldn't remember how long it had been before that. Marci had rarely spoken to them or seen them, and after Edith's death that minimal contact had shrunk even further.

"Are you going to answer my question?"

"I'm sorry Pam, what was the question again?"

"Why are you sitting on the floor in the corner? And why are you skulking around your own house?"

"I guess I do look pretty foolish."

"Just a bit."

"Well, when I entered a dark house I became concerned. I usually leave a couple of lamps on a timer. Anyway, I wasn't sure who, or what, might be waiting for me."

Pam smiled and said, "Now it's our turn to apologize. We turned the lamps off. We hadn't seen you for some time and just wanted to surprise you. Obviously we surprised you. Almost to the point of heart failure."

"Not quite heart failure, but you certainly got my attention."

They all laughed.

His curiosity showed through his query, "Now, to what do I owe this unexpected pleasure?"

"Please get up. It's a little disconcerting talking to you when you're on the floor, particularly in your own home."

"I don't know. I was beginning to enjoy it down here."

Grins all around.

He stood and moved to an armchair facing them. Before he could sit, Pam rose, took his hand and began leading him to a position on the couch.

Bill stopped and with some resistance said, "This chair is fine Pam. I'd feel more comfortable over here."

With a smile that would melt stone she answered, "Please, Bill, indulge me. It's more homey with you here between us."

"But, Pam -"

Her hurt expression cut him off. "Please, Bill."

He moved forward obediently and seated himself.

Pam sat down and with that same disarming smile said, "Thanks, Bill. That's much nicer."

He was, ever so slightly, being undermined. He couldn't ignore it and needed to take control of wherever this might be going. With formality he asked, "All right Pam. What brings you here?"

Sensing his change Pam replied, "I apologize Bill, this must seem rather clandestine. We show up without so much as a call, enter your home without an invitation, and conveniently neglect to explain why. You have every right to be concerned, upset even. Can we start over?"

She certainly seemed sincere. Bill nodded his concurrence.

She continued, "We hadn't seen or talked to you since Marci's service. I must admit we're a little guilty at not offering any help. Be it moral support if nothing else. We are family and we should have done more. Well, we're here now to see if there's anything we can do. We realize we're late with the offer, but we hope you'll overlook that, put it behind us, and let us do something."

He softened. "Thank you, Pam." Then turned to confirm; "Thank you, Pat."

As he looked at Pat, his subconscious took a step back. Had she moved closer, or was his imagination getting ahead of him. Oh well.

"There must be something we can do Bill?"

Before he could respond to Pat, Pam put a hand on each shoulder and turned him back toward her. "Yes, Bill. There is surely something we can help you with."

Imagination or not, Pam's thigh was now resting against his. Before that had registered he felt Pat's thigh against his on the other side.

Pam's tone was warm, inviting, as she pressed, "We would be glad to fix you a meal from time to time. Maybe come over and clean the house. We would even be happy to baby-sit the kids. After all, you do need some time to yourself. We just want you to know that we're here for you Bill."

Coinciding with the completion of her statement Bill felt a hand come to rest on each thigh. His temperature rose markedly as his libido made its presence "felt".

Something Pam had said, but what? He needed to be more alert. Some detail underneath demanded his attention. He strained. He couldn't find it.

"Please, Bill there must be plenty of ways we can help you." And with a very provocative softness she closed, "We'll do anything."

He struggled to regain control, but his stammering hardly made the forceful response he was after, "Th-th-there's really nothing you can do. I mean, I appreciate your offer, but I'm seeing to everything. Besides, it keeps me occupied."

Pam nodded to Pat and they rose together, as though choreographed, turned to face him and then began unbuttoning their coats. They opened them in unison and let them slide sensually to the floor.

Bill's mouth dropped open and his eyes widened. Both wore identical outfits, though the term "outfits" hardly did them justice. He could have held each of the ensembles in the palm of his hand. They stood, hands on hips, flaunting see through lace bras, lace thongs, matching garter belts and stockings, and spiked high heel shoes. The only difference was the color. Pam was in blood red and Pat in powder blue!

He looked from one to the other. Each was her own testimony to America's advanced design capabilities and the eroticism of structural engineering. Their form and proportion would have made Michelangelo proud. And, Bill had no doubt that their function would surpass their anatomical statement.

Pam invited his endorsement, "Well, Bill, what do you think?"

Hell, he couldn't think! He was being overwhelmed by months of forced abstinence. Moreover, the blood his brain needed for rapid, decisive thought was being diverted to another body part!

"I'll take your silence as a hearty approval."

He could only nod his head loosely. He felt like some mutated form of bobble headed doll.

"Which color do you like the best? We guessed at your favorite."

More nodding.

She scolded him coyly, "Well, Bill, which do you like?"

His response staggered past his lips, "I like them both."

"That answer won't make you any enemies. But then, as you can see there weren't any enemies here to start with."

With that Pam and Pat sat down on each side of him and snuggled playfully against his hips.

He had to think. Something Pam had said was the key to where this was going, but what? Between the pressure of trying to decode her words and that brain, blood, other body part issue he couldn't focus. He knew the end game was not going to be a good place. His only immediate hope was separation. He began to rise from the couch. Pam swung her leg across his thighs and straddled his waist. She then pushed his shoulders back against the cushions and kissed him. While her tongue probed his mouth Pat's tongue was licking his neck and ear. What resolve he maintained was very quickly losing the battle to two determined half naked women.

Hell, he thought, *lay back and enjoy it. You can sort it out later.*

In the next instant his shirt was off and his pants were being unzipped. Just as his pants past his knees the house phone rang. The interruption jolted Bill. It then rang several times in quick succession and the bell tone seemed noticeably louder than normal.

It wasn't requesting his attention; it was demanding it.

Bill complied, "I have to answer that."

Pam whispered, "No you don't. It can wait."

"No it can't."
He pushed the girls aside and began pulling his trousers up as he rose.

Pam cooed at him, "Not now Bill. We have a lot of surprises in store for you."
Without response he moved toward the receiver. He wobbled at first and then regained his balance. He looked over his shoulder at Pam and Pat. They were wearing their garter belts and stockings, nothing more.

You are a very stupid man, he thought.

That assertion accepted, somewhere deep inside he knew there were forces pulling him in many different directions. He had past free will shortly after he'd entered the house and was powerless to resist these influences. Each chime pulled him further from his erotic fantasy and plunged him deeper into reality. As he plucked the instrument from its base he shook his head as though casting off the last remnants of a heavy anesthetic.

"Hello."

Nothing. Actually, it was less than nothing. It was a deafening silence and it attached itself to his soul! In this moment he understood the crushing magnitude of the word VOID! It consumed all thought and all self control. He stood momentarily on the edge of an infinite abyss. Then suddenly, from the darkness came an avalanche of snapshots - each one of he and Marci - one scene hardly arriving before being replaced by another. After what seemed like a thousand offerings the process began to slow, each picture pausing long enough for recognition. Then, after a couple dozen more images the sequence stopped. There, hanging just inside his eyelids was a scene of Marci in a hospital bed. She came to life and began talking. At first she was inaudible, but slowly the sound increased until Bill could understand what she was saying.

"What ever happens, don't let my father, or my sisters, have the children. You must protect them. And if something happens to you, make certain your brother or Jeff and Donna get them."

Marci continued talking but the sound became inaudible again. After several moments the volume resumed and she was saying, "Promise me. Please promise me . . . on your Mother's grave."

He entered the scene and began to speak, "All right Marci. Your Father and Sisters will have nothing to do with our children. I swear it . . . on my Mother's grave."

His internal screen went blank and the phone went to dial tone.

There it was, that single piece of data that couldn't make it through his over stimulated body part. Of course, two beautiful naked women didn't help. But then, they weren't supposed to help. That was their intention. If it hadn't been for intervention, which he assumed came from the other side; he would surely have forgotten Marci's warning and fallen victim to this trap. Now, how to extricate himself from this snake pit?

There was a line credited to a famous comedic pair that outlined this situation perfectly. He substituted his name and paraphrased, *"Here's another fine mess you've gotten me into Bill."* He smiled as he rebutted himself, *"It really wasn't me; it was that brain, blood, other body part thing that caused all the problems!"*

Bill was off balance and shaken by Marci's sisters, but energized by the mystery confronting him. Marci had shared her concern, but not the ominous nature of this situation. Was she that fearful of his ability to act responsibly and decisively? Was she that certain he would not be the hunter, the protector the family required? Whatever the reasons, his communion with this puzzle would have to wait for a more contemplative time. Right now, he had bigger fish to fry, like how to avoid be eaten alive by these two waiting piranha?

He returned the handset to its home and inhaled deeply. Thanks to a metaphysical jab in the ribs he was now clearheaded. Clearheaded, or not, he still needed a plausible exit strategy.

As if offering an answer to his question the phone rang again. This time the chime was normal in volume and duration. Against the first ringing pattern this one seemed to Bill to be almost thoughtful. He reached for the handset. As his hand closed around the device an idea began to germinate.

"Hello."

Again there was nothing, but this time the nothing was serene. From this tranquil background a viable diversion appeared.

As Pam and Pat watched and listened, Bill launched his acting career with a troubled note, "Yes?"
He nodded to fill in the other side of this nonexistent conversation.

He resumed, more troubled, "Yes. Is she all right?"

More nods combined with a strained expression.

Now with urgency, "No. No. I understand, I'll be right there. Thank you."

He hung up and moved swiftly to the now seated Pam and Pat. He retrieved his shirt and began putting it on as Pam quizzed softly, "What is it Bill?"

"The first call must have been a wrong number, there was no one there. The second call was from the couple that is watching Bill Jr. and Molly. Molly seems to be ill. They're not sure what it is, or how serious. I'm sorry ladies, but I really must go."

This time Pat interjected, "But Bill, we were ready -"

"I know, believe me I know, and I'm sorry, but I've got to see to Molly."

They stared back.

As a conciliatory afterthought he added, "I don't know how long I'll be. Hopefully, we can resume where we left off some other time. I'll call you."

They could only watch as he finished composing himself and prepared to leave. He marched toward the kitchen. From over his shoulder came Pam's question, "What should we do about the house?"

"Just lock up when you leave. Oh yeah, please leave a lamp on. Thanks."

He was through the kitchen, almost to the garage when a voice found him from behind, "We hope Molly's okay."

He issued a loud, "Thanks," as he closed the door behind him.

He started the car and left his house and driveway quickly behind. Several blocks away he allowed himself a deep breath. What he needed now was time to think, time to sort through the events of this evening. What it all meant and how it was going to shape his and the children's future. Sure he did. Easier said than done. He was exhausted. The roller coaster ride he had just negotiated had left him drained. Instead of long analytical thought he decided he would be better served with a drink . . . maybe two. He hardly had to steer the car, it drove itself from memory to his favorite watering hole.

CHAPTER SIX

Bill's intercom buzzed.

He looked up from the report he was analyzing and punched the speaker, "Yes?"

"There's a Jeff on the phone for you."

"Jeff?"

"He won't give me his last name."

The only Jeff he knew was the Jeff of Jeff and Donna, but he rarely called and had never called the office. There was only one way to find out.

"I'll take it. Thank you, Jane."

A click and he said, "Good morning, Bill Allen."

"Bill, its Jeff."

"Jeff, it is you."

"It certainly feels like it."

It was too early for cute, but he let it go, "No, I mean I almost refused the call. Why didn't you give the receptionist your last name?"

"I should, but sometimes it causes problems for people when I call and say it's Dr. Blake. Pretty soon you've got some kind of a medical issue that you haven't told your associates about and so on."

"I appreciate the concern, but most of the staff here wouldn't notice if I came in with green hair let alone being astute enough to pick up on a possible illness. Anyway, how are you?"

"I'm fine. How have you been doing?"

"Each day is a little better."

"Bill Jr. and Molly seem to be adjusting."

"I hope that's the case. I've tried talking to them and they seem okay, but you just never know."

"Well, at least you're trying. That's all you can do."

Since Marci's death and the constant self-analysis associated with it Bill had little patience for wasted time. God knows he wasted almost all the time he had had with her – and, he hated himself for that!

Following this philosophy, he prodded, "Jeff, I appreciate the small talk, but you never call me at the office. Forgive me, but is there something in particular you wanted?"

A brief silence, Jeff wasn't used to Bill's directness. Then, "Actually Bill, I need a favor."

This must really be something. Bill couldn't remember Jeff asking him for anything. He certainly owed Jeff for the personal care and attention he gave Marci. And the way he and Donna had helped with the children, well . . . . This he could, and would do without hesitation.

"Okay."

"Before you agree so quickly, you might want to hear what it is."

"I'll do it. Assuming, of course, I have the ability."

"You do."

"Then it's settled. What do you need?"

Jeff inhaled deeply, and then spoke, "You remember when Marci was in the hospital?"

"Of course."

"Do you recall a Dr. Findley?"

Bill's face contorted slightly with concentration and then offered, "I can't place him Jeff, but most of the time at the hospital is a blur."

"Do you remember the doctor you discovered treating her after we terminated all treatment?"

"Oh, that Dr. Findley."

"Yes."

"I can see that arrogant piece of shit like it was yesterday."

"Well, he's had a hard-on for me ever since our confrontation. Now, I've got a problem and apparently the good Dr. Findley is behind it."

"He must really like you if he gets a hard-on for you."

"Bill, I'm being serious. That's not funny."

"I thought it made an interesting picture. I guess you had to be there. I know; I'm sorry, what is it?"

"My hospital privileges have been temporarily revoked. Someone filed a complaint and I have to wait for a preliminary board of review hearing to answer it. And, while you wait for the preliminary review your privileges are suspended."

"How do you know it was Findley?"

"Well, I'm not supposed to know. You are only told the nature of the complaint for the preliminary hearing. Then, after that if the board believes there is enough supporting information they will recommend a formal hearing be held. At that time, the actual complaint and the person, or persons, making the complaint is made known. This allows time to gather supporting documentation to defend oneself."

"Have you had a preliminary hearing yet?"

"No."

"Then, how do you know it was Findley?"

"A source on the inside was kind enough to inform me."

"So you believe this is over the way you handled that situation with Marci?"

"I don't know what else it could be. I never interface with him. He's the head of that department. My dealings with oncology and related areas of the hospital are always through staff physicians. That was my first and last exchange with him."

"So, you go to the preliminary hearing and end it. How long before the hearing?"

"That's the problem."

"Why?"

"Normally a preliminary hearing is held within two weeks of the complaint filing. My hearing has been postponed twice and I was told yesterday by my source that it is going to be postponed yet again. These postponements have already caused me to refer more than two-dozen patients to doctors with privileges. If this keeps up my practice will have trouble surviving."

"Can't you just use another hospital?"

"The nearest hospital that I trust my patients with is fifty five miles away. I can't justify that to my patients or myself."

"Well, doesn't the board of review realize what pressure this places on a private practice?"

"I'm sure they do, but when the complaint comes from one of their own, well . . . . The medical profession is a very tight community and hospital staffs are even tighter."

Bill was still no closer to understanding his role in Jeff's dilemma. That frustration tainted his follow on question, "Jeff, I'm very sympathetic to your plight, and heaven knows I would do anything to help you, but I still don't know how I fit into the scheme of things?"

"Well Bill, I know how much you despise Dr. Findley. And, I know how angry you were when he countermanded the order to cease all treatment for Marci. I believe you were prepared to sue him and the hospital over that issue."

"I was."

"I also remember talking you out of it."

"I suppose I talked myself out of it."

Actually, at the time, that situation had allowed Bill to act self important, self-righteous and permitted him to be a martyr at Jeff's urging. He knew inside, he neither had the balls nor the courage for the fight. It was he at his best - take credit, but don't ever extend yourself with action.

He finished with the appropriate concession to Jeff, "But you made perfect sense under the circumstances."

"I was thinking, would you consider threatening a lawsuit against Dr. Findley and the hospital?"

"Toward what end?"

"He might consider dropping his complaint against me in trade for you dropping your proposed lawsuit."

Jeff knew this was asking a lot. They had been friendly over the years, but they hadn't really been friends. He also understood that Bill felt a deep sense of obligation for how he had worked for them during Marci's illness. And, frankly he was playing to some degree on that guilt. His own sense of guilt however required that Bill have an out. Assuming, of course, he chose to take it!

Jeff played his final trump, "I realize this is asking a lot. If you don't care to do this I certainly understand. After all, this is my battle, not yours."

Bill was less than enamored with the idea of taking on the medical profession, but debts were debts. He decided to tweak Jeff a little before signing on, "I thought you took a Hippocratic Oath to heal people, not maim them?"

Jeff measured Bill's comment, and then yielded, "You're right. Deal making and treachery have no place in the medical profession. I'm sorry I asked."

Solemnly Bill closed the case, "You should be." But just as quickly he reopened it with a chuckle and a playful jab, "But I'm not!"

Confused, Jeff fumbled, "What?"

"I think it's a great idea. If I can gaff that son of a bitch and do some good for you while I'm doing it, well that's a very good thing. Where do I sign, and when do I start?"

Jeff's tone echoed his elated surprise, "I don't know how to thank you Bill. I can't tell you how much I appreciate this."

"Just call it partial payback to you, and to Donna, for all the support you've given to Marci and now me."

~~~~~~~~~~~~~~~~~~~~~~~~~~~~~~
~~~~~~~~~~~~~~~~~~~~~~~~~~~~~~

For two days Bill had called Findley's office and left messages for him to please call. Nothing! It was now time to become more forceful.

A very sterile voice answered the call, "Dr. Findley's office."

The other two times Bill had called the office he was convinced that this woman either needed a laxative or had hemorrhoids. Now he was convinced.

"May I speak to Dr. Findley?"

"I'm sorry sir, but Dr. Findley is with patients. May I take a message?"

"My name is Bill Allen. I've left messages the past two days. I wonder if you could tell me when Dr. Findley might be returning my calls?"

With ice sickles poking holes through the words she replied, "Well, sir, Dr. Findley is a very busy man."

"And I'm not?"

"I couldn't answer that sir."

"Of course you can't sweetie."

He could feel her hackles going up through the phone. Which was exactly the effect he wanted.

"I do not appreciate being called sweetie."

"And I don't appreciate being treated rudely, 'sweetie'. I've tried nice, but apparently neither you nor Dr. Findley went to nice school - so, we'll do it your way, 'sweetie'. Tell Dr. Findley, he can either speak to me or, he can speak to my attorney. I'll expect his call by noon tomorrow. If I haven't heard from him I will proceed accordingly."

If tone could kill, her reply would have buried him, "I'll see that Dr. Findley gets your message."

"Thank you, 'sweetie'"

~~~~~~~~~~~~~~~~~~~~~~~~~~~~~~

He entered Findley's office two days later at exactly 5:15 pm. The receptionist looked up from her very formal and very tidy desk.

"Yes sir, may I help you?"

"My name is Bill Allen and I have an appointment with Dr. Findley."

Her eyes widened and her expression soured even more. She scanned the appointment book for the time and name. She was visually disappointed when she found it. She swallowed her ire and said, "Please have a seat Mr. Allen; Dr. Findley will be with you directly."

Bill made an obvious effort to read her nametag and then said, "Danielle, I think we got off on the wrong foot. I'll make you a deal, I promise not to call you 'sweetie' ever again if you'll smile one time."

As she studied him, he winked and gave her a wide grin.

Obviously not the approach she expected. She looked down at her book for a moment. When she lifted her face she was smiling. "How's this?"

"Touché. I knew you had a beautiful smile."

Danielle beamed.

He smiled back and seated himself.

He'd hardly open the magazine when Danielle called to him, "Mr. Allen, Dr. Findley will see you now."

She directed him to an office door marked "Private". Bill thanked her and entered.
~~~~~~~~~~~~~~~~~~~~~~~~~~~~~~

Dressed to the nines with a smock overlay he sat comfortably behind an antique desk. The desk was hand polished oak and considerably larger than utility warranted. Bill smiled to himself at the pretense. Before Marci died, this type of glitter and subtle innuendo would have appropriately impressed him. Now, he accepted it for the statement of intimidation it was meant to be.

Maybe it's a penis thing. He blushed internally at the thought. He had never before allowed himself a free wheeling thought such as this. Was Edith reshaping his personality? Or, was the loss of Marci teaching him to meet life and its situations head-on?

Bill's temporary preoccupation had obviously gotten Findley's attention. His question indicated the concern, "Mr. Allen, is something wrong?"

Bill snapped back and focused on Findley, "I'm sorry, something I forgot to do just came to me."

"Do you need to make a call?"

"No, no. Thank you."

As he refocused on Findley he couldn't think of anything but his desk and the possible connection to his penis. *That's just great Bill. Now when you look at this man all you can see is a penis. You're becoming a very dangerous man.*

"Are you sure you're all right Mr. Allen?"

"I'm sorry Dr. Findley, I'm fine now."

"Good, now what brings you to my office with the threat of an attorney?"

No wasted time here, right to the point. Bill liked that.

"There are actually two situations I'd like to discuss with you. One concerns my late wife, Marci Allen, and the other concerns Dr. Jeffrey Blake."

Dr. Findley's expression darkened as he replied, "Well, why don't we discuss the one requiring an attorney first?"

"Very well. As you may, or may not, remember you treated my wife briefly just prior to her death."

"Frankly, I did not recall her, but my staff searched the records and refreshed my memory."

"Good, then you should know that during your treatment of her there was some question as to whether you actually had the authority to do so."

Findley took a deep breath and humbly replied, "Mr. Allen, it is true that in my zeal to fight disease I sometimes overstep the boundaries. And, in your wife's case my records would indicate that I did indeed do that - but I can assure you there was no ulterior motive other than my belief that a possible defense could be mounted. I deeply regret any additional pain or confusion my actions may have caused."

Bill studied Findley's face as he analyzed the value and intent of the statement.

Damn, he thought, *I almost think he means it. Besides, when was the last time I heard a physician admit culpability for their actions? Hell, when was the last time anybody heard that!*

Rather Findley meant it, or not, had nothing to do with the matter at hand. Plus, he's an intelligent man and he knows, by the fact that I'm here raising the issue, where this might be going. I can afford to be magnanimous before I drop the other shoe.

"I'm sure you're being sincere when you say these things Dr. Findley, but that doesn't change the facts. Your actions have been clearly documented."

A simple nod was Findley's acknowledgment.

"I'm here to tell you that I'm considering suit against you and the hospital."

Findley raised himself slightly in his chair and said, "I assumed as much, and you can make a very strong case on your behalf. I, of course, would hope that you can be dissuaded from your position, but I certainly understand it. If there was something I could do to change what has happened I would, but if your mind is made up . . . so be it."

Findley began to rise from his chair. Bill halted him with a raised hand and said, "Please Dr. Findley let me finish."

"I'm sorry, I thought you were."

"I said there were two matters. The second concerns Dr. Jeffrey Blake. It is my understanding that a complaint has been filed against him."

Findley eyed Bill quizzically before saying, "That is correct."

"It is also my understanding that you are behind that complaint."

Findley's cheeks reddened as he replied, "I don't know where you get your information Mr. Allen? All information relating to a complaint is confidential until a formal board is convened."

Bill's eyes narrowed to magnify his purpose, "Let's just say, I have my sources. I also believe that the review leading to a formal board examination has been unduly delayed creating serious economic repercussions for Dr. Blake."

"First, I have no control over when, or why, the board meets. Second, whatever the circumstances, no one wishes to cause anyone undue financial problems."

"Well, Dr. Findley, it certainly appears that way to me."

"Mr. Allen you are certainly welcome to believe what you must."

"And, finally, I think this all has to do with the confrontation we had over my wife's care."

His eyes were clear and direct, as he answered, "That is not true."

"With all due respect, that's the only response I expected from you."

"Mr. Allen, all I can do is tell you the truth. If you chose not to believe me there is nothing I can do about it. Unfortunately, any information surrounding Dr. Blake's complaint must remain confidential until it goes to a formal board hearing. It is, of course, possible that the facts will not support moving the issue to a formal hearing, but, again, I do not have the luxury of discussing it."

"A very convenient out Dr. Findley."

"Convenient out or not, those are hospital procedures."

Findley began to rise again. And again Bill's raised hand stopped him, "Please Dr. Findley, I'm not finished."

"What else is there to discuss?"

"Regardless of the truth Dr. Findley I believe I have a way to resolve these two situations. Assuming you are willing to entertain a solution?"

Findley settled back in his chair with resignation and said, "I'm listening Mr. Allen."

"In exchange for you dropping your complaint against Dr. Blake I'm prepared not to pursue any legal action against you or the hospital."

"It's not my complaint Mr. Allen."

Showing his waning patience with Findley's exercise Bill replied, "Whatever, Dr. Findley. Will you accept this offer?"

"Some people might call this blackmail Mr. Allen."

"That's such a nasty term Dr. Findley. Just as many people would call this a mutually beneficial business arrangement. Now that the semantics have been discussed, do we have a deal Dr. Findley?"

"Honestly Mr. Allen, if it were up to me alone your answer would be no. I find this very distasteful, but there are other people involved and I am compelled to present your offer to them."

"Your delicate sensitivity aside Dr. Findley, let's hope that cooler heads prevail."

Findley rose deliberately, extended his hand and said curtly, "This meeting is over Mr. Allen. Someone will be in touch regarding this matter."

Bill refused Findley's hand. Allowing that there was only one gentleman there. He just wasn't sure which one it was. He punctuated the deterioration of the conversation with a smirk, "Don't take long Dr. Findley, I may change my mind."

Bill left Findley's office and walked through the reception area. He was almost out the door when, from over his shoulder, there came an unexpected voice, "It was a pleasure meeting you Mr. Allen. Have a nice day."

He turned back. Awaiting him was the smiling face of his latest acquaintance.

"Thank you Darlene. You have a nice day too."

As he closed the outer door behind him he thought, *I wish I had another reason to come back. That's a smile worth getting to know better.*

~~~~~~~~~~~~~~~~~~~~~~~~~~~~~

The intercom buzzed on Bill's desk.

"Yes?"

"There's a Mr. Keller on the phone. He said to tell you he represents the hospital."

"Thanks Jane, I'll take it."
~~~~~~~~~~~~~~~~~~~~~~~~~~~~~

It had only been one day since he had met with Findley. Whatever their response, they were anxious to move forward. Bill composed himself, poked the outside line button and in his best business voice said, "Bill Allen here Mr. Keller how may I help you?"

"Mr. Allen, I'm an attorney, a to the point attorney. After careful deliberation, my clients have decided to accept your offer."

"A to the point attorney. That's a pleasant surprise Mr. Keller. I'll be just as brief. We have a deal."

"Thank you Mr. Allen. There'll be some papers to sign. I'll forward them to you with appropriate instructions. If you have any questions my office address and telephone will be on the letterhead. Please feel free to contact me. Will there be anything else?"

"No Mr. Keller, thank you. It's a pleasure doing business with you."

"Likewise Mr. Allen. Have a nice day."
Dial tone.

Bill laced his fingers behind his neck, tilted back in his desk chair, put his feet up on the corner of his desk and then crossed his ankles. He stared at the ceiling and announced with deep satisfaction, "God that felt good. I skewered Findley and helped pay a debt. One for the good guys Marci. Yes sir, one for the good guys."

CHAPTER SEVEN

It had been eight days since the excursion with Pam and Pat. In between Bill had dealt with Findley and attempted several times each day to reach Edith. Nothing. Between her elusive reaction when he'd asked about Marci and his need to understand how Pam, Pat and the kids were all connected he desperately needed answers - and his only quick source of information was Edith. Of course, if she would not, or could not, speak to him then he was left with a long involved treasure hunt for information.

The kids were at Jeff and Donna's. He had slugged down a couple of Scotches and now sat cross-legged on the attic floor. He stared at the Messenger XD 500. It seemed to be staring back. After several moments, with his courage as high as it was going to get and the Messenger XD 500 winning the staring contest, Bill picked up the receiver. Before he could engage the speed dial function it came alive and chimed. The surprise nearly jarred the instrument from his hand.

He punched the talk button and said, "Hello."

"Hello, Bill, it's Edith."

It was his turn to gouge back, "Oh, I thought it was Santa Claus."

"That's good Bill. I'm surprised you can remember my comment about Santa Claus considering all the Scotch you're consuming."

Before the recent events, and his banter with her, he would have leapt to defend himself. Now, with an acceptance of the absurdity of their connection and his conquest of Dr. Findley, his growing confidence accepted in stride Edith's personal thrusts.

"I figure Edith that talking to you when I'm half in the bag makes us equal."

"Well now, have we been reading up on the art of repartee?" Before he could respond she pushed the knife one notch deeper, "I apologize, Bill, I may have crossed your semantics threshold. Repartee means a quick, witty reply."

"That's -"

She sliced through his response with a final push of the knife, "Of course, I'm giving you credit for being able to read, understand what you've read, and then put into practice a series of complex thoughts."

Surrender was the only viable out, "All right Edith, I give."

Edith had never been able to accept victory graciously, "Thank you Bill, for knowing when you're outmatched."

At this point he was ready to hang up, but among the lessons he seemed to be learning daily was the one that said, "Stifle your anger and frustration in favor of the goal." This was valuable at any time, but when dealing with Edith, well . . . it spoke for itself.

"Edith, the phone rang before I tried to call you."

"I knew you were trying to reach me so I thought I'd surprise you."

"You certainly did that, I almost dropped the receiver."

"I know you've been calling what can I do for you."

Frustration showing he said, "If you know I've been calling why aren't you answering?"

"Frankly, Bill, sometimes I don't want to talk to you. There are other times I can't talk to you. Bottom line, I don't have to talk you under any circumstances if I chose not to. I understand that knowing I exist opens an infinite number of doors, and that each door leads to an infinite number of questions. Almost all of those doors are closed to both of us. I'm simply not permitted to comment on most areas that might interest you. That assumes, of course, that I have the information you're seeking, and, in most cases I don't. Where I do, I will do my best to accommodate your query. There are ground rules however that must be honored. As I've said before, I'm probably in trouble for talking to you at all and I'm not going to make it worse by violating rules I think apply. What I'm trying to say is that we're both in uncharted territory and you're not making it any easier by hounding me."

He knew she was right, but being this close to answers about Marci only magnified the weight of his quest. He needed her more than she needed him. To bypass that basic fact would have been, not only arrogant, but stupid. After digesting her words he bowed to her and the process. Proud of himself for another learning moment he replied humbly, "You're right Edith, but then, you usually are. I'll move at whatever direction and speed you dictate."

"Thank you, Bill."

There was silence on the line, almost as though she was composing herself.

He was just about to speak when Edith continued, "Before you ask, I am fully aware that I sidestepped your question about Marci last week. I couldn't have answered your questions then. I believe I can answer some of them now. If you like we can try again."

Excitedly he asked, "Is she there with you?"

"No."

"Where is she?"

"I don't know for sure."

"I don't understand."

"It's going to sound like double talk, but if she's not here then she's someplace else."

He bit his tongue and pressed on, "A worse place?"

"No, I believe she must be in a better place."

"Why?"

"Remember me telling you that once I accomplish all that I believe I am to accomplish here then I thought I'd move somewhere else."

"Yes."

"I think this is where you start. And, if she's not here then she has already passed this test to move on."

"But, she died after you did?"

Rancor and frustration vibrated Bill's ear as Edith answered, "I'm completely aware of that Bill."

"But you said that's where you start?"

Her reply was not based in comfort, "That's correct. This is where I started. She apparently was permitted to bypass this place. Before you ask, she must be ahead of me."

"I don't understand Edith."

Now his ear vibrated with torment, "It means Bill that Marci must be a better person than I am. No, Marci *is* a better person than I am. She always has been. Actually, she's always been a better person than you and I put together. And that's why I believe she is in a better place."

Edith was right . . . yet again. And this knife, turned slowly in his heart. This statement crushed him with Marci's absence, what must it be doing to her Mother. What must Edith feel to realize that the student had passed the teacher? In that instant, he recognized the anguish and humiliation Edith was meant to endure.

His head and spirit sank as he said, "I'm sorry, Edith."

As usual, Edith rebounded with spunk, "Whatever doesn't kill you makes you better," she chuckled as she continued, "and, since I'm dead already, I don't have to worry about being killed. I guess that means I'm going to get better."

Bill fumbled with his response, "I only meant -"

"I know, Bill. You don't have to explain. I appreciate what you're saying."

He moved to divert this line of discussion, "Can you communicate with her?"

"No."

"Do you know why?"

"I believe communication here happens top to bottom. Since I seem to be on the bottom then I must wait for someone to contact me. If I'm right, and Marci has passed to a higher location, then until she chooses to contact me there will be no conversation."

"But, you called me?"

"Based on what I just said, think about what you just said."

"Edith, my head is already reeling without you tossing brainteasers at me."

"You need to have some understanding of what you and I are dealing with. It helps both of us if you can figure out some of it on your own."

"I'm not sure I have the head for this."

"Suit yourself."

He waited hopefully for her to relent and explain.

Nothing.

He implored her, "Edith, please."

Nothing!

"Are you going to talk to me?"

"No."

More nothing.

"All right, Edith, I give up."

"Well?"

"Let me see. You can't communicate vertically, but you can communicate with me; therefore, our communication must be horizontal. Is that correct?"

"Yes."

The shadow of an unnerving thought began to take shape. He asked tentatively, "Does this mean that this world is below yours?"

She confirmed casually, "Or less."

"Less?"

"Remember, communication here occurs downward. I just called you , so . . . ."

"If you're right, then we are pretty low on the food chain. Not a comforting thought."

"True, but Marci has moved higher. There must be hope, even for a couple of escargot like us."

"Sounds like we're just a couple of snails rather than escargot."

"Speak for yourself. I prefer to think of myself as a cut above the norm,"

The irony of her comment caused Edith to laugh, quickly followed by his own accepting chuckle.

Lighter moment behind them, Bill resumed the inquiry, "Was that you calling the other day when I was with Pam and Pat?"

"Yes."

"Why didn't you speak to me?"

"I'm unable to talk on the phones in your world."

"You speak on this one."

"We don't know where this telephone came from, but I can guarantee it wasn't your world."

"But, you made my house phone ring on two separate occasions."

"Yes. I now know that I can, under the right circumstances, and with considerable effort, cause certain physical actions to occur in your world. That ability, however, is very limited, and requires an immense amount of energy."

"You didn't know you could do that?"

"No. Not until that incident."

"Why not?"

"You keep forgetting, this is all new to me, and, I'm learning as I go."

"Were you also responsible for that tidal wave of images that plowed into my brain?"

"Apparently."

"You didn't know you did that?"

"Not until just now."

"You almost knocked me down."

"I don't know when I initiate a mental action here what the consequences are there."

"But you told me you see events here."

"That's true, but I don't know what you're thinking. I don't have that ability. Besides, that will never happen again."

"Why?"

"I didn't know I was flooding you with pictures. It was a fluke. Now that I'm aware that I have that capacity I will never use it again."

"Why?"

"I am not permitted to offer any unsolicited information or direction."

"Why are thoughts any different from activating a telephone?"

"Those images influenced your actions. The telephone did nothing but ring. A chiming instrument can in no way direct your course of action. It might alert you, but you would be on your own to determine a resulting path."

"Even if you gave me pertinent information, why is that so terrible?"

"It has something to do with altering the time line."

"The 'time line'?"

Here was an unexpected visitor. The 'time line'?!!! As if this situation wasn't convoluted enough he was now being introduced to an area of speculative phenomenon that had baffled legitimate science for a thousand years. It had always appeared to Bill that science fiction writers were as close to understanding this theoretical field as were all the "Einstein's" that had ever lived. Now, Edith was offering a reason to believe that this hypothetical bogeyman was actually alive. His ability for logical, rational thought was Neanderthal at best, but even he was fascinated by this impossibility. He pressed forward, gently, "You mean,

as in parallel universe 'time line'? Or, as in the future 'time line?'"
"Please, Bill, I had trouble balancing my checkbook. I have no idea what any of this means. All I know is that if I, in any way, tamper with it, I can cause irreparable damage."

Oh well, he had hoped, but why should he expect Edith to have an answer when Albert Einstein hadn't.

He really needed now to move to the most troubling aspect of his inquiry. He inhaled slowly, and then asked, "What do Pam and Pat have to do with Bill Jr. and Molly?"

"I can't answer that Bill."

"What the hell does that mean? Did you, or did you not, alert me to what Marci had said regarding their contact with the kids?"

"I did."

"Well then, you don't know, or you won't say?"

"I can't say. At the risk of repeating myself for the hundredth time, remember the rules!"

"What do the rules have to do with you answering a question?"

"Everything, if my answer gives you information you can't obtain on your own."

He flared, "Christ, Edith, here we go again with the double-talk."

"Are you chewing gum?"

Now what, he thought.

He had past patience some time back, "All right, Edith, I'll play. No, I'm not chewing gum."

"Well then, that's not the problem."

"Which means what?"

"I thought maybe you couldn't chew gum and think at the same time."

"That's really cute Edith. Throwing insults at me doesn't accomplish anything, other than make you feel superior. Why don't you try explaining whatever you can?"

She backed up, but not far, and chastised him as though he were an inattentive child."Think, Bill. You're not thinking."

He shook his head in an effort to clear the underbrush blocking his concentration. He moved cautiously, but with purpose as he said, "I know you can answer questions because you have."

"Yes."

"But I don't understand why you can't answer questions about Pam and Pat?"

Nothing.

Her silence forced him to focus. The light in his brain flashed on, but dimly, as he asked,"Is it because your answer would have influenced my direction?"

"Yes."

"But you've answered questions about your world."

"That's true."

He paused to merge all the information she'd offered, and then said,"Is that because information about your world won't impact this one?"

"For the most part. There are many questions that I'm free to answer about this world because the answers will have no impact on yours. Questions about yours however are a different matter."

That dim light began to grow brighter as he pressed from a different angle,"Are you required to answer my questions?"

"Yes."

"Truthfully?"

"Yes."

"But you can't give me any direction?"

She brightened as she responded, "Good, Bill. You're almost there."

As though repeating everything aloud would complete the puzzle he recapped, "You must answer my questions truthfully, but you cannot by your answers influence my direction."

He stopped to ponder where he was at and where he was going, but it seemed he had come face to face with a door that would not open. He voiced his frustration, "How is that possible?"

With encouragement Edith replied, "Come on, Bill. You're on the edge."

Her gentle shove spurred him toward the key. It was floating just outside his reach, taunting him with its inaccessibility. His mind stretched, almost to throbbing, and ever so slowly closed around it. Almost gleeful, he spouted, "You can only respond to questions about this world with a yes or no."

With shared glee Edith punctuated his solution, "You got it Bill."

Bill beamed, as though he had just planted his foot on the summit of Mt. Everest. Buoyed by his success he prepared to launch his inquest. He opened his mouth to speak, but before a word could tumble forward the paradox behind his accomplishment rose before him. He had fought to open one door, only to be confronted by a new one. How does one launch an expeditious, well-directed, search for the truth when the forgone answers were simply yes or no? He had just extracted his foot from one pit of quicksand only now to have placed it into another!

He temporarily shut down to calculate his next step.

His delay caused Edith to ask, "Bill, are you all right?"

"Yes, I'm trying to shape my next question."
Her silence signaled her acquiescence to his dilemma.

His next move hovered over the sand. He decided; *what the hell. After what I've been through, a little blood or some lost limbs well feel like a picnic.*

He leapt forward with both feet, "Was Marci's concern about her half sisters and your husband founded?"

"Yes."

"Did Pam and Pat's visit to my home have something to do with that concern?"

"Yes."

Without gauging his next question he asked, "Why did Pam and Pat visit me?"

Nothing.

Oops. He rephrased, "Were Pam and Pat trying to harm me?"

"Didn't look like it to me."

"Come on Edith. You know what I meant."

"Sorry, Bill, but it was a great show while it lasted. It was good for me, how about you? If we weren't dealing with much bigger issues I wouldn't have rung the phone."

"Damn you, Edith."

"I apologize. Please don't begrudge me a little fun. I haven't had any since I got here."

He attempted to best her at her own game, "I suppose you'd be happy if I became a porno star?" He should have known better. Bad idea!

"You'd actually do that for your old dead mother-in-law? I'll take back all the nasty things I've said about you." She chuckled as she continued zapping at him, "That would certainly help pass the time. Oh, that's right, we don't have time here. It would fill in the blank spaces rather nicely." She was now on a roll. Stopping this snowball wasn't going to be easy, "I could also make the phone ring at those poignant, or should I say, climactic moments. I'd be glad to add my little bit for the cause. Or, I -"

He had only himself to blame for this monologue which made it that much more painful. He severed her comedic dialogue with formality, "Edith, please, can't we get back to the matter at hand?"

"Well okay, poopy drawers, if you insist."

He couldn't stand it, he almost shouted, "Poopy drawers? What the hell is that?"

"Do you ever have any fun Bill?"

"Of course I do."

"It must all have been before I died, because I haven't seen any."

"I realize Edith that your definition of fun and mine are probably different – and I'd be very happy to have that discussion with you some other time, but I've made a breakthrough and I'd like to pursue what seems to be a mystery to me and no one else."

With feigned agitation, she said, "Oh, all right, the answer is no."

He blinked his eyes with confusion and said, "The answer to what is no?"

"Your question, Bill."

"What question?"

"Your question about Pam and Pat."

"Damn it, Edith, you've got me so twisted around I can hardly think."

"Good."

He scrambled to regain his footing. Finally his original question squeezed between his anger and exasperation, "You mean the one about Pam and Pat harming me?"

"Yes."

"So, they weren't trying to harm me."

"Yes."

His revisited confusion filtered through his question, "They were trying to harm me?"

"No."

"Well, which is it Edith?"

"Bill, it's not my fault you can't phrase your questions correctly. One last time, 'yes, they were not trying to harm you.'"

Now what. Thanks to Edith, his brain was a pretzel. He stopped to reformulate.

Edith interjected, "Bill, let's stop here."

"But, I have so much more to ask you."

"I know, but you're going to waste precious time attempting to shape questions towards a yes or no answer. Why don't you work on it and we'll start again when you're better prepared?"

She was right. It made him mad when she was right, but it was the best course of action.

"Okay, Edith. I should be ready in a couple of days."

Nothing.

He kicked himself mentally, *remember stupid, there is no time there. That*

means nothing to her.
"I mean I'll call when I'm ready."

"Fine, Bill. We'll talk later." She couldn't depart without a little needle, "In the meantime, let me see some fun from you."

"Sure, Edith. Anything to keep you amused."

She laughed as she disconnected.

CHAPTER EIGHT

It had been four days since his groundbreaking discourse with Edith. Every day since, he had toiled to structure a system of inquiry that would be both expeditious and fact-finding. The more he attacked the problem however, the more entangled he became with its difficulty. The question of format alone was enough to stymie him, but when the issue of brevity was added it was nearly unmanageable. After all, neither one of them knew how long this inter-worldly connection would last. Not only the technical aspects of the link i.e. the power source, whatever the hell that was, and the medium in which the signals were being transmitted, but the issue of discovery as well. Edith had been very clear, if she was discovered communicating with Bill's world the penalties, though undefined, would be far less than desirable. It required him to garner every pertinent piece of information as quickly as possible. He was beginning to feel like the proverbial dog chasing its tail; however, to his way of thinking the dog was closer to achieving its goal than he was to achieving his!

He eased his car into the garage, closed the door and dragged himself toward the mudroom door. Bill opened the door to darkness. He froze!

The children were not an issue. They were with Donna. Jeff was at a medical seminar somewhere in Europe. Who knew; who cared. Donna gladly volunteered to watch Bill Jr. and Molly. "Besides," she had said, "I love kids, and ours and yours all get along so well together. They're really very easy."

Bill would have argued the "easy" part, but not with the person that took that load off his back.

With the children crossed off the concern list he could return to the moment. And, here he was again, faced with the two lights out at the same time probability riddle ... not likely!

Are the sisters here again?

Instead of calling them Pam and Pat he had begun referring to them in shorthand as the "sisters". He could never remember seeing them apart and it seemed to him that when they chose to accomplish something they did so together. Besides, to Bill, they were physically interchangeable. From his last encounter with them he was certain their most sensuous body parts were very definitely interchangeable! That was a vision he would not soon forget.

If they are, Edith will get that x-rated diversion she's after. An encore performance by that tandem would melt the polish off the furniture. Edith can ring every damn phone on the block, it won't matter. Not only do they have twice the moving parts than I'm used to, they move them in such delightful directions. I now know what "silly putty" feels like!

But if it was the "sisters", how did they get in? He'd changed the locks after their last visit.

Well, dopey, you can stand here in the dark with your dick in your hand or you can put one foot in front of the other and find out what's waiting for you.

He took a deep breath and prepared, again, to do his imitation of stealth. He moved through the mudroom and kitchen without incident. With considerable pride he started into the family room. Bill was about to take his second step when, *don't forget you moved that chair to clean a spot on the carpet.* Too late! His foot caught the leg of "that" chair. The tumbling move that ensued would have scored an 8.5 at the Olympics. That is, until he took out an end table, a lamp, and various shapes, sizes, and values of knickknacks. After his collision with the furniture the tumbling move that had started as an 8.5 was downgraded to a .5 and he was disqualified from further Olympic competition!

Bill lay on the floor doing another one of his now famous imitations. This one was his classic variation of the pretzel. He was attempting to rub several throbbing areas of his body at the same time when he spouted, "God damn that hurt!"

The word "hurt" had barely passed his lips when a lamp came on. The temporary blindness that followed only added insult to injury. He blinked his eyes in quick succession to clear the spots, and then scanned the room quickly for anyone or anything else waiting to do him further harm. Sitting in Bill's favorite stuffed armchair sat a man with his hands comfortably clasped in his lap. As he stared with amusement at Bill's sprawled carcass he said, "Are you all right Bill?"

Surprise was quickly replaced by inquiry; then anger as he fired back, "Of course I'm not all right Frank; I could've broken my neck."

Frank chuckled as he replied, "Why didn't you turn on a light?"

"First, why the hell are you sitting here in the dark? Secondly, you might try getting off your ass and helping me up."

Frank moved to accommodate Bill's demand. He assisted Bill to that favorite armchair and then seated himself on the couch.

The questions were lining up as Bill tried unsuccessfully to rub the pain from his body and the mounting anger from his mood. The anger with himself for his swan dive could be dealt with later over a Scotch. His anger with Frank's unannounced and clandestine visit would need more immediate action.

Frank was Edith's second husband and father to the "sisters". He was half a dozen years younger than she. His history prior to entering Edith's life had always been a mystery. He had taken Edith's substantial inheritance from her first husband, Marci's father, and through careful and vigilant investment in the stock market had built a significant fortune. Amassing wealth apparently cancels a mysterious history, because no one seemed interested in Frank's roots after they looked at the family bank account . . . not even Edith!

Frank had always been a little too smooth for Bill's liking. His envy of Frank's financial wizardry and his general distrust of Frank's demeanor had caused Bill on several occasions to remark to Marci, "Wealth and greed have allowed Frank to rewrite his past; or, should I say, cancel it altogether." This would prompt Marci to rebuke him with, "You're just jealous, besides he takes very good care of my Mother."

Bill eyed Frank skeptically and cautiously. His tone had a definite edge as he asked, "How did you get in here Frank?"

Frank replied casually, "I have a key."

Bill fired back suspiciously, "You have a key?"

Just as casual, "Yes."

"Where the hell did you get a key?"

"The girls gave it to me."

Bill started to pounce but stepped back with the thought, *what will I gain by exposing the fact that I changed the locks.* He paused before thinking, *Nothing. You're supposed to be learning, stupid, don't tip your hand. Play it out and see where it leads.*

"Oh, I didn't know they had one?"

"I guess Marci gave it to them. They didn't say."

Next point of inquiry, "What are you doing here Frank?"

"Before I get to that, let me apologize for sneaking in here and surprising you. I was going to call first, but the girls said they had surprised you and you seemed to get a big kick out of it. With all that's happened lately I thought I'd surprise you too. I've clearly overstepped the bounds and I'm sorry."

Bill smiled inside; *I'll just bet they said I got a big kick out of it. Not quite as much as they had in mind however.*

"It's fine Frank. I've had a long day and I overreacted. Let's just put it behind us."

"Okay."

"Now, why are you here?"

"Pamela and Patricia said that when they saw you they offered to help with cooking, cleaning, and the children. Is that true?"

"Yes."

"They said they hadn't heard from you."

"I've been very busy Frank. There's a lot to deal with since Marci died and I just haven't had the time to call."

"They were concerned that you questioned the sincerity of their offer?"

Bill chuckled to himself, *not likely. When you care enough to get naked I'd say you're pretty damn sincere.*

"No, Frank. They seemed very sincere to me. Sincerity is not the issue, time and scheduling are."

"They, and I for that matter, feel bad that we haven't offered sooner, but we wanted you to have the time and space to deal with the issues."

"Frankly, Frank -"

They both interrupted Bill with laughter. Then Bill said, "I'm sorry for laughing Frank. That just sounded strange."

"That's okay Bill, I know what you meant."

"Anyway, Frank, what I was about to say was that I really haven't thought about it, one way or the other."

"They're quite sensitive Bill, and they didn't want you to be angry because they hadn't inquired sooner."

Another inward chuckle and, *Sensitive is not the first word that came to my mind. They might be considered sensuous or sexual, possibly tactile, maybe even downright carnal, but definitely not sensitive. No, Frank, sensitive doesn't do it!*

"You can assure them Frank that I'm not upset or angry. I've just been busy."

"In that case, Bill, I'm here because they thought they weren't persuasive enough and that I might be able to convince you."

Any effort on Frank's part to discuss Pam and Pat in serious terms had now deteriorated in Bill's brain to a collage of he and the sisters together. And, almost any word Frank used to describe their intent opened a door to numerous declining meanings.

It wasn't an inward chuckle this time, it was more like a sidesplitting inward laugh, *if they had been any more persuasive Frank, the three of us would be the next porno hit! No, Frank, your daughters do not lack persuasive powers.*

"It's not a matter of convincing me, it's as I said, simply time and scheduling."

"Can we expect to hear from you soon?"

"Just as soon as I get around to it."

"The cooking and cleaning can wait, but you really need some quiet time to yourself. We'd be pleased to watch William and Molly for you any time. And for as long as you need. A day, a week even a month if that works for you."

Here it is with the children again, Bill's antenna went up. Marci's directive concerning the children, Edith's confirmation of that directive, the sisters mention of the children, and now Frank with a more than extended offer to care for the children. An apparition rose before him. It was Marci waving a large red flag and shouting, "The children Bill, protect the children!"

Frank interjected, "Are you all right Bill?"

Bill shook his head to drive Marci from in front of him, and then said, "Of course Frank. Why?"

"You seemed distant, preoccupied for a moment."

"Sorry, Frank, it was nothing."

"Honestly, Bill, it's this type of behavior that has us concerned about you. That's why we think you need some time to yourself."

You're concerned about me . . . my ass! There is something very wrong here, and your concern has nothing to do with me.

Frank was an imposing man, both physically and intellectually. Bill realized at this moment that he had never looked Frank directly in the eyes. He had always spoken to some other point of reference when conversing with him. Did he have the balls necessary to take on the Franks of this world? He didn't know. What he did know was that he better have; and now was the time to find out!

Bill's stare glowed forcefully as he sprang, "What is this sudden fascination with my children?"

The fire and determination in Bill's query froze Frank. This was a Bill he'd never seen before. This was probably a Bill that no one had seen before. He needed to revise his estimate of this man and respond accordingly.

He tried humble and confused first, "I'm sorry, Bill, I don't understand why you feel that way?"

"Well, let me see Frank, maybe it's because months have gone by without a word from you or the girls. Maybe it's because neither you nor the girls have ever acknowledged me, or the children, on birthdays, holidays, or any days. I think it's natural to question your timing and your motives. So, I ask again, what's the sudden fascination with the children?"

Humble and confused didn't work, so Frank moved to wounded and falsely accused, "I resent the intimation that our caring for the children is anything other than a genuine desire to see to their safety and welfare."

"You can resent all you want Frank, but do me the courtesy of answering the question."

Frank's head and eyes fell slightly forward, signaling a change in course. When he raised them up his face had hardened with resolve. He measured Bill, then said, "Very well, Bill. We believe you are incapable of caring for the children."

"We, being you and the girls."

"Yes."

"And why not Frank?"

"You neither have the emotional stability or the financial resources to create the environment necessary for their well being."

"You know something, Frank. Before Marci died I would probably have agreed with you. Today, however, you're dealing with a different animal."

"Please, Bill, sell that to someone that doesn't know you. You are an emotional cripple, a self-absorbed drunk that can hardly take care of yourself let alone two developing human beings. And, though, you are currently financially solvent, within a short period of time, you will be nearly destitute."

"I am perfectly capable of satisfying the monetary needs of this family."

Frank laughed in his face, then said, "Your Scotch bill alone would bankrupt most small countries. You have numerous outstanding debts. Were you a corporation, your best chance of survival would be a friendly buy-out. No, Bill, your future is dismal at best."

"Where do you get your information Frank?"

"I have my sources."

"They're wrong Frank."

"You can believe anything you like Bill, but I know the truth."

Before Marci's death Bill would have fired back in angry defense. Now, however, he realized that Frank was driving toward an end game. His rage and pomposity would only permit Frank to mask and dilute the finish line.

He returned calmly, "Well, Frank, I guess we're at a standstill. I'm here and you're there. It would appear there's no middle ground."

"That's where you're mistaken Bill."

"How so?"

"We can do this the hard way. Or, we can do this the easy way."

"All right Frank, I'll bite, what's the hard way?"

"I can sue for custody of the children on the grounds that you're an unfit parent. You will resist temporarily, but given time, money and the forces I can bring to bear you will not prevail."

"Okay, Frank, I can't wait, what's the easy way."

"If you turn over custody to me and the girls I am prepared to reward you quite handsomely."

"How?"

"I can make your life financially secure. In addition, the girls are prepared to offer you earthly delights that you haven't begun to dream of. Between the two, you should be a very contented man for the rest of your days."

"Just when will all of this happen?"

"Just as soon as you agree to my custody terms."

"How do I know you won't, in some way, harm the children?"

"I will assure you, in writing if need be, that they will not be harmed in any way and they will never want for another thing for as long as they live."

"And you have the ware-with-all to guarantee such a thing?"

"And more, if necessary."

Bill still didn't know why, but he now knew the battle lines. He was learning, albeit, slower than he would have liked, that time can be your friend or your enemy. Under no circumstances can an outcome be assured, but buying some time would permit the luxury of planning and hindsight. If, however, Frank forced a decision now, it would eliminate any possibility of contingency planning and lessen Bill's position substantially.

"I must admit Frank; you've given me something to think about. I need to step away and and take a more orderly view of your offer. I don't know what it will be like without the children in my life. There's also the issue of how Marci would want me to proceed."

"I can arrange liberal visitation rights if you so desire. That should soften the loss issue. As far as Marci is concerned, you should be more concerned about your interest than hers. After all Bill, life is for the living. She's gone, and her supposed desires regarding the children are meaningless. With all due respect Bill, she doesn't deserve the grotesque, drunken mourning you're giving her. Save your loyalty for someone more worthy, like yourself."

Bill boiled over inside, *that last comment will cost you Frank. I'm not sure what, but I can guarantee a substantial amount of pain. And her interest in the children? Oh, Frank, if you only knew, she may yet have the last word!*

"I'll need some time to think this through."

"How long?"

"A week should do it."

"All right Bill, you've got a week."

"Thank you, Frank."

"One last thing Bill."

"Yes?"

"Don't try and get cute. I have a number of methods to insure your compliance. None of them are pretty."

Keep it up you son-of-a- bitch. The more you threaten me, and this family, the more determined I am to cut your balls off.

"You've made yourself clear Frank."

Frank moved forward and extended his hand. Bill reciprocated. As if punctuating his threat, Frank squeezed Bill's hand with force.

Deal sealed, Frank turned on his heal and left.

As the front door closed Bill tried to shake the stinging from his hand and said aloud, "You might want to remember Frank, there's no honor among thieves."

CHAPTER NINE

How long could Bill hold Frank at bay? Not long he'd bet. Frank hadn't even bothered to veil his threats. This alone was enough to prove to Bill that Frank was perfectly prepared, and capable, of doing whatever was necessary to achieve his end. Frank's untimely appearance had accelerated Bill's already compressed investigation timeframe. He hadn't passed Private Eye 101 yet. This development would require him to catapult directly to his doctoral thesis on surreptitious skullduggery within days.

First order of business, call in sick for the next week. He didn't have time to work, be James Bond and deal with Edith too. Next order of business, where to start? Oh, yes, who to start with? Hell, his head was already spinning. This wouldn't do. Good spy work required the best brain food. When it came to brain food he took a back seat to no one. Between field study and the rigors of comparative analysis he could say, without fear of contradiction, that his mental acuity was exponentially accelerated by the ingestion of three large rock glasses of well-aged single malt Scotch! It not only calmed his nerves, it leveled his thinking and greatly increased his intuitive powers.

Next stop, his well-stocked liquor cabinet. Three drinks later and his course of action was clear. He was off to his home office. Seated in front of his keyboard and oversized screen he eyed respectfully the greatest tool ever invented for the capture and accumulation of data . . . the computer! He bowed reverently as he laced his fingers together and stretched them for action. Waiting for him was the great equalizer, a weapon unparalleled in history, a tool that permitted him to slay his Goliath . . . the "information highway"!

Speed Dialing the Dead

Everyone has an expertise. Bill's was an uncanny ability to make a computer sing. Since he was a boy it had been his Stradivarius.

He gently depressed the "on" button. Instantly "his" special instrument tuned itself. It came alive with color, and then poised itself, waiting for the maestro to create a symphony. "His" baton had the shape of a mouse. His hand closed slowly around it. He took a deep breath, smiled with growing confidence at the task before him, and then made a caressing downward movement with his forefinger.

It would be several hours before his hands slowed to a blur. Only then, would he stop to stretch his overloaded synapses and replenish his "brain food".

~~~~~~~~~~~~~~~~~~~~~~~~~~~~

It had been two days since Bill began his search. He had stopped for brief intervals of food, Scotch, sleep and toilet duty.

He had farmed the children out to Donna under the guise that he was suffering from a mystery virus. His concern, of course, was for their health and the only way to insure that was to be quarantined.

Donna offered the appropriate compassion, "Are you sure you don't need something Bill. A prescription, food, anything?"

"Thank you Donna. Everything is being delivered. Watching Bill Jr. and Molly takes a great load off and permits me to rest."

Donna scolded playfully, "Well, if you need anything you'd better call."

"I will."

~~~~~~~~~~~~~~~~~~~~~~~~~~~~

Bill sat before his alter. He mused to himself, *is the attic floor an appropriate seat for a shrine? And, can I really call a telephone a shrine?* He pondered the incongruity briefly and decided he could call it anything he wanted. After all, by his definition, this particular instrument had become a shrine, plus, a rose by any other name . . . .

His first pass at the Internet had yielded some puzzling information. From that data he had developed a list of questions. He had intentionally kept the list small. Too many questions would only serve to scatter his inquiry. Moreover, experience told him that the response to a particular query would probably open other avenues of investigation. He pulled the crib sheet to his side and reached to depress Edith's name on the speed-dialing menu. He touched her key ever so lightly, as though too much pressure would diminish his chances for connection, and then waited as the unmistakable ratcheting began.

Three rings later, "Hello, Bill."

"Hello, Edith."

"Are you ready to ask me more questions?"

"Yes."

"Fire away."

Bill inhaled deeply and wondered at the task facing him. An old saying worked its way to the surface of his mind. He couldn't remember it exactly, but paraphrased it went something like; *the longest journey begins with the first step.*

Well, here goes, "Did you know that Frank came to see me?"

"Yes."

"Did he come to harm me?"

"No."

"Will he do me harm if I don't abide by his wishes?"

"Yes."

"Will it be physical, mental or economic?"

Silence.

"Sorry Edith. I'll get the hang of this eventually."

She chided, "We don't have eventually as an option. Let's hope it's sooner rather than later."

"Point taken. Let me rephrase. Will it be one of the options I gave?"

"No."

"But you said he'll do me harm?"

"Try thinking Bill."

He stopped. Was he up to this maze of twisted logic? He had to be. He stood, stymied by the hedgerow in front of him. And then, from the top of its wall the tip of an idea stared down at him. He stared back. The idea tumbled over the edge and fell on him!

"Will it be all the options I gave you?"

She replied with delight, "Yes, Bill."

He made a fist as he concurred, "All right."

Lifted by his correct turn in the maze he moved cautiously forward, "Would Frank ever harm the children?"

"No."

"Would your daughters harm them?"

"No."

Having gained answers to the immediate peril Bill could now move on to broader areas of inquiry.

"Can you predict the future?"

Some moments went by before Edith replied, "Yes."

Her delay was too conspicuous. Was she giving him a clue? A way in which, because of the structure of his question, she could relate some unintended misdirection by her answer? He stopped again, confronted by the next turn facing him.

Edith pressed impatiently, "I said yes."

He snapped back with frustration, "I heard you Edith. I'm thinking."

"I thought I smelled something."

He scolded her, "You just can't help yourself, can you?"

She snickered as she said, "Sometimes I can't. You make it so easy Bill."

"I'm doing the best I can."

"I know, Bill. I get frustrated for both us. Believe me, I want you to get the information just as much as you do, and I understand the constraints we're working under."

Suddenly another thought fell off the top of the hedgerow and hit him between the eyes. He took another cautious step, "Do you know the future?"

"No."

"Damn it, Edith. You just said you could predict the future."

"I can Bill, but so can you."

"Again with the double talk."

"You're like most people Bill you don't understand what you say. Just because you don't understand my answers doesn't make my answers wrong. It just makes you stupid."

"There you go again Edith with the snotty remarks."

She laughed openly as she said, "One man's snot is another man's truth."

"Please, Edith, I'm trying so hard."

"Yes you are, Bill, but you need to be more specific when you're asking questions."

He reluctantly relinquished her point, "You're right."

"I'm going to try and explain it to you. I can do this because you already have the information and my explanation will not change the outcome. Ready?"

"Yes."

"Can you predict the future?"

"Of course not."

"Wrong. You can predict the future. Anyone can predict the future. Knowing for sure what the future will bring however is a totally different circumstance."

"You're splitting hairs."

"Quite the contrary. And, it is this subtle distinction that you need to deal with when you attempt to gain information from me."

Knowing that Edith was correct and being able to calmly accept the truth of her statements were two different issues. It wasn't her fault. The blame rested clearly on his inability to stretch his mind to her limits. He felt pummeled, beaten down by his own lack of intellectual flexibility.

Bill's silence spoke volumes to Edith. He was a man in turmoil - dejected and demoralized, fighting himself as much as the circumstances around him. She was in fear, for the first time, of losing him as an ally. Yes, an ally. He didn't know it, but she needed him as much as he needed her . . . maybe more. Sure, he had his own axe to grind, and, when he knew the complete story he'd want a much bigger axe! She, on the other hand, had been given this metaphysical opportunity to extract a most deserved vengeance. Bill was to be her unknowing accomplice, her sword of retribution. This thought of impropriety, let alone the act she was propagating, would cost her dearly. Only the purest of ideas and actions were entertained in this plane of existence. To Edith, some things must be done . . . regardless of the price! Without Bill however, this opportunity would be no more than an idle wish. She moved to shore up her unwitting gladiator, "That was a nice piece of logic on your part."

"What?"

"That question about the future."

Slightly off balance by this departure he replied, "I'm not sure what you mean?"

"Without me knowing about the future you can eliminate an entire field of exploration. That will cut your effort in half."

He *had* done that . . . hadn't he? He knew there was a reason for that approach but until just now he hadn't identified it specifically.

With a brighter side showing he responded, "I thought you'd appreciate that."

"Well, I do. Nicely done."

"Thank you, Edith."

Patchwork complete she proceeded to close the deal! "The last time we spoke you had a question for me but I don't remember what it was?"

Bill scanned his notes. There it was; next item on his list. He asked anxiously, "Have you communicated with Marci?"

"That was it. I knew it was something important. Short answer, yes."

Agitation framed is reply, "What?"

"Yes, I have communicated with her. Or, should I say she has communicated with me."

"Damn it Edith, you know how important that is to me. Those should have been the first words out of your mouth. Instead, you conveniently forget to mention it."

Feigning a psychic wound she said, "That's not fair Bill. You had an agenda and I simply followed along. In the process I misplaced Marci for a while. After all, I did ask."

Bill responded curtly, "You're unbelievable Edith."

"Well, thank you Bill. I appreciate the compliment."

"That's not what I meant."

"I know what you meant Bill, I was just trying to lighten the mood. You're off being poopy drawers again. So shoot me, I got distracted."

"I suppose I'm going to be stuck with this poopy drawers tag now?"

"You are when you act like a poopy drawers."

With his irritation showing Bill said, "That's great. By the way what in hell does poopy drawers mean?"

"When children act cranky because they've shit in their pants that's what you call them."

"You mean I act like a cranky, messy child?"

"You see, Bill, sometimes you *can* figure things out."

His anger was near boil-over, but he stopped. There was no use fueling Edith. After all, she had little to do but aggravate him. And, even he had to admit she was getting rather proficient at it. The answer here was not to give her the stage, but to stay focused and pointed.

"Back to the point, you've been in contact with Marci?"

She had done a masterful job of pumping him up and then quickly followed that with subtle diversion. Now, she had only to set the "hook". The artful punctuation that would keep him tied to her.

Edith answered, "Yes."

"Can you tell me what she said or must I put everything in question form?"

Silence.

More silence.

Finally Bill spoke, "Edith, are you there?"

"I'm sorry Bill, but something is happening here. I think we are about to be discovered. I've got to go, try me tomorrow."

"But, Edith, I need to -"

The line went to tone in the middle of his sentence.

He stared at the receiver. He raised it high. His anger told him to slam the unit down on its base. He paused to reconsider. Was venting his anger worth shattering the Messenger XD 500? Was his anger worth destroying his only possible connection with Marci? He gently reset the receiver, then raised his head and yelled, "Damn you, Edith! This isn't fair."

From the other side Edith smiled smugly. Of course, she didn't have a face to smile with, but if she had, the satisfaction of her successful manipulation of Bill would have covered it.

CHAPTER TEN

Bill's cell phone chirped. He pulled it from his pocket and scanned the incoming number. There were only two people that knew his cell number, his brother and Donna. His brother typically called him at home and Donna when there was an issue with the kids. He didn't recognize the incoming caller. In another life these constant departures from the norm would have concerned him. Now however, if it weren't for the unusual he'd have no life at all.

Bill shrugged his shoulders and connected, "Hello."

"Hello, Bill, it's Frank."

He did not need this now! But then, why not, when it rains it pours.

"Yes, Frank. What can I do for you?"

"Just wondering how you're coming with your decision?"

"It's only been three days Frank. I thought we decided on a week?"

"We did, but I don't understand why it should take a week."

"Regardless, Frank, I've got a week."

"Why delay the inevitable?"

"At the risk of repeating myself, I believe I've got a week which would give me four more days."

Frank's tone hardened as he pressed,"Bill, why are you being so stubborn. You know, in the end, I will prevail."

It was time to make himself felt. Bill's rebuttal was confident and sharp, "Frank, we had an agreement. I suppose there was a time when my word was questionable, but now, it means something. Does yours?"

There was a brief silence while Frank regrouped. Here was that "new" Bill again. Pretense would now be a thing of the past! His response bordered on rage, "I'll have the contract in your hands four days from now. I expect you to sign it."

In the heat of a confrontation polite and pleasant was the ultimate insult. Bill proceeded with his best imitation, "Thank you, Frank. I appreciate your consideration."

Frank slammed the receiver down!

Bill smiled, *this being a man stuff is not easy, but it sure makes you feel good.*

He had been shopping when he received Frank's call. He had immediately terminated his search for the perfect prepackaged dinner. There was no such animal. A dinner that combined convenience, variety, price, and taste was the stuff of which myths were made. A quest worthy of Merlin the Magician!

He had sped home to confer with Edith. He could no longer rely on Frank honoring their timetable - which meant, that Frank might move against him and/or the children at any moment. He needed to know the players, the playing field and, their probable intentions in order to develop alternative scenarios - and, he needed this matrix of information now!

He sat cross-legged on the attic floor with a large Scotch on one side and his crib sheet on the other. He stabbed the speed dial button for Edith. It rang . . . and it rang . . . and it rang. Nothing!

Where the hell are you Edith? I need you . . . now!

He disconnected and tried again. The same results!

Third time is the charm. Wrong. The same results . . . again!

He placed the receiver on its cradle and reached for his high protein diet. In one continuous swallow he finished the first course. Since he had anticipated a lengthy conversation with Edith he had brought a cooler filled with ice and a near full bottle of "protein". In a blur of motion he reconstituted his rations and polished off the second course. He paused to reconnoiter his situation? When in doubt, raise your energy level! Halfway through the assembly of the next course the phone rang. He almost dropped his glass as he fumbled for the phone.

"Hello, Edith, where have you been?"

"I was in the middle of something and couldn't answer."

"I was getting frightened that our connection was lost."

"Not yet."

"The situation is heating up here and I need your input."

"I know."

"Then, you heard Frank's call?"

"Yes."

"Did you expect this?"

"Yes."

The questions regarding Frank were banging into the back of each other in his head. He groped to take control . . . then stopped.

"Before I go on Edith, I need to know about Marci."

"All right."

"Must I ask yes or no questions?"

"Nothing in our communication will change the direction of your world. Ask what you like. If I think it's a problem I won't answer."

"Very well, how is she?"

"She's fine."

Slightly agitated he pushed, "That's it?"

"Bill, I told you before, an entity's condition here can not be described in terms that relate to your world. 'She's fine'. That's the best I can do."

"It seems so . . . so inadequate."

"It is, but it will have to serve for the purpose of this conversation."

"Was there anything else?"

"She doesn't want you to worry about her. She's in a very good place. She loves you and is concerned for the safety of you and the children."

"Is that all?"

"There was more, but it had to do with issues regarding her and I."

"I don't understand?"

Edith's reply was cross, "Of course you don't understand. That's because it's none of your business."

"I just thought there'd be more."

"Bill, you're acting like a dope again. From this side, I gave you quite a bit. If you weren't so self centered you'd cherish what you've got."

He was contrite as he responded, "I'm sorry. This is all on such a grand scale. It's so overwhelming, and there are so many things I want to tell her."

Edith softened as she said, "I understand, Bill, but just accept what is and be thankful for it."

"I'll try to be less impatient."

"Let's move on Bill."

"Right." He took a deep breath, followed quickly by a swig of Scotch, and then said, "Did you or Gil meet Frank first?"

Silence.

"Oh right, sorry. Did you meet Frank first?"

"No."

"Then, Gil met him first?"

"Yes."

Gil was actually Guilford, but Guilford was so outgoing and laid back he had become Gil as a teenager. He was Edith's first husband - an inventor, engineer type that worked for a defense contractor. Gil held the patents, in conjunction with his company, on several major radar/sonar components that had revolutionized the tracking of enemy ships, submarines and aircraft. These patents and their residual royalties had made he and Edith wealthy. Not richest in the world wealthy, but wealthy enough that had he stopped working they couldn't have spent all the money before they died. He was a devoted husband and father. Caring, kind, and considerate of Edith and Marci to a fault. His loss had gaffed them deeply and they spoke of him softly and eloquently until their own deaths.

"Was Frank a business associate of Gil's?"

"No."

"A social acquaintance?"

"Yes."

"From your country club?"

"Yes."

"Gil knew Frank approximately one year?"

"No."

"Approximately two years?"

"Yes."

"Did you know Frank approximately two years?"

"No."

"Approximately one year?"

"Yes."

"Were you all friends?"

"Yes."

"Close friends?"

"Yes."

Bill was pleased with himself. He had established a baseline for Frank, and his relationship with Edith and Gil. He had done so under the constraints of Edith's ability to answer. It was now time to get serious!

"Gil died from wounds sustained during a hunting accident?"

"Yes."

"I read the police report that was filed after the inquest. At first blush, it seemed straightforward. The investigation concluded that Gil was climbing over a waist high split rail fence when he fell and his shotgun discharged into his chest. Because of the severity of those wounds he bled to death before help could arrive. Is this a fair representation of the conclusion of the court?"

"Yes."

"I did some research on Gil, his proficiency with guns, and his hunting prowess. It is my understanding that he was a firearms instructor in the Army. Is that correct?"

"Yes."

"Also, that he had been an avid hunter for approximately fifteen years?"

"Yes."

"I find the conclusion of the court rather curious. I am admittedly not a hunter, and my experience with firearms is limited at best, but it seems strange to me that a man with Gil's background in both firearms and hunting would make, what appears to be, a beginner mistake. Did anyone find fault with the ruling?"

"Yes."

"Was it you?"

There was a conspicuous lapse in time before Edith said, "No."

There it was again. This obvious pause before she answered. Edith was clearly sending a message.

"Should I take your delay in responding to indicate that there is more involved than a simple no?"

"Yes."

That's great Bill, you've managed to decipher the signal, but where do you go now?

His delay caused her to ask, "Are you still there?"

"I am Edith. I'm trying to structure my next question. Do you mind giving me a few moments?"

"Of course not."

He was faced, again, with a turn in the maze. When in doubt . . . drink. He took a substantial swallow of Scotch. He savored its smokey flavor as it glided down the back of his throat. Just as the "smoke" cleared the next question for Edith formed before him.

"You did not find fault with the ruling then, correct?"

"Yes."

"Do you now?"

"Yes."

"Because you have information now that you did not have then?"

"Yes."

"You said someone else had problems with the court ruling?"

"Yes."

"Someone outside the investigation?"

"No."

"Someone within the investigation."

"Yes."

"In law enforcement?"

"Yes."

"Was there more than one person?"

"No."

"A person on the investigating team?"

"Yes."

Did that person have contrary evidence?"

"No."

"Was this differing opinion like mine?"

"Yes."

"But based on more experience than mine?"

"Yes."

"Did that officer believe there was foul play?"

"Yes."

"Did that officer believe that Gil was murdered?"

"Yes."

"Do you now believe that Gil was murdered?"

Another conspicuous lapse in time before Edith replied, "Yes."

"Have you seen Gil's murder?"

"No."

"Can you explain why you've changed your mind?"

There was a pause, and then, she said, "I'm trying to decide if I can explain it to you. And, I believe I can without causing a rift in time, or whatever I'm in jeopardy of causing. I cannot see the past before I died. I'm led to believe that once I've moved to a higher plain that I will then be able to do so. But, as I just said I cannot now. Therefore, when I relate information regarding that incident it is based on what I can remember. The same would be true if you were trying to describe something that occurred in your past. I can, however, look into your world since my death. It is from that point that I have information that changes my view. Does that explain the appearance of contradictions?"

"Absolutely."

"Good."

"If, Gil was murdered, do you know who did it?"

"No."

"Let me rephrase that. Do you think you know who did it?"

"Yes."

"Is it someone we both know?"

"Yes."

Sometimes you work very hard to get somewhere, only to find, that it's not where you want to be. Bill had just arrived in that place. The next question had to be asked, but he wasn't at all sure he wanted the answer. When in doubt . . . no, a drink wouldn't help now. How about Plan B? What the hell was Plan B?

I'll have to create a Plan B. Okay, I've got it.

Plan B felt like, "jumping off a cliff". So, Bill jumped off the cliff, "Is it Frank?"

"Yes."

There in the wings appeared the elusive Mr. Murphy with a giant kettledrum and a giant cushioned mallet. Sporting an impish grin, that only he could, he slowly raised the mallet above his head. Then, with the force of Paul Bunyan, he slammed the mallet down on the surface of the drum. The enormous percussive sound one would normally expect from such an instrument combined with such a force was replaced by a wink from Mr. Murphy and a giant "thud"! He giggled as he whispered to Bill, "Be careful what you ask for."

Bill swallowed, trying hard to push his heart back down his throat. He was only partially successful.

"I was afraid you were going to say that."

"Sorry."

"Do you have any proof to support that belief?"

"No."

"I was afraid you were going to say that too."

"Sorry again."

"Not your fault." He took another swallow of Scotch and then said, "Edith, I've got some research to do and I need time to deal with this latest bombshell, do you mind if we quit for today?"

"Not at all, Bill. We've just overcrowded your plate."

The sound of disconnection punctuated Edith's closing.

He swirled the Scotch in his glass and stared at the motion as though his "tea leaves" would offer up a solution. None came. If he and Edith were correct . . . well, Frank was going to be more of a problem than originally anticipated . . . much more. He wouldn't need a plan for confrontation he would need a Battle Plan!

CHAPTER ELEVEN

Bill had gotten the names of the investigating officers off the police report. Gil's death had been so long ago - would anyone remember, were the officers still available, and, if they were, would they even care? After several phone calls and several rude responses he had finally been connected to the office of Captain Maureen Romano. At first, she had been too busy to accommodate questions regarding an investigation that was over twenty years old. After Bill's lengthy explanation of the case and his interest in it Captain Romano agreed to pull the records and call him back. Of course, when he pushed for expediency he almost lost her.

"Do you have any idea how busy I am Mr. Allen?"

Bill pleaded.

"And you say this case is how old?"

More pleading.

"And you want the information when?"

If only she could see her way clear to try, he would be eternally grateful? Little did she know how much eternity was actually involved?

"I'll see what I can do and call you back."

~~~~~~~~~~~~~~~~~~~~~~~~~~~~~~
~~~~~~~~~~~~~~~~~~~~~~~~~~~~~~

The house phone rang. He looked at the caller I.D., but didn't recognize the number. Hell, that might be a good thing. He really wasn't ready to talk to someone he knew.

"Hello."

"Mr. Allen, this is Captain Romano."

It had only been two days. Damn, she was fast. This was more than an unexpected surprise.

Excitement skirted his reply, "Yes, Captain. So kind of you to get back to me."

"I don't have a lot of time. I've got a meeting with the Mayor shortly, so I'll make this brief."

"I appreciate whatever time you have Captain."

"I found the case, and I did work on it. I was just a rookie. I had only been assigned to that squad one-week prior. Back then; no one wanted a woman on the police force, let alone, one with a Master's Degree in Criminology. I was the token female in the good old boy network, an experiment that everyone wanted to fail. To assist my failure the Chief put me with the crustiest son of a bitch he could find – Sergeant Jerry Kiminski. Jerry and I eventually became partners and friends. Normally they would have referred you to him, but he was retired and died last year."

Bill interrupted, "I'm very sorry Captain."

"Thank you Mr. Allen. He taught me most of what I know today and I miss him. Anyway, it all came back to me when I started reviewing the file. It was a very straightforward case. The gentleman in question had fallen while trying to negotiate a short wooden fence. Everything pointed to an accident so that was the ultimate report that was filed. The inquest concurred; end of case. What can I add?"

"It is my understanding that you weren't convinced that it was an accident?" Captain Romano hardened, "And just where did you get that piece of information?"

"From Mr. Watson's wife."
The pause was thick . . . quicksand thick!
Finally Captain Romano responded, "Mr. Allen?"

"Yes."

"Where do you figure in all of this?"

"I'm Mrs. Watson's son-in-law."

"And?"

"Some recent findings indicate that it may, in fact, have been more than an accident. I'm not a professional Captain Romano, but based on these recent findings, and comments by Mrs. Watson, I'm inclined to lean toward foul play. Obviously, I would like to know why a professional went against the conventional wisdom."

"First, Mr. Allen, if Mrs. Watson heard me expressing a view contrary to the final report she overheard a private conversation. My personal feelings do not enter into a report based on an investigation of the evidence."

"Captain, I'm more than willing to stipulate that your opinions have nothing to do with a formulated statement based on the evidence at hand. Nevertheless I would still like to hear that opinion."

"All right Mr. Allen, but if you share what I'm about to say with another living soul, I will not only deny it, I will bring charges against you for crimes we haven't invented yet. Am I making myself clear?"

"You have made yourself very clear Captain Romano." As Bill continued he smiled, "And you can rest assured, I will never share your comments with another living soul."

Bill chuckled to himself with the irony, *If only you knew Captain.*

"Very well, Mr. Allen. The reason I questioned the accident theory was that the scene of Mr. Watson's death was perfect."
"Perfect?"

"Yes, perfect . . . too perfect. It was so perfect it looked to me as if it had been staged."

"Sergeant Kiminski obviously disagreed."

"I'm not sure of that either?"

"I don't understand."

"Jerry listened to what I had to say, but he never said whether he agreed or disagreed. All he said was that we had a hell of workload and unless there was clear-cut evidence pointing us in another direction we didn't have the time, or the manpower, to continue the investigation. Now, before you say another word, let me say, in retrospect Sergeant Kiminski was absolutely correct."

"Just one more question Captain Romano?"

Impatience undercut her reply, "All right Mr. Allen, but that's it."

"Thank you, Captain. Had you pursued the matter was there a particular person that might have been of interest?"

"No. We looked at the other people in the hunting party, but they were off in other locations and not within a half a mile of Mr. Watson at the approximate time of death."

"Was one of those other people a Frank Turner?"

"As a matter of fact it was. Is that significant?"

"No, he was a long time family friend and I've seen his name before. I'm sure it means nothing."

Bill knew that Captain Romano had stretched pretty far in sharing this skeleton with him. He also knew that she was finished with him and any further discussion of this matter.

He bowed to her figuratively, "Captain, you have been more than forthcoming. I only hope that life will present me with the opportunity to reciprocate your candor and kindness. Thank you for your time."

Acknowledging Bill's appreciation she closed, "You are welcome Mr. Allen. I wish you success in bringing closure to this matter for Mrs. Watson. Goodbye."

As he replaced the receiver he said aloud, "Edith, I hope we can both get closure on this mess. We're going to need a lot of luck and a lot of quick thinking."

~~~~~~~~~~~~~~~~~~~~~~~~~~

Scotch in hand, Bill seated himself on the attic floor. He pushed Edith's button. The irony of that act amused him.

Actually, after all the shit she's given me, I'd rather pull her chain than push her button.

She answered on the second ring, "Hello, Bill. Any headway?"

"No real headway, but I got some information that I believe ties Frank pretty tightly to Gil's murder."

"Really?"

"I talked to one of the investigating officers on Gil's supposed accidental death, and - wait a minute, why am I telling you this, you could watch it all."

"And I did."

Angst penetrated his reply, "Why do you let me start when you know about the conversation already?"
~~~~~~~~~~~~~~~~~~~~~~~~~~

"You did a great job Bill, why not let you crow a little."

"Thank you Edith, but we have bigger fish to fry."

"All right Bill, what now?"

"I've been thinking Edith -"

She cut him off with, "There you go again, doing the right thing. Be careful, when you overwork a muscle you don't use much it can be painful."

"You know Edith, a few days ago that would have pissed me off, but that's part of what I've been thinking about. Now that I've determined Frank probably killed Gil I figure you want Frank's ass as much as I do - me, for the kids and my own self-preservation, and you, for Gil. So, you need me as much as I need you. In that case, I suggest you start treating me like an ally rather than the awful step-child."

There was a brief silence before Edith responded, "You know Bill, I can't decide if I liked you better as the self-absorbed rectum that you were or the man that you're about to become. Give me a minute . . . ."

Another brief silence and then she finished, "You were certainly easier to jerk around before, but I think I'm going to like the 'man' better. Having said that you've got an ally."

Treaty negotiated, and signed, Bill moved forward with his army of one.

"I don't see any choice but to go on the attack with Frank. Do you agree?"

"Absolutely."

"Can I win?"

A conspicuous pause and then, "Yes."

"I assume your qualified yes means there are extenuating circumstances?"

"Yes."

"Is it fair to say that your qualified yes is based on my recognition of the skills of our enemy and a well drafted battle plan?"

"Yes."

"In that case, here we go. I'm sure you know that I've spent days gathering information on Frank and his life."

"I do."

"With the aid of my computer I have literally taken him apart and put him back together. I can probably tell you what he eats for breakfast. With that in mind, I need access to his house." Bill finished with a little well placed needle, "Oh yeah, I just remembered, it use to be your house too?"

"Now who's being cute?"

"I've had a good teacher. Some of the shit you've been throwing at me must have stuck?"

Her reply seemed to indicate that she was much happier dishing it out than taking it, "We're allies Bill, remember?"

"All right Edith, I'll stop, but you have to admit you owe me."

"If that's all it takes, then I will admit Bill that I have been overly zealous in my quips at your expense."

"Thank you Edith, I appreciate your apology. Now, the big question, can you get me in the house?"

"Yes."

"Past the security system?"

"Yes."

Bill had already obtained the schematics and operational specs for the alarm system. If he could get in one time he could reset the programs to allow him his own code and complete access to the residence. Of course, he would have to disable the software that recorded the entry data. It wouldn't do to have the day, date, and time of admittance recorded on a printable report for all to see. He had also gone into the city records and captured a complete set of drawings for Frank and Edith's home. They included architectural, electrical, and plumbing layouts. That was all well and good, but without the ability to bypass the security safeguards it was for naught. He was now at that crossroads, that being, the preset code that Frank, Pat and Pam used on a daily basis to enter and exit the premises.

He sighed, pictured Edith standing before him and said, "I'll need the password, correct?"

"Yes."

"Do you know it?"

There was that signaled pause and then her reply, "Yes."

He was beginning, slowly; to understand the unspoken system they had developed to modify a "yes" or a "no" answer. Edith was no doubt bending the rules, but technically she was within the letter of her law. She was only answering his questions with a "yes" or "no".

He thought briefly, and then he had it, "You used to know the password and if Frank hasn't changed it you still do?"

"Yes."

"Did he revise codes and passwords often?"

"No."

"Well then, we'll have to hope he's stayed true to his course. We don't have a choice for now."

"I agree."

Bill had predicted this path for the determination of the security system key. His script was meant to narrow the options quickly. Of course the entire process was trial and error, extremely slow and cumbersome.

"Here goes, Edith. Is it a name?"

A pronounced pause, and then, "Yes."

Already with the side step. There had been an old quiz show called "Password". One player would offer a word in an attempt to induce the other player to choose the selected game word. The best players were those that calculated the closest clue words and, were also able to think like their partner. Bill felt as though he were in a new and slightly different version of that contest. The major difference being that he was competing for considerably higher stakes! It was also noteworthy that his playing partner was dead and in some other dimension.

Thinking like Edith was going to introduce some interesting wrinkles. He was only now learning to think for himself, God knows where thinking like Edith would lead him.

What the hell, "Is it a person's name?"

"No."

He started to chastise her but stopped. In her own slightly twisted way she may have saved him a substantial slice of time, but where to now? He tested the water, "Is it an animal?"

"Yes."

"Living?"

"No."

"It's the name of a dead animal?"

"Yes."

"Do I know this animal?"

"Yes."

Well, he had tested the water; it was now time to jump in with both feet. He began a barrage of questions. Bill fired them at her in rapid succession, as though he was inventing a language of short hand. Edith was more than up to the task. Her yeses and no's came bouncing back so fast that a bystander would have been unable to separate the questions from the answers.

Twenty minutes later and almost out of breath, Bill said to her, "McTavish?"

Mc Tavish had been Edith's West Highland Terrier. Her "Westie" had been all white and the love of her life. Bill had always thought she treated that dog much better than the rest of the family. McTavish had died a little more than a year before Edith. He had been given a cremation befitting the head of a Scottish Clan. His ashes now rested in an urn shaped like a doghouse on the mantle over the walk-in fireplace in the expansive Turner family room. When Edith had spoken of McTavish she had referred to him as her dearly departed friend. When she did so around Bill he would work his way behind her and give Marci the finger down the throat motion indicating his need to vomit. That had always gotten him several days of detention in their guest room and meals less than desirable for human consumption.

"Yes, Bill, you got it."

"Is it spelled McTavish?"

"Yes."

"Is it case sensitive?"

Silence

"Does that mean you don't know?"

"Yes."

"No matter that's a minor glitch. We've done good Edith, a real day's work, thank you."

Pride surrounded her reply, "Thank you, Bill."

"I've got a lot to do if I'm going to be prepared for the next step. If you don't mind, let's call it a day."

"Break a leg, Bill. Call me tomorrow."

"Goodbye, Edith."

~~~~~~~~~~~~~~~~~~~~~~~~~~~~

Bill sat in his car waiting for dusk to slowly blanket the surroundings. He was dressed in black clothing and a black ski cap. Black tennis shoes and a darkened face completed the ensemble. He felt silly wearing this attire, but every military movie he'd ever seen had always shown the commandos in camouflage and the like. Who was he to argue with Hollywood? He was also carrying a small duffle bag, his own "second story" kit, filled with a mixture of tools, lubricants, and gloves. In order to avoid notice, or any connection with the Turner compound, he had parked a quarter of a mile away. The horizon became gray as Bill exited his car and started working his way along an access road that led between the backs of several mini estates. He moved stealthily between the trees and bushes that lined the dirt lane.

He had intercepted e-mails from Frank to two separate people saying that he and the girls would be out of town on business for two days. E-mail to one person would have alerted Bill to the possibility of a vacant house; two however, were all the confirmation he needed to take his show on the road. Why the girls were traveling with Frank on business was another mystery, which given time, and other circumstances, would be worth further analysis. That review would have to wait its turn. He now stood, overlooking a white split rail fence which surrounded Frank's lavish estate.
~~~~~~~~~~~~~~~~~~~~~~~~~~~~

He scanned the two hundred and fifty feet of landscaped yard between him and the house. Frank's home, of more than six thousand square feet, sat comfortably on slightly more than six acres of land. Directly behind the main structure were a large pool, hot tub, and substantial leisure space with build-in barbecue and bar. On the few occasions Bill had been to Frank and Edith's he had always mused to himself and Marci about why her Mother and stepfather needed a recreation area the size of a small amusement park. Marci had always accused him of being jealous and had then gone on to explain that Frank's business required entertaining groups of clients. Marci had been right about the jealousy part, but then she was usually right about most things. The question that had never been answered to Bill's satisfaction however was what exactly was Frank's business. Between Edith and Marci the flip response had always been, "Oh, he has something to do with financial investments." His even more flip rebuttal, "You mean he invests in massage parlors?" had always met with a long and painful scolding.

Dusk had come, and was now almost gone, replaced by the front side of night. The near darkness signaled the commencement of his journey. He climbed over the fence and walked purposefully toward the house. He continued through the pool area and up the two steps to the back entrance of the house. Beside the double doors at shoulder height was a wall mounted phone style keypad with a red glowing light above it. Even though there was now little external light he had no trouble seeing the internally lit keypad. To prepare his mind and body for the coming gauntlet, he inhaled slowly and deeply. He reached and typed the magic word, "McTavish".

Nothing.

Again, using all lower case.

Nothing.

Again, using all upper case.

More nothing.

He whispered out loud, "Shit!"

Frank, you sneaky bastard, you changed the code. What now poopy drawers?

He hated that nickname given to him by Edith, but even he had to admit, in this instance, he deserved it. He had put most of his eggs in the "McTavish" basket. It could be anything. And now, he'd have to wait until Edith saw Frank or the girls actually input the code – then, he and Edith would have to play their guessing game until he eventually got it.

That could take weeks. Do you really think you've got weeks?

That very cagey Mr. Murphy peered around the corner of the house and answered the question for him, "You'd better circle the wagons Bill. I'm not sure you've got one week, let alone 'weeks.'" In his finest imitation of the late W.C. Fields Mr. Murphy continued, "Another fine mess you got us in 'poopy drawers'. You seem to have a penchant for doing things backward Bill. Good luck . . . ." He giggled aloud and faded into the night.

Bill stared at the corner of the house just occupied by Mr. Murphy. Shook his head to chase away the vision and wondered, *is there really a Mr. Murphy, or am I just going crazy, or is he my inner self playing devil's advocate?*

Whatever it was, something told Bill that underneath all the banter, there had been a pearl. A seed waiting to blossom . . . but what? He stood, fixed in place, straining to make that seed grow. Suddenly . . . . He reached and typed in, "hsivatcm". The red light went off and the door unlatched.

Frank, you crafty son-of-a-bitch you reversed it!

As Bill pushed the door opened and crept into the house somewhere behind him a disgruntled Mr. Murphy said, "You could at least say thank you Bill. Or, were you the one that thought of 'backward'? See if I help you again?"

Thinking he heard someone behind him Bill stopped, looked over his shoulder, and listened.

Must have been my imagination.

As Mr. Murphy again faded into the night he issued, "Your imagination my ass. You ungrateful mass of protoplasm, I'll remember this the next time you need some help . . . 'poopy drawers.'"

Bill had the house layout indelibly stamped in his mind. Led by the low level light from his flashlight he moved swiftly through the rooms and directly to Frank's office. He seated himself in front of Frank's computer screen and keyboard. Since Frank's office was in an interior room Bill didn't hesitate to switch on the desk lamp beside the computer. Frank's processor was a high-speed version of a popular brand . . . a very high speed version. Bill depressed the on button and within seconds the screen was alive with color. Now came the next turn in the maze . . . the password. There it was, screaming at Bill, a blank box asking for the "password". He had spent a considerable amount of time and effort gaming the possibilities. Most people were habitual in their selection of code words. So as not to forget the specific word or phrase, they either reused the same word or phrase over and over, or they chose a close variation thereof. Bill's first choice would have been "McTavish" but due to Frank's twist he entered "hsivatcm". No response. Since Frank seemed to like names Bill began typing in all the family names he knew. He even tried "Edith". After several minutes of failures he was back to square one.

Where to now . . . poopy drawers?

Then in a flash, he smiled and typed in "McTavish".

No response.

He muttered aloud, "Damn, I was sure that would do it."

And then, another flash, Bill launched, "Would you have the nerve to do that Frank?"

Bill typed, "Gil".

No response.

And then with a broad grin, "You would have the nerve to do that, just not that simple."

He typed quickly, "Guilford."

Frank's desktop filled the screen, along with twenty-five or thirty icons. As the screen painted, Bill said with pride, "Got you, you sneaky piece of shit!"

Savoring the moment, he leaned back in Frank's desk chair and exhaled fully. He dropped back forward and said to the screen, "Look out, Frank, here I come."

For the next two hours and forty minutes Bill did his Stradivarius thing. His fingers danced as he composed a concerto that captured every detail of Frank Turner's secret life – credit cards, bank accounts, business associates, recipes, names, addresses, phone numbers, etc. Along the way there were a considerable number of"oohs","ahs", and"oh nos". When he had finished capturing all pertinent information he created a special file and saved it to a disk. He beamed as he removed the disk from the CPU and deposited it in his duffle bag. He then deleted any trace of his activity in Frank's computer. He turned off the computer, wiped his fingerprints from the keyboard, and then rose from the desk chair. He returned the chair and everything else he had touched to their original resting place. He switched off the lamp and exited Frank's office for a brief tour of the other rooms.

Thirty minutes later, after a complete mapping of the first floor, second floor, and basement he stood before the rear door of the house. The thought of referring to the downstairs as a basement caused him to chuckle. Its decorations and furnishings were so upscale he would have been content to live there. It was almost another home.

His final piece of work now lay before him, reprogramming the security system. For five minutes he typed rapidly and efficiently. Any record of his entry was now gone. And, any future visits would go unrecorded. He even programmed his own entry code, one that would remain invisible to all, but the most gifted security software programmers. His final touch, his *piece de resistance*, his cherry on top, was his choice of code words.

As he entered the letters that comprised his key he looked up and said to the ceiling, "I hope you appreciate the beauty of this?"

He looked back at the security pad and winked as he tapped in these three letters, "Gil".

He exited the house, reset the security system and walked across the lawn. As he climbed the fence and started toward his car that impish Mr. Murphy peeked around the corner of the house and said, "You know what Bill, I like your style. How could I stay mad at someone with your sense of irony? Go get 'em 'poopy drawers'"

CHAPTER TWELVE

With a Scotch in one hand and a list of questions in the other, Bill seated himself on the attic floor.

Damn this floor is hard. Why don't you get yourself a pillow to sit on?

The next question to himself would have been, why didn't he move the phone to a different location with an easy chair? He didn't ask it because he had long since decided he wasn't tampering with whatever cosmic forces were at work and moving the Messenger XD 500 even one inch might cut off his connection with Edith. No, the pillow was a good idea, but that's where comfort would end in favor of utility.

A couple of swallows of his high protein food, a deep breath to compose himself and he was ready to reach out for Edith. He tapped her speed dial button and waited.

She clicked in with, "Hello, Bill."

"Hello, Edith. Have you been watching my adventures?"

"I have. Not as exciting as sex, but good enough to keep my attention."

"I'm glad I'm keeping you occupied."

Edith ignored his comment and moved on, "What exactly do you have in mind for Frank?"

"Why?"

"Based on what I've seen, you're preparing for an extensive campaign. So, what are you planning?"

"I haven't decided yet."

"I don't believe you."

"I'm not done accumulating information yet, and besides, I wouldn't tell you anyway."

"Come on Bill, share with the other children."

"No, Edith. Let's just say I'm going to surprise you."

"All right, poopy drawers, have it your way."

"Are you done pestering me?"

"Probably not."

"Nevertheless, I have a few questions."

"You won't share with me, so why should I share with you?"

"Come on, Edith. I'm running up on a deadline, I don't have the time for this."

Like a petulant child whose fun had been interrupted she replied, "Oh, all right, what are they?"

"When I toured your home and tried to match up the floor plan with the square footage I found a discrepancy. There's about an eight hundred square foot difference in the lower level of the house and the actual rooms that show on the lay out. Am I missing something?"

"Yes."

"Is this missing space undeveloped?"

"No."

He reached for confirmation, "It's not part of the foundation?"

"No."

"It is developed space?"

"Yes."

"Hidden?"

"Yes."

"With a defined entrance?"

"Yes."

"Do you know the location of the entrance?"

"Yes."

Bill stopped to review the lower level in his mind. A hidden entrance would have to be expertly concealed as part of the décor, meaning, it blended in so perfectly with the actual wall surface that it took very detailed inspection to discover it, or, it would have to be shielded by a piece of furniture or the like. The downstairs was almost large enough to be someone's principal dwelling. There were two master suites complete with lavish bathrooms, a large family room/game room combination, a full bar, and a complete study. He eliminated the master suites and bathrooms immediately. Guests, in their normal use of the suites might inadvertently stumble on a secret doorway – and, there was too much plumbing and too many immovable fixtures in the bathrooms to make them a viable alternative. Besides, it would be inconvenient to explain to visitors the need for a concealed opening.

He began the process of trial and error, "Is it in the family/game room combination?"

"No."

"Would it be part of the bar area?"

"No."

And finally, "The study?"

"Yes."

He couldn't remember the furniture arrangement in the study. Any thought of specific pieces had been lost to his impression of the overall size of the downstairs and its general furnishings. Even the missing space hadn't become an issue until he had arrived home and began a direct comparison. This would obviously require another visit to Frank and Edith's to ascertain entry strategies and the exact location of the secret doorway.

"Can I assume that if I find the entrance to the missing space that it will have its own security system?"

"Yes."

"Do you know the code?"

"No."

"But that doesn't make any sense Edith?"

Silence.

"You have to know the code?"

Silence.

Another turn in the maze had just risen up to confront him. He searched the top of the hedgerow for answers. Surely an answer was waiting to fall on him? All right then, where the hell was Mr. Murphy when you needed him?

He grumbled to himself, *I guess you're on your own . . . stupid!*

He took a large mouthful of Scotch. Slowly swirled it around the inside of his mouth. Having milked the bouquet and the smoky flavor from every last drop he allowed the fluid to slowly slide down his throat.

With half the Scotch still to swallow it hit him, like a shovel between the eyes. Its simplicity and clarity jarred him. The subsequent distractions caused him to gulp too much, too fast. The liquid collision with his throat and windpipe rebounded with an aria of coughing.

Somewhere in the midst of his fit Edith ventured, "Are you all right?"

Between the throat clearing and hacking he managed to squeeze, "I'll be fine, something went down the wrong way."

"I was concerned, you sound awful."

Embarrassed by his whooping he moved to change the subject, "Was this area build after your death?"

"No."

"It was there when you were alive?"

"Yes."

Confirming her previous admission Bill asked, "And you didn't know the code?"

"Yes. That is correct."

There it was, he need only ask the question. "Did you know this area existed while you were alive?"

"No."

"And that is why you don't know the code?"

"Yes."

He'd successfully negotiated that turn in the maze, but the next turn was about to open "Pandora's Box".

"Someone else knows the entrance cipher?"

"Yes."

Mr. Murphy's head peeked up over the attic stairs. His head swiveled from side to side until he found Bill with his eyes. Bill's next question was beginning to form on his lips when Mr. Murphy yelled, "Be careful what you ask for, you might not get what you want."

Bill paused and turned his head as though there was something buzzing at his ear. He shook it off as Mr. Murphy slowly dissolved and asked, "Frank?"

A conspicuous pause and then, "Yes."

Her clue pushed him forward, "More than one person in the family?"

"Yes."

"Your daughters?"

"Yes."

He was becoming frightened by where this was leading. He had no choice, he had to know, he closed his eyes and continued, "All three?"

"No."

"Pam and Pat, but not Marci?"

"Yes."

He sighed with relief, and said, "Thank God."

"God has nothing to do with this."

His head was swimming from the possibilities - there were so many coming at him from so many different directions his brain felt like a train wreck. He couldn't begin to ask questions until he had an intended course. At this point there was none. This turn had left him confused and nearly speechless. He needed to gather himself. Unfortunately, time was becoming his worst enemy. Frank's deadline was fast approaching and he still couldn't see the top of the mountain he was climbing.

He scrambled for a safe harbor, even though he knew it was temporary, "Edith, I need to deal with these revelations. I'll talk to you as soon as I have a better grasp of the situation."

She replied with quiet resolve, "I understand. Call me when you're ready."

He didn't wait for her to disconnect. He was gone.

~~~~~~~~~~~~~~~~~~~~~~~~~~~~

He stood overlooking the white split rail fence behind Frank's house. Frank and the girls weren't due to arrive at the airport until late afternoon. He had verified there arrival by checking airline schedules and passenger manifests. With normal flight delays, and ground transportation, they should be home by early evening. Due to his possible discovery, enhanced by the daylight, it had taken him nearly thirty minutes to traverse the quarter of a mile from his car to this spot overlooking Frank's backyard. He would have preferred to wait until after dark to attempt entry, but the bombshells presented by his conversation with Edith required action – and with Frank and the girls returning today he had no choice, it was now, or possibly never.

He started to squeeze between the split rails of the fence when a sound out of sync with the surroundings stopped him. He froze with his leg through the fence and about to touch the ground on the other side. His eyes searched and found a man motoring around the corner of the house on a large mower. Fortunately for Bill the man was oblivious to anything, or anyone, other than the music from his headset or any immediate obstructions to his intended path. Bill quickly pulled his leg back and crawled to the cover of a group of bushes. He breathed slowly, and deeply, as he calculated his alternatives. It was a short list . . . a very short list. He could wait, in the hope, that the lawn service would complete their work expeditiously or he could leave. He waited.

At one point in the mowing pattern the mower rumbled down the back fence line and actually passed within ten feet of Bill. At that moment
~~~~~~~~~~~~~~~~~~~~~~~~~~~~

Bill slid deeper into the bushes and dropped to his belly. After that close call the driver's path took him closer and closer to the house. After twenty minutes he drove down the other side of the house and out of view. Shortly thereafter the distinctive growl of the motor stopped. Bill waited a few minutes to confirm the completion of the lawn mowing chores and then left the cover of the bushes. He was about to negotiate the fence again when around the far corner of the house came four jump-suited workers. He scurried back to his protective niche.

Anger flaring he thought, *How fucking long is this going to take?*
Not long, it would seem. He stared in awe, as they became a swarming hive of activity. They moved through the backyard as though a world record time hung in the balance. Within fifteen minutes they had trimmed, pruned and edged the entire one and a half acres of landscaped surroundings. Their artistry complete, they sauntered back around the far side of the house.

Bill waited ten minutes, then an additional ten minutes, to be certain they were finally finished and gone. He eased himself out of his hiding place and one more time began negotiating the fence. Half way through he stopped. Partly from habit and partly expecting some new interruption. When there was none he finished squirming through the rails and walked to the back door. He punched in his own entry code, entered the house, closed the door behind him and stood silent for several moments to gather himself. Sensing nothing out of the ordinary he moved to the lower level stairs and descended to the family room. He turned on the wall lighting and walked to the study. He entered through the open door, switched on the overhead fixture and began scanning the wall surfaces. Somewhere behind a piece of furniture or a break in the wall covering was an entrance. He walked the wall line sliding his hand across the wallpaper in the hope of feeling a break, a slightly protruding surface, or anything indicating a demarcation from the norm. He traveled the room with no success. The only other item of promise was the bookcase. It filled half of what should have been the outside wall. It had eight shelves, was almost six and a half feet high, and was full of books.

Who the hell has time to read this much? No one. It's got to be here.

He began pulling one book at a time from the case and then replacing it. Typically, one book was the trip for opening a barrier or it was the trigger to a device that would open the barrier. He finished the entire bookcase and nothing had happened.

He shook his head with frustration as he thought; *it's in this room. Edith said it was. So where is it stupid?*

He examined the exterior of the bookcase for a switch, button or lever. He even pulled a chair over and search the top . . . nothing.

Its here, damn it, I know it is.

If it wasn't the books then it had to be part of the case. He began pulling each and every volume from its interior to search the insides. He gave great care to their order. These were Frank's publications. Just one misplaced title would alert him to tampering. Bill investigated a shelf at a time. He emptied one, then another, scanned the inside panels and then reset them. He was nearly finished and his frustration was mounting. He was in the process of replacing the hard covers on the lowest shelf when something suspended his effort. He replayed the entire process for each previous shelf from top to bottom, but what was it? He pushed the last books into position on the far right side and reached for the six books directly above. He withdrew them slowly and set them aside. He inspected the hole that was left behind. The inside panel was clean and so was the wallpaper behind.

Wallpaper?

That was it! The entire case had a wooden back. He shouldn't be seeing wallpaper. He reached through and polished the wall with his hand. A square notch had been cut from the bookcase backing and the wall covering had been tinted to look exactly like the back panel. As his fingers glided across the wall surface he felt a slight protrusion. He peeked through the opening. The swelling blended perfectly – and, combined with the low light level behind the cabinet it was nearly invisible to the naked eye. It was so indistinct he had to brush it twice to be certain it was actually there.

I've got to give you credit Frank. If it hadn't been for Edith knowing it was here I never would have found it.

Then he smiled and said out loud, "But I did, you sneaky son of a bitch!"

He pressed gently on the magic button. There was a muffled whirring sound and the bookcase parted in the middle and swung open. Looking back at him was a recessed panel that had been exposed when the bookshelves parted. And there, was the same style keypad Frank had used for the house security system. He immediately began typing in names. He even tried "Edith", but no luck. He scratched his head as he pondered alternatives.

Mr. Murphy poked his head around the study door opening and said with a smirk, "I guess you'll need a lot more luck Bill. Who knows maybe you'll back into the right code again. You seem to be good at backing into things."

He then giggled and stuck his tongue out at Bill. Bill turned as though someone or something had blown on his ear. He looked back at the doorway, but too late, Mr. Murphy had already dissolved.

Now, where was he? *The code you dummy.*

Whether the blowing on his ear was real or not, it made his ear itch. As he reached to scratch his ear a thought pushed its way forward. As it took shape Bill said aloud, "Would you really do that Frank? Would you reverse the house entry code?"

He smiled and tapped in the word "McTavish". Another muffled whirring sound and the portion of wall in front of him slid to the side to reveal a door and doorknob. He reached, turned the knob, but the door was locked.

The way you've secured this room Frank there must be an atomic bomb inside.

This turn in the maze was easy. Bill reached for his duffle bag and withdrew some lock picking tools. He inserted two in the key slot and began manipulating the tumblers. Within seconds they fell in place. He turned the knob and pushed the door open to a pitch-black room. He reached around the opening and felt down the wall for a switch. There were three. Once found, he depressed them and the room came alive with light. He blinked his eyes to focus. What he saw caused him to blink them several more times to convince himself that what he was looking at was real!

His mouth fell open and his eyes widened as he surveyed the room. He was savvy to the ways of the world, alternative life styles and the like, even considered himself open minded, that was, until now, what he was viewing not only stretched the envelope, it broke the seal! This was the ultimate sexual fantasy store. There were tables, chairs, devices hanging from the ceiling, wall mounted restraint systems, and each item had several variations. Around the walls were hung men and women's uniforms - some leather, some vinyl and some lace. All of the uniforms came in different colors and styles. Also hanging on the walls were whips, chains, handcuffs and numerous other items, which Bill was unfamiliar with. But then, he was unfamiliar with half of the paraphernalia his eyes landed on. In one corner was a complete video set up, with cameras, playback equipment and special lighting. In another corner was a bathroom, the door to which was standing open. The main room was spotlessly clean and each piece no matter how large or small was displayed from its own resting place. It felt like a perfectly merchandised retail store. Bill leaned back against the wall, overwhelmed by the magnitude and extent of what this area represented. After a complete tour he settled into a large desk chair behind a formal desk that could be in any CEO's office in the country. Against the wall behind him were bookshelves and file cabinets. The shelves housed what appeared to be a couple of hundred photo albums. He rose from the desk chair and jimmied the locks on the file cabinets. Neatly cataloged by names and dates were rows of videodisks. His head was swimming. Not in is wildest dreams, would he have imagined this. Hell, not in his wildest nightmares would he have imagined this! He returned to the photo album cabinets and withdrew several leather style scrapbooks and reseated himself. He opened the first book cautiously, expecting some unforeseen fate to befall his intrusion. Each book held approximately thirty clear vinyl photo pages. Each page had between six and nine photos in ordered display.

Twenty minutes later Bill replaced the albums. He had witnessed still life's of Frank, Pam, Pat, and a multitude of unidentified persons, in and out of costume, using more tools and apparatuses than were used in the inquisition, and bent and contorted to every imaginable sexual position. He was, at first, reviled, but then like the proverbial moth, he was drawn to this perverted flame. He couldn't wait to turn the page to see what new and different deviation had been fostered. As he scrutinized each new photo he would subconsciously tilt his head to one side or the other in an attempt to understand how the human body could bend to that position. He would also cringe or wince when some painful act was performed. When the "girls" were engaged in some particularly erotic act he could be heard to coo a sympathetic, "Mnnn." He was greatly entertained by the "girls", even stimulated, but that was quickly reversed at the sight of a flaccid or erect Frank. Bill always thought his own penis was rather gnarly; however, all he could do when examining the panoramic views of Frank's organ was issue a distinct and repugnant, "Ugh."

From the desk, he moved to the file cabinet to see what other information he might garner from this living compilation of the Kama Sutra. He opened the drawer and began scouring the rows of names and dates associated with the disks. He didn't need to view these records; his concern was for names and dates of interest. After the photo albums there was no need to see more, besides, he was nearly numb from the volume of activity, after all, there were only so many things you could put in so many places. Adding motion and sound would only be beating this dead horse. He was shuffling through the second drawer when a passing name caught his eye. He flipped back several tabs and withdrew the particular video. As he read the name and date an avalanche of emotions crushed him. He was shaking with fear and anger as he moved to the playback unit. He withdrew the disk from its plastic holder and inserted it in the machine. He hit the start button and watched a new horror unfold before him. It lasted for five and a half minutes. During those minutes he would be changed forever. When it stopped he ejected the platter and attempted to replace it in its holder. His hand was shaking so badly it took several attempts to accomplish the task. He filed it and closed the drawer. He meticulously replaced everything as he had found it, reset the desk chair and checked the settings on the equipment. It wasn't necessary to wipe his prints since he had been wearing surgical gloves from his entry to the house. He calmly went to the bathroom, kneeled before the toilet, and threw up! When there was nothing left to regurgitate he pulled a towel from his duffle and wiped his mouth. He rose, washed his face and hands, wiped down the sink and commode and returned to the main room. He sat down on the floor and sobbed . . . uncontrollably. After several minutes he slammed his fist on the floor. His course was now defined; they had defined it for him. There would be no turning back. Weak from catharsis, he struggled to rise. Once risen, he retraced his steps and left the house.

He knew in his heart there was a piece of him left behind. He also knew that he would be returning soon to claim it!

CHAPTER THIRTEEN

Bill's first order of business was to shortcut Frank and his deadline. If Frank believed that Bill was ready to yield to his demands then it would make it easier for Bill to massage the timetable. One way to accomplish that would be to beat Frank to the punch. He tapped in the phone number for the Turners. Of course no one answered, they would just now be landing at the airport, so Bill waited for the appropriate tone and said, "Frank, it's Bill. I'm prepared to discuss turning the children over to you, Pam and Pat. There are a lot of details to work out so get back to me at your convenience."

There, Frank thinks he's won.

A false sense of security had to accrue to Bill's benefit. Secondly, he had given no indication that he knew that Frank and the girls were out of town. When Frank called back tomorrow Bill would wait a day to return the call. With his original message indicating his willingness to surrender the children Frank would not be concerned about the extra day. If Bill played his cards right he could turn that extra day into a week, and a week would give him the time he needed to activate his plan.

After a quick dinner, and a couple of drinks, Bill arrived at his seat of honor in the attic. Before he could reach for the Messenger XD 500 it rang.

He removed the receiver and said, "Hello, Edith."

"Hello, Bill. You've been having quite a day, you must be exhausted?"

"You've obviously been watching."

"Of course, you're better than my favorite sitcom."

"I'm always happy to help you pass the time. Oops, I forgot there is no time there. Anyway, you know what I mean. And, you're right I am exhausted, but you know what they say, 'There's no rest for the wicked.'"

Edith chuckled as she replied, "I'd hardly call you wicked Bill, but if you're going where I think you're going with Frank and the girls, you might earn you're first merit badge."

"And just where do you think I'm going?"

"It will suffice to say, you have to fight fire with fire. Remember, I can't influence your path. Once you choose it however, I can then comment on it."

"Well, that's what I'm here to find out."

"I don't understand."

"I've got a lot of questions for you. Until I get them all answered I'm not committing to any particular course of action."

Her tone was filled with glee as she said, "Well, what are we waiting for? I can't wait to see how this turns out."

"I'll bet you can't. Why do I think you have your own ulterior motives invested here?"

"Please, Bill, would I do that - not here anyway, I'm not permitted."

"Whatever, Edith. Let's get started."

"Okay."

"I know you didn't know about the secret room when you were alive. Did you know about Frank and the girls activities when you were alive?"

A pause, then, "No."

That tell tale pause. "Did you believe there was something going on when you were alive?"

"Yes."

"Did you ever confront Frank with you're beliefs?"

"Yes."

"Did you confront the girls too?"

"Yes."

"Did either of them admit to it?"

"No."

"And though they wouldn't confirm your suspicions you were still convinced they were involved in some unseemly practices?"

"Yes."

Each "yes" answer from her permitted Bill to insert another factual piece into an otherwise disjointed puzzle. He was gaining momentum and, with Edith's assistance he would soon have the appropriate pallet and brushes to complete the painting.

Buoyed by his progress he veered slightly and said, "Are most of the other people I saw in those photographs business associates of Frank's?"

"Yes."

"Would it be important for me to know who the other people are?"

"No."

"Would I be correct in believing that he uses these sexual encounters to influence business decisions?"

"Yes."

"Does he use the photographs and videos to blackmail these individuals?"

"No."

"Would he?"

"Yes."

He needed to shift gears and gather background to reinforce the evidence he was gathering. "I know Frank's a murderer, but I can't bring myself to comprehend how a person, no matter how despicable, can surrender his daughters to clients in such a way."

Silence.

"Were the girls teenagers when he began these practices?"

"No."

"Well at least he waited until they were adults?"

"No."

"What kind of gibberish is this?"

"I'm just answering your questions."

"If they weren't teenagers, and they weren't adults . . . ." As the horror of the only possibility left wrapped itself around his heart Bill closed his eyes, clenched his fists, and tightened his jaws. How low could a human being stoop? The question was its own answer. Frank was not a human being; he was some kind of animal. Bill had never encountered evil . . . until now. This was, "the belly of the beast" incarnate! As gut wrenching as it was, he needed to close this topic and move on. Anger and desolation filled his closing, "My God, Edith, you mean they were children when this all started?"

"No."

"What?!!!"

Silence.

He was relieved on one hand that the girls had not been prostituted, but knocked down by confusion on the other.

"As you're prone to do Edith, you've lost me."

"I'd suggest you think Bill. When you've exhausted all your presumed possibilities then what's left must be the answer."

"That's easy for you to say Edith, but I'm left with nothing."

Here it was, another turn in the maze. From over top of the maze hedge line that impish Mr. Murphy peered down and said, "I can't help you Bill, because you're helpless. Try listening to what the lady just said to you. If that doesn't work, you can give up, or, there are always the Scotches of the world. Either way, I'll be out here waiting."

Mr. Murphy stuck his tongue out through a very broad grin and dissolved.

Bill replayed his questions and Edith's answers in his mind. The second time through an idea began forming. He took a big swig of Scotch while he massaged it. She was right ... it was obvious. That was the problem ... it was too obvious. He was so invested in a particular scenario that, when it didn't fit the facts, he couldn't see the forest for the trees!

Discovery intertwined his query, "Do you mean the girls are responsible for this?"

"Yes."

Now what, asshole? This throws a wrench into your thinking.

He confirmed this new position, "So Frank was not responsible for setting up the sexual workshop?"

For the first time Edith embellished, "Frank's a murderer, not a pimp."

Leave it to Edith to capture the moment with as few words as possible. This would require him to take two steps back. The focus of his plan had been aimed at Frank. With this latest tidbit an adjustment would be in order. But, even though the girls had extreme sexual appetites, did they deserve the same treatment as Frank? He thought not, but if he'd learned nothing else in this exercise, it was to keep digging until all germane information was uncovered.

"That's the first time you've given me an answer other than a yes or no. I thought you couldn't offer direction?"

"I didn't give you direction. You already knew the answer; I just put it in context. The rules haven't changed yet."

"Should I assume they will?"

"You never assume."

"All right, Edith, enough of the word games."

Silence.

He continued, "Is there anything else I should know about the girls that is relevant to my exploration?"

"Yes."

He launched his frustration, "Shit, Edith, what now?"

Silence. The effect noted, she then said, "Bill, I just answer the questions. Why do you insist on blaming me for the answers? I have no control over what, or how, you request information."

He inhaled deeply. She, of course, was right again.

"Edith, you threw me a curve. I know, I asked for it, but I need to retrace my steps and determine where I go next. Can I call you back after a nap and some dinner?"

"Of course."

"Thank you, Edith. I'll talk to you later."

They disconnected.

~~~~~~~~~~~~~~~~~~~~~~~~~~~~~

Bill was repositioning himself before the phone when it rang.

"Hello, Edith."

"Hello, Bill. Feeling better?"

"I am. Thanks for the break."

"You've been on a fast track. You need to slow down."

"I appreciate the thought, but that will have to come later. Can we resume now?"

"Yes."

"As best I could, I reviewed our conversation. I need to review a point we made before."

Silence.

"You stated earlier that you had confronted Frank and the girls regarding their activities. Is that correct?"

"Yes."

"You were a very wealthy woman Edith. Is that a fair statement?"

"Yes."
~~~~~~~~~~~~~~~~~~~~~~~~~~~~~

"As a matter of fact, Gil left his fortune to you. The only exception was a rather substantial trust that would be divided by Pam, Pat, and Marci on their respective fortieth birthdays. Is that correct?"

"Yes."

"Would it also be fair to say that your financial position was considerably larger than Frank's?"

"Yes."

"I read your will Edith. Marci had a copy here at the house."

"Yes?"

"You left everything to Frank, Pam and Pat; except for a token to Marci. Is that correct?"

"Yes."

"If I remember correctly, that was because you were adamant about her marrying me."

"Yes."

"After your death your -"

She severed his thought, "I was wrong, Bill."

"Excuse me?"

"I was wrong about you Bill."

"Thank you, Edith."

"Silence."

He had come to know her well. This was a major admission. Thank you was enough; it was better left alone. He restarted, "After your death your estate was divided in accordance with your will. Correct?"

"Yes."

"You made Frank, Pam and Pat very wealthy people. Correct?"

"Yes."

"You are a tough woman Edith, and knowing -"

She sliced through his statement, "Come on, Bill, I'm only as tough as I have to be. I have always been fair."

"Relax, Edith. If you'll let me finish?"

Silence.

"Very well then. Knowing what I know about you, I am inclined to believe you threatened the three of them with something. Is that correct?"

"Yes."

"Did you threaten to disown them if they didn't curtail their activities?"
"Yes."

"Well, here we are, Edith. I believe bullfighters call this the moment of truth."

He paused before igniting the fuse, and then asked, "Did you die of natural causes Edith?"

"No."

"Were you murdered Edith."

"Yes."

Expecting a particular response and getting it, are two vastly different circumstances! His exhale was long and slow.

"Was it Frank?"

That poignant pause, and then, "Yes."

Her pause had opened the door and Bill rushed through, "The girls too?"

"Yes."

Betrayal is a tough pill to swallow, but from your own family . . . from the people you believe will protect you no matter what. He hurt for her, "I'm so sorry Edith."

"You needn't be. As a matter of fact Bill, I'm rather proud of you."

With puzzlement he replied, "Proud?"

"Absolutely. You uncovered the truth. Granted, I'm along to help, but you did the heavy lifting."

"But, Edith -"

"No buts, Bill, if I were there I'd kiss you."

"Edith, please."

"Are you blushing Bill?"

He stammered a response, "No, Edith, of course not."

"That's what I thought Bill. Don't worry I won't tell anyone that your mother-in-law has a thing for you. Besides, Marci already knows and she doesn't mind."

"Marci knows that you'd like to kiss me?"

"Sure. We communicated just before you and I spoke."

"And you didn't tell me?"

"I'm telling you now."

"What did she say?"

"She said she has always loved you and still does."

He started to speak, but the lump in his throat wouldn't let the words past.

"Are you still there?"

He forced a raspy, "Yes," as a tear rolled down his cheek.

"I thought you'd be happy to hear from her?"

"I am Edith. It's just . . . it's just . . . I thought she hated me?"

"Why in the hell would she hate you?"

"When I wouldn't help her end her life she called me all sorts of names and I thought she hated me."

Edith chuckled as she offered, "She did, but women have a short memory when it comes to the men they love. She's proud of you too. She can also see the man that your becoming; and, I stress the word man."

The tears were now cascading down his cheeks. He tried wiping them with his sleeve, but they were coming to fast. He looked down at the damp spot on his trousers: simply shrugged, and then smiled. His joy grew with each drop that crashed into his lap. When the puddle was large enough he knew he would explode with happiness. After all, why the hell should he care about a little salt in his lap, his life finally had meaning.

"Bill, are you all right?"

He couldn't speak. In an instant his months of anger and isolation came crashing down on him. Just as instantly, the self-hatred, the loathing for everything he'd represented was washed away. He pulled the phone to his side so Edith could not hear him weeping.

She heard something in the distance, but what, "Bill?"

Nothing.

She yelled, "Bill, are you crying?"

This he heard. He pulled the phone back and choked out, "Yes."

"What's the matter?"

"I love her so much."

"She knows that. She always did."

"But I didn't show her when it counted."

"It still counts Bill. It always counts. Women know these things. Gil is here somewhere and I'm going to find him."

"I'm sorry, Edith."

"What for?"

"I'm so concerned about myself, I didn't even think how you must feel about Gil."

"It's fine, Bill. Don't concern yourself, besides I have more to tell you from Marci."

His excitement blanketed the receiver, "What?"

"She's afraid of what you might be planning? She just wants you to protect the children, no more."

His purpose was no longer split. Edith's disclosures had now placed the girls on the same shelf as Frank. They would be dealt with in the same manner. Everywhere he went women were demanding equal treatment. Well, he was an equal opportunity avenger . . . the girls would get their share!

His tone changed along with his demeanor, "You can tell Marci that I'm going to protect the children the only way I know how. And, in the process, I'm going to settle some other scores too. You can call it two birds with one stone, or, in this case, three birds with one stone."

"Are you going to kill Frank and the girls?"

"I didn't say that Edith."

"I heard what you didn't say Bill, and I believe you are very artfully sidestepping the question."

"You can believe whatever you want, just make sure to tell Marci when you communicate that I'm going to protect the children."

"It won't work, Bill. We both know what your intentions are."

"Well then, you're both smarter than I am. Regardless, we're all going to have to wait and see . . . aren't we?"

"You can't -"

He amputated her statement, "Edith, this conversation is over. I'll talk to you soon."

He gently placed the receiver on its cradle, took a large swallow of Scotch, and smiled.

As he rose to leave the phone rang.

He faced it, came to attention and saluted, "Edith, I know you can hear me. Save the battery, because I'm not going to answer. The die is cast."

As he turned to exit the attic the phone stopped ringing . . . .

CHAPTER FOURTEEN

Bill had extended the children's stay at Jeff and Donna's. Jeff and Donna had been a godsend. Without them he would never have been able to concentrate on the components of his plan. He spoke to Bill Jr. and Molly everyday, but the separation was wearing on all of them. Each day he justified that separation with the need for their future welfare and safety. And, indeed that would have been enough, but he knew that equal retribution was demanded for the past heinous acts committed against Gil and Edith. He hadn't known Gil, and his regard for Edith had only recently become more than a casual mention, but their deaths convinced him to what extent the Turner's would go to accomplish their goals.

Each day, his conversation with Molly tore at his heart, "Daddy, when can we come home? Don't you want us anymore?"

"Of course I want you. I love you and Bill more than anything."

"But we've been here a week and we miss you and our fish. We want to come home."

"I know sweetie. The fish miss you too. I'm taking good care of them until you get back. In another week we'll be together again and I won't ever let you go. Now, put your brother on the phone."

Those conversations were tearing him apart, but better some temporary pain than what could be expected if Frank and the girls had their way.

He also spoke to Donna everyday, "Donna, I can't thank you and Jeff enough for what you're doing for me and the kids. When this is over I'll try and make it up to you."

"You concentrate on what you're doing and when it's finished we'll talk about how you can make it up to me. In the meantime, I'm here for you Bill, remember that."

~~~~~~~~~~~~~~~~~~~~~~~~~~~~

Bill answered the house phone, "Hello."

"Hello, Bill, it's Frank."

"Hello, Frank, how are you?"

Agitation filled Frank's reply, "I returned your call yesterday. Why haven't you called back?"

"I'm sorry Frank, but I didn't get your message. You're the third person today that said they called me and left a message. I have a call into the phone company to find out why I'm not getting messages."

Considering the fact that everyone has problems from time to time with phone service Frank could hardly deny the possibility. Temporarily mollified he continued, "Well, all right. I thought you were ducking me."

"Frank, I called you a day before my week deadline, that doesn't seem to me that I'm ducking you."

"Well, I suppose not, but I'm anxious to get this matter settled."

"Send the paper work over. I'll review it, along with my attorney, and get back to you with any questions. If there aren't any questions I'll sign it immediately."
~~~~~~~~~~~~~~~~~~~~~~~~~~~~

Frank barked back, "Wait a minute; that could take a minimum of three days and as long as a week. We never discussed the need for an attorney. I don't like this at all Bill."

Bill's tone became more formal . . . much more formal, "First, Frank, would *you* ever sign an agreement without having an attorney review it?" He didn't wait for a response before launching, "I think not. If you would, then you're not the businessman I think you are. Second, this is not a bushel of wheat that I'm surrendering . . . it's my children! Would you have given Pam and Pat away? And, if you had, would you have done it without guaranteeing their future welfare? Again, I think not. But if you would then you aren't the father that Edith and Marci thought you were."

Question that you piece of shit and you give away your real colors. You won't, and we both know it. So, stick it up you ass Frank!

There was a pause before Frank responded. When he did his voice was more contrite, "Since you put it that way, Bill, I suppose it makes more sense. Pam, Pat and I are just excited to get started giving Bill and Molly a new life. I guess it's clouding my thinking."

"All right, Frank. Send the agreement over so I can get started. I'll get this accomplished as fast as I can."

"You'll have it tomorrow."

"Thanks, Frank. Goodbye."

The dial tone in Bill's ear was Frank's goodbye.

~~~~~~~~~~~~~~~~~~~~~~~~~~~~

Two days later Bill called Frank. It was time to instill anger in the negotiations. An angry adversary was an off balance adversary. An angry adversary was not a quick and cognitive thinking adversary. Bill smirked to himself; he was almost starting to enjoy this war bullshit . . .
~~~~~~~~~~~~~~~~~~~~~~~~~~~~

well, almost. He was smart enough to realize that one slip and a lot of lives would be in jeopardy!

On the fourth ring Pat picked up the phone,"Turner residence."

"Hello, Pam, how are you? It's Bill."

In a very seductive tone she said,"Well, hello Bill. This is a pleasant surprise. Are you calling to set a date to finish what we started at your house?"

"Not yet, but soon. I'm actually calling to speak to Frank."

"I'll get him for you. We're anxious to get together again. By the way, this is Pat, not Pam."

He knew that. The wrong name was just a simple way of keeping the girls slightly off balance. Siblings hated to be compared, rivalry would do the rest, he completed the dig,"I'm sorry, Pat. You sound just like Pam. But, I'm sure you hear that all the time."

With a hint of annoyance she said,"I'll get father for you."

While he waited he hummed a military march. Something by Sousa he thought. Regardless, he was in a military mood.

Frank picked up and said,"Hello, Bill, what's that you were humming? Was that a march by John Phillip Sousa?"

"I don't know Frank. I heard it on the car radio yesterday and I can't get it out of my head. That ever happen to you?"

Frank wasn't in the mood for small talk,"What do you want Bill?"

"Well, Frank, you're not going to like this, but I found out today that my attorney is out of town for several days. His secretary called me when she got the agreement. I had forwarded it this morning by messenger."

Anger danced down the line as Frank snapped,"You're right, Bill, I don't like it at all. You just keep wasting time."

In his most charming voice Bill answered, "Frank, I went through the document as soon as I received it. I expressed it to my attorney today and now I'm calling with the news as soon as I got it. It doesn't seem fair of you to say I'm wasting time."

"I don't give a damn, I want this process moving."

"His secretary assured me he would get on it as soon as he returned."

Frank had reached the fuse point that Bill had hoped for, "We're going out of town the day after tomorrow on business for four days. That agreement better be here when I return. Playtime is over Bill. Have it here when I get back, do you understand?"

Smugly Bill thought, *I knew you were leaving town Frank. I read your e-mail.*

His reply oozed maple syrup, "I certainly do Frank. Now, you have a successful business trip and don't worry about a thing. I'll see that the agreement is completed for your return."

Frank slammed the receiver down!

Bill smiled. It was a broad, self-satisfied smile. As he gently returned the handset to its cradle he began humming that Sousa March again.

~~~~~~~~~~~~~~~~~~~~~~~~~~~

Frank couldn't have been more cooperative if he'd tried. It would take Bill a good two days to bring all the pieces together. Frank's unwitting participation in his own downfall was a very helpful surprise.

When Bill thought of the irony he joked to himself, *when this is over Frank, I'll have to send you a thank you note. But, you probably wouldn't understand, and if you did you wouldn't appreciate it. Just my way of saying, "Fuck you, Frank!"*
~~~~~~~~~~~~~~~~~~~~~~~~~~~

~~~~~~~~~~~~~~~~~~~~~~~~~~~~~~

Two days later, his electronic shopping list complete, Bill scripted the dance with the Turner's. No assault plan worth its salt was ever initiated without a completed task timeline. It, along with contingencies for the unexpected, was then tested, retested, and each and every detail committed to memory.

The following evening he prepared to leave his home. If successful, this visit to Frank's would put in place the final preparations for his own personal D-Day. He had verified Frank and the girl's arrival at their business destination. He had confirmed their rental car pick-up, drop-off date, their check-in, length of stay and checkout date at the nationally known downtown hotel. Hell, he even knew their suite number and what they were having for meals, in and out of the hotel. He needed a backpack to carry all the miniature equipment. He placed it and the other items of need in the trunk of his car, exited the garage, and drove to that spot down the access road from the Turner's house. Face blackened and regaled in night camouflage he gathered his assault tools. With a duffle bag in each hand and the pack strapped to his back he began the trek to that white split-rail fence. His movements were slowed by the considerable weight he carried. His consolation - if the job were completed as planned, the return trip would be with a substantially smaller load. Twenty minutes later he stood before his point of demarcation. He was confident, prepared, and excited with the task at hand, but like any rookie he was nervous. He now knew what a rookie, standing at home plate waiting for his first pitch in a World Series felt – or, what a pro golfer felt when he addressed his first tee shot in his first Master's Tournament. He swallowed hard and placed his gear on the other side of the fence. Over this hurdle, he secured his supplies, carefully moved to the backdoor, dialed in his security code and entered the house. Not sure he had breathed since he left the fence he paused to take several deep breaths. He set the alarm on his watch. He had eight hours to complete the placement and evaluation of all the electronics and surveillance devices. There were several lamps on in the house. They were obviously meant to dissuade intruders. Bill chuckled at their intention and thanked Frank for lighting his way to the lower level. Through the bookcase and into the inner sanctum Bill set about placing his toys. He silently thanked the electronics industry
~~~~~~~~~~~~~~~~~~~~~~~~~~~~~~

for their numerous wireless innovations. Had he needed to hard wire the cameras etc. required for his scheme the job would have been impossible. Stealth was difficult enough but physical wiring would have surely led to exposure and subsequent discovery. No, thanks to wireless and miniaturization, his probability of success was considerably higher. Six hours gone he took a break for a sandwich and cold drink. As he sat, replenishing his reserves he scanned the room. He could see nothing out of the ordinary, nothing that wasn't already there. He rose and traveled the room. He placed himself in every conceivable position ... nothing. Only his trained eye could begin to make out the minute edges or corners that now existed. It would take a specific, detailed search to uncover his interior decorating. And, he knew that when the Turner's were using this room that would be the last thing on their minds.

He finished his repast and placed the wrappers and drink container into one of the duffle bags. He resumed his charge. Within an hour he was finished. He toured the room, retrieving any and all evidence of his visit. He started to leave, stopped, and then moved slowly to the tape cabinet. He opened the appropriate drawer and leafed through the disks until he found the one that compelled his revisit. He read the label. He ran his fingers across its surface and hung his head in despair. After a few moments of silent reflection he replaced it. He closed the drawer, left, what he was now calling "ground zero", and worked his way back through the house.

Outside, he inhaled deeply from the clean night air and whispered to himself, "Can we ever put Humpty Dumpty back together again?"

As he drove home the sun was beginning to meet the day.

Back home, he undressed and retired. Not the physical activity, but the mental and emotional strain of the past hours and days had completely drained his reserves. After four hours of much needed sleep he rose to a long hot shower and a steeping cup of coffee. Sometime after the biggest breakfast he'd had since Marci's death he seated himself in the commander's chair at command central. He reached forward and initiated a main console housing nine mini screens. He then flipped a switch that turned on a low level light that he left there specifically to check the operation of the nine cameras. There, displayed for him in living color, were nine different views of "ground zero". The images were clear and concise. Better than he had hoped for and better than he required for their intended purpose. Pleased with the equipment, and himself, he turned the low level light off first and then the multi-screened console.

He then swiveled his chair ninety degrees and faced his computer. With phase one complete, he now set about phase two and beyond. His first order would be the manipulation of each and every one of Frank's financial accounts. Once Bill had the mechanisms in place he could configure Frank's holdings to anyone, and anywhere, within seconds. Once he had gutted Frank he would gladly do the same for the girls. There were also dummy accounts to create and a detailed, but complex array of paths connecting all of the shadow transactions. It was vital that an "expert" be able to follow the convoluted trail that Bill was creating. Of course, the key to Bill's success would be allowing someone else to follow the designed course and not be able to decipher the keys that he had invented underneath.

After that would come the appropriate alibis. Not complicated defenses, but defenses that were real . . . believable. Ones that would prove, under close scrutiny, that no matter what had actually occurred, nothing could be attributable to him.

With very little sleep, and a day later, he turned off his computer and bellied up to a tall Scotch. Half way through his reward the house phone rang. He was annoyed that someone would interrupt his *serious* drinking. Grumbling to himself he raised the receiver and groused, "Hello."

There was no one there, which only served to sour his mood further. He replaced the receiver and resumed his tasting. Moments later the phone rang again.

He repeated everything as before and said loudly, "Hello."

Again. No one.

Could this be . . . no, there was nothing for them to discuss - at least, not yet. After a brief argument with himself he decided to be certain. He walked the steps to the second landing. He had taken one step on the upper level when he heard a phone chiming in the distance. He trudged the stairway to the attic. The Messenger XD 500 was announcing

Edith's arrival. He sat down, retrieved the handset and said, "Yes, Edith, what do you want?"

"Hello to you too, Bill."

"I'm sorry Edith, but I'm tired."

"As well you should be. You've been a busy little beaver."

"Spare me the cute analogies. What is it?"

"Nothing from me. I'm delighted with what I see so far."

"Then, what?"

"It's Marci."

That got his attention, "What about her?"

"She's very concerned about what you might do to Frank, Pam and Pat. She wants you to reconsider."

He started to reply and stopped. A very salient point jarred him from Marci's entreaty. He thought a moment longer and then inquired of Edith, "Wait a second Edith, does she know you talk to me?"

Silence.

He waited.

Silence.

"Edith, you can stop with the silent shit. I asked you a question and I know you have to answer. So, answer me."

"Yes, Bill, she knows."

"I thought no one was allowed to know or you'd be in trouble."

"That's true, Bill."

"If she doesn't tell will she be in trouble too?"

"Probably."

"Why the hell did you tell her?"

"I didn't."

"You mean she knew it?"

"Apparently."

"Edith, I don't want something to happen to her over this."

"Let me see if I understand this? Fuck Edith, as long as Marci's okay."

"That's not what I meant and you know it."

"Nevertheless, Bill, it's all moot at this point, nothing's going to change. She asked me to relay her concerns and I've done that. Do you have a reply or not?"

He was weary, that was all he knew, and all this outside crap was just adding to the pile. His reply reflected his frustration, "Here's what you tell her Edith. If she's not happy with the way I'm handling this, she can come back and take care of it herself."

Edith laughed and said, "That works for me Bill. I'll tell her next time she contacts me. Although she probably already knows."

"Now if we're done Edith, I'd like to have another drink and go to bed."

"Sweet dreams, Bill."

The line went dead.

He ambled down stairs, fixed himself another large Scotch and went to bed. There was a very real possibility that this would be his last chance for substantial rest until this was over.

CHAPTER FIFTEEN

He had two days until Frank and the girls returned home. Between brief naps, food breaks, and the continuous dress rehearsals, the hours sped past. The equipment required for this stage could be held in one small duffle bag. Each item was placed in the carrier to allow quick identification and removal. Bill located the bag on a kitchen counter near the garage entry. This allowed for retrieval on the run. Staging complete, he need only wait for the Turner's unknowing cooperation and notification from the warning system he had installed at "ground zero". He sat at his computer replaying the nuances that would ultimately complete the end game. Each day that Frank and the girls had been gone he had called and left a message. Nothing specific, a simple, "Hi, how are you, hope all is well, talk to you soon." This was to establish his overall regard for the Turner's and concern for their general welfare. Next, he placed a message on his answering machine that he had been called out of town suddenly on business. When Frank returned and the agreements weren't there he would definitely call Bill. This ploy should keep Frank angry and focused on Bill – and, not as likely to discover any miscues that Bill might have left behind. He had gone over every step of his "ground zero" set-up and was convinced he'd left nothing to chance, but keeping Frank occupied was part of the insurance built into every good battle plan.

One hour after the projected return of the Turner's Bill's phone rang. He had his machine on speaker so he could screen his calls and remain anonymous. While his recorder played, caller ID confirmed Frank's telephone number. When his message was complete a very irate Frank Turner exploded his return, "Where the hell are you Bill? The agreement isn't here. I've had enough of your bullshit; if that paper work isn't here by tomorrow at noon you're going to be a very unhappy man!"

Bill had a broad grin as Frank slammed his receiver down. He carefully erased Frank's message. He wanted no record of angry discourse between himself and Frank. His relationship with the Turner's must appear to any outside review as one of close and caring relatives. As he listened to the blank recording for the second time he spoke aloud, "Sounds like you're pretty angry Frank. Gee, that's too bad. I wonder what I can do to make it worse? I'll try and think of something. By the way Frank, fuck you!"

Approximately one and a half hours later Bill picked up his phone and dialed the Turner's. He had the call rerouted through another city to confirm his trip. On the third chime Pat answered, "Turner residence." "Hello, Pam, it's Bill."

Anger filled her reply, "This is Pat, Bill. Can't you get our voices straight?"

"I'm sorry Pat, you sound so much alike. I'll get it right one of these days."

Still miffed, she moved forward, "I don't recognize the number, where are you Bill?"

"I'm out of town at the moment. I got Frank's message."

"Father's very angry at you Bill."

"It would appear so. Put him on please."

Before she could put the receiver down he yelled, "Oh, Pat."

"Yes, Bill."

"I was hoping we could get together in a couple of weeks?"

A brief silence and then in a much lighter voice she said, "Pam and I would like that Bill."

"Oh, I'm sorry Pat, I didn't make myself clear. I don't want to see Pam too. I just want to see you."

Another silence, and then, "I don't know if I can do that. Pam will get upset."

"Do we have to tell her?"

She bubbled as she said, "I suppose not."

"Good, I'll call you soon."

"I can't wait."

She was gone and Bill was left to applaud yet another well placed distraction.

He was a few bars into that Sousa March when Frank interrupted angrily, "Again with that damn march. Where the hell are you Bill?"

"I got called out of town on business. I wasn't sure what day you were coming home so I left the message on my answering device."

"Where the hell is the paper work?"

"I assume by your anger that it's not there."

"You're damn right it's not here. And if I don't have it by -"

Bill cut him off, "Whoa, Frank. When I left town yesterday my attorney guaranteed that you'd have the agreement today for your return."

"Your attorney's a liar."

"That may be, but until you called I had no way of knowing that it wasn't there waiting for you."

"Well, I don't believe you."

"Suit yourself, Frank – but until I talk to him I won't know what's happened."

"I suggest you speak to him now."

Bill was ready for this response, "When I got your message I tried to call his home. He wasn't there. I then tried his cell. I got his voice mail. I left messages in both places to call me immediately."

Ultimatum inflated Frank's anger, "I'm tired of your crap Bill."

Bill smiled, it was time to push Frank one more step off balance, "You know what Frank, I'm getting tired of your crap too. You're the only one that's right here. If things aren't just the way you want them then, I'm stalling, or, I'm being cute, or who knows what! You've got two choices, wait until I talk to my attorney, or proceed with whatever dastardly thing you're going to do to me. Because, Frank, I don't give a shit anymore. I've had your orders up to my eyeballs."

Silence.

Bill continued, "Well, Frank, what's it going to be?"

More silence. Then, in a firm, but contrite tone Frank said, "I guess your attorney may be to blame for this. I want this settled Bill . . . now."

"That's fair, Frank. As soon as he calls me I'll call you. Don't get upset if it's not until tomorrow morning. It's getting late, and he may wait until tomorrow to get to me."

"All right, Bill. I expect a call no later than noon tomorrow."

"You'll have it. Good night, Frank."

The line went to dial tone.

Bill knew that Frank was beginning to weigh other options. He also knew that it would take Frank several days to move against him. So, Frank had nothing to lose by being magnanimous. If Bill were telling the truth then this would all be resolved before it would be necessary to apply other means of compliance. Either way, Bill's strong rebuttal and/ or Frank's other options have again kept Frank otherwise occupied.

Bill was very pleased with himself. He was becoming a rather accomplished adversary. He was going to make Marci and Edith proud yet!
His outspoken punctuation completed the moment, "By the way, Frank, I don't have an attorney. The documents have never left my house. Oh yeah, Frank, fuck you again!"

~~~~~~~~~~~~~~~~~~~~~~~~~~~~

The day before Frank's return Bill had sent e-mails to Frank's four closest friends. He had initiated them from Frank's traveling laptop. Each was filled with the general topics that friends discuss. Nothing out of the ordinary, or was there? Mixed in among the dialogue was a very subtle remark that Pat had been acting strangely lately. This remark would mean nothing until placed in context of the upcoming events. If asked by an investigator, one, or maybe two, of Frank's friends would be unable to recall anything out of the ordinary, but all four not recognizing something different would be an astronomical impossibility. Of course, Bill had blocked Frank's e-mail account from receiving any return e-mail. He had also blocked all of the Turner's phones from receiving any incoming calls or messages. This had been done in such a way that anyone attempting communication, via either media, would believe that their messages had been saved and recorded. At the appropriate moment Bill would release any and all such communiqués with their times and dates. They would show as if they had actually occurred in the appropriate time frame and the Turner's lack of response would be simply that, a lack of response. No one would be the wiser and events would appear as usual. He put a mental check mark next to this latest line item on his battle plan.

He smiled as he thought; *Talk about slight of hand, magic has nothing on science and technology.*

~~~~~~~~~~~~~~~~~~~~~~~~~~~~

His permanent residence had become "command central." He left for food or bathroom breaks, nothing else. He had even relinquished Scotch and contact with Edith until this was complete. Each would be an unnecessary distraction until this was an intriguing piece of history.

He waited for his "early warning system" to call him to arms. Twice the system had alerted him to an entry into Frank's inner sanctum. Both times it had been Frank alone. He needed all three together at "ground zero".

He waited.

Nothing.

The following day, just before noon, he called Frank. Several rings and Pat answered, "Hello, Bill."

He continued playing his trump cards, "Hello, Pat."

She cooed back, "You recognized my voice."

"I now have a reason to know who I'm talking to."

"That's sweet, Bill."

"Sweets to the sweet."

Pat was warmed by Bill's intimacy, but her tone reflected her concern at being discovered by Pam. She deflected the conversation, "I see you're back in town."

"I am. I returned early this morning. I need to talk to your father."

"I hope we can get together soon? I'll get father."

"We will. Thank you."

While he waited he hummed his favorite march.

Frank interrupted a particularly vigorous passage, "Hello, Bill."

"Hello, Frank."

"What's going on now?"

"I finally spoke to my attorney. It was just twenty minutes ago."

Forcefully, "And?"

"He was out of town. His Mother died. The funeral is today and he will be returning tonight."

"How convenient for you."

Bill growled back at Frank, "Do you want me to continue, or would you like to end this call now?"

Frank retreated slightly, "You can go on."

"He apologizes for the delay, but hopes everyone understands. He will finish reading the agreement first thing tomorrow and have it in your hands for final review the following morning." Before Frank could respond Bill set the hook, "Before you say anything Frank, should I call him back and tell him not to bother?"

Moments passed before Frank spat his response, "You have until the day after tomorrow Bill. If I don't have that agreement then nothing you do will matter."

As Frank jammed the receiver on its cradle Bill smiled and said aloud, "Oh, I think I can do something that will matter Frank."

Bill sat waiting. For hours nothing occurred. He stood and left for a sandwich. Half way out the door the alarm buzzed and all his screens lit up in living color. He repositioned himself before the monitors. It was Pam, alone, dressed in high heels and a see through negligee.

He strained his eyes to focus and thought, *you dope, why didn't you buy those high-resolution cameras? I could see a birthmark with those.*

She moved to the video cabinet and removed a disk. She placed it in the replay unit.

As she moved about the room Bill realized that she was by herself and would continue to be. He reached to turn the system off. His hand stopped mid-way as Pam moved to a wall and removed a phallic device. She kicked off her shoes and slowly pulled the negligee over her head. Any thoughts of terminating this session had moved way down Bill's list of priorities. He sat back in his chair and kicked himself, again, for not buying those high-resolution cameras.

She moved again to the playback unit, engaged the disk, and then climbed onto Frank's desk. She lay down on top, and began watching one of her homemade movies. As the show continued she used the vibrator in ways Bill could only have fantasized about.

He felt guilty invading Pam's privacy. Particularly this privacy! He didn't feel guilty enough however to stop watching. As a matter of fact, he was so entranced by the eroticism unfolding before him he lost all awareness of anything he was doing. So much so, twenty minutes later when she brought herself to orgasm he joined the party!

She got off the desk, dressed, turned off the video equipment, washed the vibrator, replaced it on the wall and exited the room.

Gee, Pam, not even a goodnight kiss. Just leave me hanging here . . . so to speak.

His joke was an effort to cover up all the negative emotions backing up in his brain. The truth of the matter was, he felt like shit! He looked at the mess in his lap and thought, *You can try and justify this performance with the excuse that you haven't had any sex since Marci died; or, you can make up some other phony reason. None of it changes the fact that this puts you side by side with them. Knowing what you are about to do, you still sat here like some sleazy peeping Tom and watched her. Retribution has its place, but be careful, you may not like what you're becoming.*

He turned off the equipment, and then rose to clean himself and change clothes.

~~~~~~~~~~~~~~~~~~~~~~~~~~~~~~

It was early the following evening and there had been no additional entry to Frank's basement hideaway. Time was pushing toward Frank's deadline and with each passing hour Bill's options were narrowing.

He had been sitting before the darkened screens for hours, waiting . . . and waiting. He sifted through alternative scenarios that would respond to Frank's hostile takeover. Somewhere in those deliberations he dozed off.

A buzzer sounding in the distance jarred his consciousness. He pulled his head forward from its resting place on the back of the chair, rubbed his eyes and blinked the sleep away. That annoying sound was the warning alarm announcing visitors to Frank's inner sanctum. He turned it off and glanced at the clock . . . one thirty five a.m. He focused, but could only find Pam and Pat on camera. They were moving around the room collecting equipment and other assorted devices.

Come on Frank, where are you? Don't let the girls have all the fun.

As if responding to Bill's script, the door opened and Frank strode in. The three began a conversation about what sexual preferences were the satisfaction du jour. As the girls disrobed Frank retired to the bathroom.

Well, here it was . . . D-Day. Or, in this case . . . D-Night! Bill took a deep breath and typed on his keyboard, "Initiate." From four pinhole nozzles located strategically around the ceiling came a fine mist. The gas was odorless, colorless, and invisible to the naked eye. Bill timed the process on his watch. Twelve seconds and the, now naked, girls folded
~~~~~~~~~~~~~~~~~~~~~~~~~~~~~~

to the floor. He smiled at the efficiency of the gas and waited for Frank to return.

Two minutes later a naked Frank re-entered the room. He saw the girls huddled on the carpet. He moved toward them. Halfway there he went limp and collapsed also.

Bill had approximately four hours before the effects of this particular nerve recipe wore off. He nearly leapt from his chair, donned his combat uniform and raced toward the kitchen entrance to the garage. As he passed through the door he reached and retrieved that "special" bag that had been waiting for him. In his car, and away from the house, he drove within all speed limits. A speeding ticket from a late night officer would ruin his timeline - not to mention the damage it would do to any required alibi. He found his special spot down the road from Frank's and eased his car to a stop. Face and hands blackened he strode to that white split-rail fence behind the house. It was a moonless night. He smiled; even the moon was cooperating. Within seconds he was across the fence and to the backdoor. A few more seconds and he was inside and moving to the lower level. He entered the office, opened the bookcase and tapped in the security code. When he heard the locks release he cautiously opened the inner sanctum door. A very angry trio could be waiting for him. They were not. They were on the floor where he had last seen them.

After a sigh of relief he dropped his duffle bag and examined the scene. He still marveled at the sheer erotic beauty of these sisters. It was no wonder that they were able to lure Frank's clients into their web. He knew first hand how persuasive they could be. Enough of that, they were carnivores, and these particular carnivores, given the opportunity, would eat their young. Bill had decided that extinction was the appropriate end for these particular animals. He began making it so!

Two and a half hours later he stood back and surveyed his work.

Frank was naked and hung one foot off the floor by his wrists. Bill had whipped his back to a bloody serrated pulp.

Pam, also naked, was lying, spread-eagle, and face up on a table. Bill had rammed a large battery operated phallus into her vagina until the trauma had caused substantial bleeding. He had left the vibrator inserted in the pool of blood to demonstrate the depraved nature of the act. He had then tied her to the table by each wrist and each ankle with silk cords.

He had dealt with her as gently as possible under the circumstances. He was still conflicted by their shared "climax." She had been an unknowing participant, but he owed her some deference based on that communion. He was struggling with what sort of deference, but in a show of ambivalent respect he slowly slid the back of his hand across her stomach and then one breast. He shuddered, for at that moment he felt more disgust for himself than her. In a final tribute he bent close, kissed her cheek and said, "I'm sorry Pam. I wish there was another way."

He then moved back to Frank, stood before his hanging carcass and said, "One last time, Frank . . . fuck you and the horse you rode in on!"

The pain that Frank and Pam had been subjected to might have bothered him more if they had been alive to feel it. He had injected them with large doses of a narcotic cocktail. They had both expired before he had finished brutalizing them.

He had other things in store for Pat. He had injected her with a mild sedative; one that would leave her system quickly and leave no trace of its existence. He had also given her a less than lethal dose of that same narcotic cocktail. For the sake of this charade he needed to establish her drug use also. He made sure her fingerprints were on all pertinent devices and surfaces. He also made certain that traces of Frank and Pam's blood were conspicuously displayed on her skin. Knowing that she would likely wake before his plan was complete he laid her comfortably on her back on another table.

Bill then set about leaving drugs and associated paraphernalia on Frank's desk. He also stashed additional drug supplies in his desk and the medicine cabinet in the bathroom. He then traveled the room one last time in search of any telltale signs of his presence. Satisfied with his handy work he then set about removing every piece of surveillance and warning equipment. Removal complete, he then sat in the middle of the floor and ran his checklist. He could afford to leave nothing to chance. One inadvertent mistake and he would be extinct too.

He had one last task to complete and that was to remove all photographic and tape evidence that could link him or anyone he knew to the Turner's and their sexual proclivities. He moved to the photo albums and removed the one album that was questionable. From there he went to the video file and searched out the disk that had shaken him so badly when he had first seen it. During that search he came across three other disks that displayed a name that staggered him. He removed one of them and quickly viewed it in the playback unit. He trembled as this new player performed before the camera. How does one deal with the unthinkable?

My God, he thought, *this is impossible. I can't believe it.*

It hadn't played thirty seconds when he reached and jammed the stop, and then the eject button. No more data was required to foster his next step. The good news . . . he was learning to think on the move. The rough outline of a strategy to combat this new component was quickly put in place. He left the other two disks where they were, removed the two he wanted and placed them safely in his duffle bag. Comfortable with his clandestine efforts, but constricted by these new developments he left the room and reset the code. He smiled as he left knowing that Pat could not leave unless he unlocked the door or someone else broke it down.

He moved through the house carefully hiding drugs and drug apparatus throughout the Turner's belongings. He placed them so they would be very difficult to find for the average person, but not too difficult for a trained investigator.

He left the Turner Home just as the sky was graying for dawn. Back in his car he slumped in his seat with the relaxation of accomplishment. He drove home with one last nuance to put in place. If he were correct, this little tidbit would wrap his entire scheme into one neat package . . . with a big red bow on top.

Back in "command central" he seated himself before his console. He had one final function to perform, but before he initiated that final directive he needed to erase any record of his entry and changes to Frank's security system. He typed the delete command and hit enter. That done, he held his hands over his computer keyboard, inhaled deeply, and then typed in a preset command to the security system, "Open door." Those many miles away the security system that controlled the back door to the house unlocked the door. Thirty seconds later the alarm sounded and the security company was notified of a possible break-in. When an analyst phoned the residence and got no answer his security procedures would require a call to the police. Being the top home security organization in the country they followed the script to the letter!

The residual beauty of this gambit was that no one could prove that a burglar hadn't opened the door. And, to make it even more convincing, Bill had left scratch marks around the lock face to indicate that special tools had been used to Jimmy the lock tumblers. He had also made certain the bookcase had not engaged when he left the office. And finally, he had set the inner sanctum security panel to flash a blinking red light. An open bookcase led to a red warning light, which fronted a concealed room, which could only be entered via a larger than normal door, which, when broken down would lead to a very strange set of circumstances.

When the police arrived and encountered the open back door, protocol would demand a very complete and thorough search of the house. They would eventually encounter Bill's scripted path. The rest, as they say, should be history!

He rose and fixed himself a very large Scotch. He'd earned it. Now the really tough part . . . the wait. He would have no way of knowing that his "script" had been followed until this incident was confirmed by the newspapers, a T-V newscast, or some other reporting agency. Two more large Scotches and he fell into bed. It made no difference that it was nine o'clock in the morning. To Bill, it seemed like he'd been up for months; and, in one sense he had! After months of torment a giant weight had been lifted from him. Without the need to support the accumulated load of the Turners' and Marci his mind and body had simply folded in on itself.

CHAPTER SIXTEEN

He woke after five hours of sleep. This would normally have been insufficient to recharge his batteries, but he had slept so deeply and peacefully it felt more like twelve hours. Famished, he literally engorged a huge brunch and several cups of coffee.

Somewhere in the middle of stuffing food into his mouth he thought, *Killing people really makes me hungry. Maybe it's just killing the right people that makes me hungry?*

Sated, he retired to his favorite easy chair to chart the aftermath.

First order of business would be to mount all the surveillance equipment and paraphernalia in, and around, the house. If someone checked his credit card accounts, the purchase of security supplies could be easily explained if he had used the items to secure his own home and family. That work order would take two days to complete.

Next, the children were coming home day after tomorrow. That would require a space in his schedule for grocery shopping.

Then, he needed to clean and straighten the house. There must be no evidence that he had been involved in anything out of the ordinary.

That was the short list. The long list was yet to be determined.

He rose, put on an everyday outfit of jeans, tee shirt, and tennis shoes and headed out for the nearest supermarket. An hour later he was back home and packing away the spoils of his shopping spree.

One order of business down, he then spent the next two and half hours beginning the placement and mounting of his own personal security system. After a good start and a tiring back he settled down with a large Scotch to watch the local evening news. With twenty minutes of the broadcast gone, and still no report regarding the demise of Frank and Pam, Bill was less than encouraged with the results of his handiwork. The female anchor was just about to go to credits when she stopped and said, "This late breaking news just in, local investment broker and financier Frank Turner and his eldest daughter were found late this morning dead in the basement of their home. His other daughter was found alive and has been taken to the Morgan County Regional Hospital, where she remains in satisfactory condition. For more on this and other breaking news join us at eleven tonight."

Bill rose with a broad smile, went to the phone and called the Morgan County Regional Hospital.

"Morgan County Regional Hospital, how may I direct your call?"

"I'd like to speak to a Miss Pat Turner please."

"One moment please, while I direct you to patient information."

A few moments and, "Patient information."

"Yes, I'm trying to reach the room of a Miss Pat Turner."

"Just one moment please."

After a few more moments, "I'm sorry all calls to that room are currently being held."

"May I leave a message?"

"At the tone please leave your message for Miss Turner."

At the tone Bill said, "Pat, its Bill. I just saw the report on the evening news. What can I do? Call me."

Obligatory concern noted for the world and still sporting that broad smile he replaced the phone on its cradle.

~~~~~~~~~~~~~~~~~~~~~~~~~~~~

Two hours later Bill's house phone chimed. He picked it up and said, "Hello."

"Bill, I'm so glad it's you. Thank you so much for calling."

"What's going on Pat?"

"I'm not sure. Father and Pam are dead. I was found unconscious and brought here to the hospital. I'm waiting for father's lawyer now. In the meantime he's instructed me to say nothing to the police. I'm so scared; I don't know what to do."

"Listen to Frank's attorney. In the meantime, if there's anything you need let me know. Otherwise, call me when you know more."

"Thank you Bill. It helps just knowing you're out there."

"Talk to you soon."

As that broad smile returned he hung up the phone and thought, *I wonder if I would have been this good at chess?*

Done temporarily with Pat, he retired to his den and watched for the second time the two disks he'd retrieved from Frank's files.

Both videos had shaken him. Albeit in different ways; but very deeply just the same. He now had the time to see where each fell in the general scheme of things.

As he watched the first he became more and more saddened and disheartened, as though his life was being systematically torn from
~~~~~~~~~~~~~~~~~~~~~~~~~~~~

his body. By disk's end the impact of what he was viewing had taken control and he hung his head and cried. Worse case, it would change who he was forever. Best case, he was furious at himself for not inflicting excruciating pain on Frank and Pam before allowing them to die. After fifteen minutes of bouncing between the best and worse case scenarios he ejected the first disk and inserted the second.

As he watched the second he became more and more enraged. The best case was bad. The worse case was horrible. Another ten minutes bouncing between best and worse case scenarios left him emotionally spent.

Would the desolation to his family ever stop?!!!

It would, and he was going to stop it!

He prepared a water glass full of his favorite high protein diet and retired to the attic.

As he seated himself on the floor the phone rang. He retrieved it and said, "Hello, Edith."

"I thought you'd stopped talking to me."

"It's been difficult finding the time. I've been busy."

"Haven't you now. Where do you find the energy?"

"When it's for the right cause, you find it."

"I particularly enjoyed your little soiree with Pam. Too bad she didn't know you were watching. She would have enjoyed it a lot more."

"Can we dispense with that Edith? I'm not proud of that particular moment."

"Like I said before Bill, it helps me through the slow periods. I'll not mention it again, but I thank you for the diversion."

"I have something much more important to discuss with you."

"The answer is, no, I haven't seen my esteemed relatives yet. I don't know where they are, but if they're here with me then I'm lower on this food chain than I thought."

"That's nice to know Edith, but that's not what I need to talk about."

"Oops, sorry Bill, I got carried away. What is it?"

He paused, inhaled deeply, and then asked, "Did you know about Marci, Frank and your daughters?"

"I assume you're referring to that sexual encounter?"

"Yes."

"I didn't know about it until I watched it on that disk with you."

"Can you tell me anything about it?"

"As a matter of fact I can."

"Do we need yes or no questions to proceed?"

"Not for this. You've already made your own history and nothing I can say will change that."

There was a moment of silence before Edith continued, then she began, "This has to be difficult for you, and I understand. When I watched that disk I was reviled and sickened too. How my husband and daughters could do such a thing overwhelmed me. Worse, I didn't know anything about it. Believe me, if I had, I would have done something. I thank you for squaring that account for both of us."

"After what we've been through, I now know that you would have exacted your own form of retribution. Thank you."

"Before you ask. You need to know, Marci was not a willing participant. She would have died first. She loved you and the children too much to have ever willingly allowed that to happen."

His heart lightened. Now, however, he was forced to face the fact of what she must have endured. How was he to deal with not being there for her? Maybe, if he had been the "man" of the family she would have shared what she had felt with him. Maybe, if he had been anything more than a self-centered piece of shit he could have retaliated when it counted.

How do you live with yourself now . . . asshole?

He put his hand over his mouth to stifle the rage he felt for himself and the pain of her suffering. It didn't help . . . he started to sob through his fist.

"Bill, are you crying again?"

Nothing.

"It's all right if you are. You're crying for both of us. It turns out, she was the best thing in both of our lives and we let her down."

The silence lay like a coffin between them.

Finally, Edith spoke, "You need to know that she had been drugged before they raped and sodomized her. She was incapable of preventing what they did."

"Why did they do it to her?"

"They wanted to bring you, her, and the children into their sex club. She wouldn't hear of it and threatened to expose them. In order to keep her quiet they staged that scene to blackmail her. As an added incentive they threatened to kill you and the children if she ever told a living soul. True to her word, she never told a living soul."

"But I could have done something."

"No you couldn't. You know what they were capable of. Stop blaming yourself. She doesn't blame you. To her, that was the only available option. You might disagree, but she protected the people she loved."

An idea suddenly rose before him like an onrushing train. An idea so horrendous he tried to sidestep it. It didn't work . . . the train hit him anyway! As his rage began to resurface the question that had to be asked leaked from his lips, "Edith, how did Marci die?"

"You were there Bill, she died of cancer."

"Don't get cute with me Edith. You know what I mean."

"Yes Bill, I do."

"Well?"

"I told her I wouldn't tell you."

With force he pressed, "Do you think I care what you told her?"

"Bill, please."

"No, Edith, I need to know."

"Very well. They had her killed."

"Did you say they had her killed?"

"Yes."

"Who actually killed her?"

Silence

"You can't tell me because of the future issue?"

"Yes."

"Very well, we'll get to that. Why didn't she want me to know?"

"You can't bring her back. She saw no purpose in you knowing how she died, other than to cause you more pain."

"Tell her that losing her is as much pain as I can feel. All you've done is further justify the retaliation."

"I will."

"Knowing that Frank and the girls had her killed, begs the question . . . who, and how? I think I now know, but let's move to the other disk first."

"Before we start, you need to know that I can't expound on that situation other than to say yes or no. Answers regarding that may impact the future."

"I understand, Edith."

Before he proceeded he stopped and thought, *How far must I cast this net?*

"Did you watch the second disk with me?"

"Yes."

"Were you aware of Jeff Blake's involvement with Frank and the girls before then?"

"No."

Even when you know the answer to a question compulsion forces you toward confirmation. He inquired, coldly, but firmly, "Was Jeff Blake responsible for Marci's death?"

"Yes."

His spirit sunk further as he thought, *I've had every other negative emotion and character trait thrown at me – why not betrayal too?"*

"Was it the cancer Edith?"

"Yes."

"Do you know how he gave it to her Edith?"

"No."

"Does Marci?"

"No."

If Jeff was involved in Marci's death, what about Donna? He had entrusted the children's care to her. Had he willingly handed them over to the keeper of the Lion's Den? He became frightened as he asked, "Is there anyone else involved in these murders?"

"No."

"Was Donna Blake involved with Frank and the girls too?"

"No."

He exhaled loudly as he said, "Thank God."

"She loves the children Bill. They are perfectly safe in her care."

"Thank you, Edith."

He had half a glass of Scotch remaining. He downed it in quick consecutive swallows.

"Are there more details I need to know Edith?"

"Yes."

"Can it wait; I'm dealing with a lot right now."

"Yes."

"Thank you, Edith. I'll talk to you soon."

"You're welcome, Bill."

He started to disconnect, but Edith's shouted, "Bill", in the receiver stopped him.

He recovered, pulled the unit to his ear and said, "Yes, Edith?"

"You need to know."

"What?"

Strength and conviction underpinned her remark, "What you did wasn't moral, but it was right."

"I've already had that wrestling match Edith. I'm not sure which one of my selves won . . . the good guy, or the bad, but I appreciate you saying that."

"You're always right defending your own. If you're not, I'm going to spend an eternity here!"

"I don't want you spending any more time at that level than you have to."

"Don't be too hard on yourself Bill. Goodbye, for now."

Warmth and softness permeated his closing, "Good bye, Edith."

They disconnected in unison.

Well, I guess I'm not done yet. There's still one more carnivore that needs to be extinct.

CHAPTER SEVENTEEN

When he'd finished with Edith he trudged downstairs for a fresh drink. Refill in hand, he flopped into his recliner to await the late news. He pushed back, took a sip of Scotch and pondered, briefly, the solution to the Jeff Blake predicament. Just past scenario number two the strain of recent days combined with his fear for Marci's welfare began to crash his already depleted reserves.

A ringing in his ears jarred him from some other place and some other time. His eyelids crept open. They closed instantly; there was nothing out there that required his attention. He floated between the reality of here and the warmth of that distant reverie until that nagging tone won the battle for his attention. Without opening his eyes he fumbled for the telephone. After a minor collision with his drink glass, and then the lamp, his hand mercifully landed on the receiver.

He raised it to his ear and mumbled, "Hello."

"Bill, is that you?"

More mumbling, "Yes. Who is this?"

"It's Pat. Are you all right?"

"I think so. What time is it?"

"Ten o'clock."

"Oh, good, I haven't missed the late news."

"Bill, its ten o'clock in the morning, not ten o'clock at night."

Recognition jolted him, "What? His eyes shot open as he finished, "It's not night time?"

"No, Bill, its day time. Are you sure you're all right?"

He pushed the recliner forward hoping that the exertion would clear his head. He'd slept for almost twelve hours. He hadn't done that since high school. Recovery was in order as he said, "I'm sorry Pat. I was up very late and I'm not with it yet."

"You told me to keep you updated."

"Well?"

"I'm out of the hospital, but now I'm in jail."

In feigned surprise he offered, "In jail, what for?"

"They haven't pressed charges yet, but father's attorney believes the principle charge will be murder."

"Murder?"

"Yes."

"How do they get that? There's no way you'd murder Frank and your sister."

"The attorney said not to discuss it with anyone, so I can't say anything more."

"I understand. If there is anything I can do just call me."

"I'm so afraid Bill. I don't understand what's happening. None of this makes any sense."

Squirm you bitch. After all you've done to the people around you; you deserve everything you're going to get. My only regret is that I can't pronounce the sentence.

"I'm sure everything will work out Pat. They'll get to the bottom of this. You just remember that I'm here for you."

"Thank you. I hope you know that I had nothing to do with trying to take Bill Jr. and Molly from you?"

He smirked as he replied, "Of course, Pat. I know you wouldn't do anything like that. Besides, the important thing now is to get you home where you belong. Now, you keep your spirits up and call me if you need anything."

"I will. Goodbye, Bill."

"Goodbye, Pat."

As he replaced the receiver he thought, *So far, so good. If everyone will just stay on script Pat's going to be a very unhappy lady.*

A quick shower, then a late breakfast and Bill was fueled for the rigors ahead. He headed for the attic. Edith might have information that could close the door on a loose end that was bothering him.

Seated in front of the Messenger XD 500 Bill consolidated his thoughts and picked up the receiver. He reached to tap Edith's speed dial number, but before he could, she said, "Hello, Bill."

He almost dropped the phone with surprise. He chided her, "Damn, Edith, please don't do that. You scared the hell out of me."

"Just like to keep you on your toes."

"Your concern for my alert behavior is touching, but I have a few questions for you."

In an upbeat tone, almost childish, she poked at him, "Oh goody, who are we going to kill now?"

"Edith, I'd prefer to say that I'm settling scores . . . not killing people."

"Very well, Bill, but a rose by any other name is still a dead person."

She laughed gleefully at her little joke.

"When you're done playing, Edith, I do have questions."

"I thought you'd grown out of those poopy drawers. Exterminate a couple of people and you lose your sense of humor. I was considering inviting you to my next wake but, if you can't enjoy the fruits of your labor, what fun would you be?"

"How are you going to have another wake? In case you hadn't noticed you're already dead."

"That's more like it Bill. Now you're getting into the spirit of things."

She cackled at her pun and then said, "Did you catch that Bill? Me being a spirit and all."

"Yes Edith, unfortunately, I got it."

"As for my next wake, you'd be surprised what I can do."

"I assume your obvious depression means that you approve of what I did to Frank and Pam?"

"You could say that. Me, I'd say I'm as happy as pig in shit. Now, back to my original question, whom are we going to kill now? As if I didn't know."

"I don't know that *I'm* going to kill anyone. I'd just like to clarify a few points."

She snickered like a petulant schoolgirl as she said, "All right Bill, fire away." Edith cackled at she continued jabbing at him, "Get that Bill, *fire away?*"

Exasperated, he pressed, "Are you done fooling around?"

"I suppose I'll have to be. It's clear that you're not in a playful mood. What can I help with?"

"Are you familiar with a Dr. Findley?"

"Yes."

"How about when Jeff Blake asked me to intercede on his behalf with Dr. Findley?"

"Yes."

"Was Jeff telling me the truth about the reason for him losing his hospital privileges?"

"No."

"In other words, Jeff lied to me about Findley's involvement."

There was that blatant pause and then she said, "Yes."

"Does that mean that either Findley wasn't involved or that Jeff misrepresented the reasons for the hospital inquiry?"

"Yes."

"Very well Edith that gives me what I needed to know."

"You mean we're done?"

"For now."

"Aren't you going to tell me what you have in mind?"

"No. Because I'm not sure myself."

She giggled with glee as she offered, "If you'd like my opinion, I think you should kill him."

"I don't want you're opinion."

"How about if I said, settle the score?"

"Won't make any difference. I'm still trying to decide what to do."

"How about if I said -"

With annoyance and exasperation red lining, he cut her off forcefully, "I understand Edith. You'd like me to kill him."

"I certainly would."

He paused, then said, "Say goodbye, Edith."

"Come on poopy drawers."

Sternly, "Edith."

"Oh, all right. Goodbye, Bill."

"Goodbye, Edith."

~~~~~~~~~~~~~~~~~~~~~~~~~~~

It was early afternoon when Bill exited the front door of the house in search of his daily paper. Like most homeowner's, the whereabouts of his daily "Tribune" would be somewhere between his yard and the neighbor's. Which neighbor's yard was always a toss-up? He was dressed in his favorite hole infested jeans and a sweatshirt that had long since lost the name of his favorite football team. He played the age old game, "If I were a newspaper where would I hide?" As he rummaged through the bushes in search of that answer an unmarked sedan pulled to a stop in his driveway. A very large uniformed man exited the driver's side of the vehicle. Moments later a woman exited the passenger side. It was sunny, and without his sunglasses, the best he could do was squint in the visitor's direction. The woman walked around the car and said, "Mr. Allen, Captain Maureen Romano. How are you?"

As they shook hands Bill said, "Captain Romano what a pleasant surprise."
~~~~~~~~~~~~~~~~~~~~~~~~~~~

She nodded in the direction of her companion and said, "Mr. Allen, this is Detective Arnold with the homicide division."

They shook hands and exchanged pleasantries.

"To what do I owe the pleasure of your visit, Captain?"

"May we step inside Mr. Allen?"

"Of course, Captain."

As they entered the house Bill offered, "Excuse the way I'm dressed, I wasn't expecting company."

She replied graciously, "Don't apologize, your dressed just like the detective and I on our days off."

They all chuckled.

"May I get either of you something to drink?"

"No thank you."

"Please sit down. Make yourselves comfortable."

Everyone seated, the Captain began, "Are you familiar with the current situation surrounding your father-in-law and your sisters-in-law?"

"No more than what I've seen on the news."

She began to speak but Bill's raised hand stopped her.

"I'm sorry, that's not completely true Captain. I have had two brief conversations with Pat Turner. Primarily to discuss her general condition and to see if there was anything she needed. We didn't discuss any details. Her attorney had instructed her not to discuss the case with anyone."

"Do you mind answering some questions?"

He smiled and said, "As long as I don't need an attorney?"

She returned the smile and countered, "Is there any reason you might?"

He laughed, "Not that I know of."

"Very well then, if I may, I will proceed?"

"By all means Captain."

"We believe Frank and Pam Turner died somewhere between 3:00 AM and 6:00AM of the morning before yesterday. Would you mind telling me where you were during that time frame?"

"Of course not. I was here at home, either in bed or working on my computer. When I can't sleep I get up and work. I have a couple of projects from the office that I bring home with me."

"Can anyone corroborate that?"

He laughed, "Not likely. My children have been staying with friends and I'm a recent widower, so I stay home at night, all night."

"Were you close with the Turner's?"

"After my wife died we grew apart. Then, recently they had expressed an interest in reuniting the family."

"Any particular reason for this new interest?"

"I believe they wanted to be more involved with our children."

"Not you?"

"I suppose, but I think because of my wife they wanted to reconnect more with the children."

"Do you know of anyone that would want to harm the Turners?"

"No."

"Can you think of any reason for someone wanting to harm them?"

"No."

"Are you aware of anything out of the ordinary that might shed light on their deaths?"

"I'm sorry Captain; I'm not exactly sure what you're looking for?"

"It's normal in a death such as this that we eliminate all possibilities."

"I can't think of anything."

Bill's expression became contemplative and quizzical. He started a sentence, "There was . . . no, I'm sure it was nothing."

Captain Romano pressed, "What was it Mr. Allen? Let us be the judge of its importance."

"I don't want to make a big deal over nothing."

"Please Mr. Allen; let me decide how meaningful it is."

With feigned reluctance he proceeded, "Well . . . okay. The last couple of times Frank Turner and I spoke he commented that Pat Turner had been acting out of sorts. When I asked what that meant he simply said that she had been different lately. We decided it was probably one of those woman things. That time of the month or something."

"Was there anything else?"

"No. That's why I hate to even mention it. It was nothing."

"That's fine Mr. Allen. I appreciate you sharing that, and you're probably right, it wasn't anything." She paused briefly and pulled a pad from her coat pocket. The pad had writing on it. After a quick glance she said, "Do you know a Dr. Jeffrey Blake?"

"Of course. He's been our family doctor for years. He was personally involved with my wife's care before her death."

"Was he a friend of the Turners?"

Bill smiled inside as he thought, *they found the disks.*

"I don't think so. He may have been, but I don't ever remember he, or they, ever mentioning each other. Why, is that important?"

"No, Mr. Allen. We have some information that they may have known one another. We're just trying to close all the circles."

Captain Romano glanced at Detective Arnold. He shook his head slowly from side to side. She looked back to Bill and said, "If there's nothing else you can think of Mr. Allen that's all we have for now."

She reached into her coat pocket and withdrew a card. As she handed it to him she said, "If there's anything else that comes to mind please call me."

"I will Captain."

They all rose together and walked to the front door. As Romano and Arnold were about to leave Bill asked, "May I ask a question, Captain?"

"Certainly."

"I'm an amateur when it comes to police procedure, but isn't it a bit unusual to have the Captain of the department investigating a particular case?"

Detective Arnold smiled. Captain Romano's glare removed Arnold's smile. She looked back to Bill and replied, "It is Mr. Allen, but I made an exception. It wasn't long ago that you inquired about the death of a Guilford Watson. Frank Turner as it turns out was a friend of his. When Frank Turner's name crossed my desk the coincidence was too strong to ignore. I'm involved because of my history with Frank Turner."

She smiled at Detective Arnold and continued, "I'm sure Detective Arnold would be much happier if I stayed out of his investigation."

Arnold started to speak, but her raised hand stopped him, "You don't have to be nice Detective, I'd feel the same way."

Arnold's grin offered the respect that the Captain had clearly earned by this acknowledgement.

"Does that help, Mr. Allen?"

"It does Captain, and I'm sorry to interfere."

"It was a fair question and one that deserved an answer. I doubt that you'll be hearing from us again regarding this matter. Thank you for your assistance Mr. Allen."

"Thank you Captain; Detective."

As they exited the house Bill thought, *she's a person I could like under other circumstances.*

The officers entered their vehicle and drove off. As they did, Captain Romano turned and said, "What did you think of him Lou?"

"That's a loaded question Mo."

"Come on Lou, one old cop to another."

"Since you put it that way. He's either the smoothest son of a bitch alive or he's telling the truth. He didn't duck a question. He was straightforward and admitted openly that he had no alibi as to his whereabouts. We've got nothing linking him to this and a lot putting Pat Turner in the wrong place at the wrong time. What's eating at you?"

"Nothing, I guess. I agree with you Lou. I just hate coincidence. It's just too neat, life isn't that organized. When it is, it has a very distinct odor to me."

CHAPTER EIGHTEEN

Bill hummed to himself as the line connected and began ringing. On the third ring a melodious voice answered, "Dr. Findley's office."

"May I speak to Dr. Findley please?"

"May I say who is calling?"

"My name is Bill Allen."

"Mr. Allen, how are you?"

"Is that you Danielle?"

"Yes."

"I'm sorry; I don't know how I could forget your lovely voice."

With a flirtatious tone she replied, "That's very nice of you to say Mr. Allen. Let me see if Dr. Findley is available."

"Thank you, Danielle."

The line went to music and Bill began humming again. Somewhere in the middle Danielle announced, "Mr. Allen?"

"Yes."

"I'm sorry, but Dr. Findley says he has nothing to discuss with you. If there is anything you'd like to say, he suggests you speak to the Hospital Board or his lawyer."

"I understand Danielle. I wonder if you would do me a favor?"

"If I can Mr. Allen."

"Please tell Dr. Findley that I understand why he refuses to speak to me and that I owe him an apology. The last time he and I met I was basing our conversation on what I now believe was misinformation. I would appreciate the opportunity to discuss this matter further with him."

"I'll try Mr. Allen, but Dr. Findley seemed adamant."

"Thank you, Danielle. I'm sure you'll do your best. I have a feeling that you can be rather persuasive when you want to be. Do you have my number in case Dr. Findley chooses to speak to me?"

"Thank you, Mr. Allen. I have your number here on caller identification. You have a nice day."

"And to you also, Danielle."

~~~~~~~~~~~~~~~~~~~~~~~~~~~~

Bill had set about alternative scenarios for dealing with Jeff. Somewhere into scenario number three his phone rang. He answered, "Bill Allen."

"Mr. Allen, John Findley here."

"Dr. Findley, so nice of you to return my call. I'm not sure I would be as gracious if the circumstances were reversed."

With a chill, Findley responded, "That's nice Mr. Allen, but how may I help you?"
~~~~~~~~~~~~~~~~~~~~~~~~~~~~

"Let me first apologize for my conduct during our last conversation. I was less than receptive to your position and more than brutish in my dealings with you. In my defense, I believe the entire situation had been misrepresented to me. As a matter of fact, I believe that I was lied to regarding your personal motivation and the hospital's business motivation in that incident."

"That's all well and good Mr. Allen, but I fail to see how I can help you now?"

"I know I'm asking a lot, but I wonder if you could meet with me so that I might explain?"

"I hardly see the value of such a meeting."

"If you'll let me buy you dinner at your favorite restaurant I think I can clarify this situation. If I don't, worse case, you'll still get a good meal."

Silence was Findley's temporary response. Then, with less chill, he said, "Very well Mr. Allen. I'll have to check my schedule with my receptionist. If you'll call my office tomorrow she will set the time and place with you."

"Thank you Dr. Findley. I will see you soon."

With a, "Goodbye Mr. Allen," Findley broke the connection.

Two evenings later Bill sat, Scotch in hand, waiting for Dr. Findley to join him for dinner.

Into his second swallow he saw Findley weaving his way through the dining room. As he approached the secluded booth Bill rose and extended his hand.

As they shook hands Findley spoke, "I'm sorry I'm late Mr. Allen, I had an emergency. Did someone on my staff inform you?"

"They did. Thank you, Doctor. They were very polite and efficient."

They sat down and Findley motioned to a waiter. The waiter arrived within moments and said, "Good evening Dr. Findley, may I get your usual?"

"Yes George, thank you." Findley turned to Bill and asked, "What are you having Mr. Allen?"

Bill raised his glass and offered, "Another one of these please."

George was gone as anonymously as he had arrived.

"I hope you'll find this restaurant acceptable Mr. Allen?"

"I've heard a lot of nice things about it. I'm happy for the opportunity to finely try it."

Findley measured Bill and then said, "Now, Mr. Allen, what's this all about?"

"Please, call me Bill."

More measuring, and then, "Very well, Bill."

"I need to know why Dr. Blake was being called before the Hospital Board."

Before Findley could respond Bill continued, "I know it's confidential, but I hope you'll believe me when I say it's vital that I know."

"I'm sure this is important Bill, but I can't release that information." George arrived at that moment with the drinks.

Drinks in hand, they toasted to, "Better days," and settled back.

"If I were to guess the reasons for the inquiry would you confirm the correctness of my hypothesis?

Findley studied Bill's face. Several seconds went by before he said, "Very well, Bill, guess away."

Bill smiled and said, "Was it drug related?"

Findley chuckled as he replied, "Do you read minds Bill?"

"No, why?"

"Then, who are you?"

"Just an angry man that doesn't like being lied to."

Findley's chuckle was now reduced to a broad smile, "Remind me never to lie to you."

"You don't seem the type Dr. Findley. Now, what's the answer?

"Yes."

"Can you expand on that?"

"No."

"If I know the details, I think I can solve both of our problems."

"Both of our problems?"

"Yes. I'm sure you and the hospital want him out of there. Not that you won't have him removed at some point anyway, but I'm sure you would prefer sooner than later – and with our legal system, it could be much, much later. Secondly, I helped create this mess by being an unwitting accomplice, so I'd like the opportunity to correct my gullibility."

"Bill, we've all been lied to. No one holds you responsible for Dr. Blake's behavior. Is it really that important to you?"

Bill measured Findley before saying, "Let's just say, I'm holding myself responsible for Dr. Blake's conduct – and yes, it is important to me. Ever since my wife died, I'm finding lots of things more important than they used to be."

"All right, but if you say I said this, I'll deny it."

"I won't, but if I do, you should."

"We suspected Dr. Blake of stealing drugs from the hospital."

"Could you prove it?"

"No, but we were very close."

"Close only counts in hand grenades and horseshoes. It would have taken a long time to get him. Now that I have this piece of information I believe I can solve our problem quickly."

"Now it's my turn to ask a question . . . how?"

Bill leveled his eyes at Findley and replied, "You're just going to have to trust me Dr. Findley."

Findley returned the stare and smiled as he said, "Call me John, please."

At that, a vaporous Mr. Murphy peered over the table's edge and whispered, "Did I just see a white flag? It was probably a figment of my imagination." He giggled and then dissolved!

"Thank you, John. By the way, in case you were wondering, we never had this conversation."

John's response was a raised glass.

As their glasses clinked together they sealed the deal!

~~~~~~~~~~~~~~~~~~~~~~~~~~~~
~~~~~~~~~~~~~~~~~~~~~~~~~~~~

The children were back home where they belonged, so that detail was in place. He had just completed the installation of the last pieces of his home security system, so that component of his alibi was complete. He was pleased and more relaxed than he could remember. Life was good, almost normal, or at least more normal than it had been since Marci's losing battle with the cancer. The only aggravation left to deal with was good old Dr. Blake. He had taken to calling him Dr. Blake instead of Jeff when he discovered the "other" Jeff.

Bill had made a copy of the disk that showed Dr. Blake, Frank, and the girls in one of their sexual encounters. In case the authorities ever searched his house he had sealed the original in a weatherproof container and buried it in a flowerbed in the back yard. It would not do for him to be connected with the forthcoming events. Of course, if things went as planned there could be no connection, but better safe than sorry. He now placed the duplicate in a plain brown envelope, with a clasp seal, in anticipation of its delivery to Dr. Blake. Dr. Blake didn't know it, but he was about to commit suicide. Between the pressure that would be applied by the police when he was connected to the Turners by the other disks and the weight of an unknown person having delivered him this disk, the overwhelming fear of exposure would set the stage for a very convenient suicide!

~~~~~~~~~~~~~~~~~~~~~~~~~~~~~~

Bill had entered the below ground garage where Dr. Blake had his office. Mid afternoon in an office building would see few people coming or going. Between the camouflage of the parked cars, the poor lighting, and the lack of prying eyes it provided Bill with the perfect cover for his task. He found Dr. Blake's vehicle and knelt between his car and the one next to it. Within seconds he had bypassed the lock and disengaged the security system. He laid the brown envelope on the driver's seat, locked and closed the door, and whispered to himself as he left the scene, "Fuck you, Dr. Blake."
~~~~~~~~~~~~~~~~~~~~~~~~~~~~~~

~~~~~~~~~~~~~~~~~~~~~~~~~~~~~~

The following day Bill was seated before his computer finishing a project for work when the house phone rang.

"Hello."

"Bill, it's Pat."

"Are you okay?"

"Not really. They've just charged me with the murder of Father and Pam."

He smiled as he excitedly replied, "But how, why?"

"They say my prints were everywhere. I was in a locked room that could only have been locked from the inside and their blood was all over me."

"Should you be telling me this?"

"Father's attorney said not to discuss this with anyone but I don't care. He's an old fart and I'm so scared Bill. I know you won't discuss this with anyone."

Oh, you can bet on that sweetheart.

"Of course not. Is there anything else?"

"Apparently, almost all the monies in Father's and Pam's bank accounts were withdrawn the day of the murders and more than half of it was deposited into my accounts."

"You said half. Where is the remainder?"

"I don't know. The police think I've done something with it."
~~~~~~~~~~~~~~~~~~~~~~~~~~~~~~

He grinned as he thought; *I know you don't know Pat. That's because the remaining funds are in an unmarked account in Switzerland. And, by the way, only I have access to it.*

"What does your attorney say about all of this?"

"He just keeps saying that it's all very damaging. I think he believes I'm guilty. I didn't kill them Bill and I don't know what happened to their money. This is all so confusing and I'm so frightened. What am I going to do?"

Gee, Pat, you could always plead guilty. That would make things easy for all of us.

"I know its difficult Pat, but have faith. I'm sure your attorney will figure out something."

"I don't know Bill. He mentioned bringing on a well-known defense lawyer today. He said, since he only does corporate work, I need a qualified defense attorney to represent me."

"I know its tough Pat, but it'll work out. I'm behind you. If you need anything let me know."

Thank you Bill, it helps just knowing I have your support."

"Take care. Goodbye."

"Goodbye, Bill."

He replaced the receiver and chuckled as he spoke aloud, "I'm behind you Pat. Pushing you as hard as I can . . . toward the edge of the cliff."

CHAPTER NINETEEN

The children were at school. He had three hours before he had to pick them up. This was not a routine, but Bill had two more days before he had to return to work, so while he could he was interfacing with them as much as possible. He owed them that. They had been patient and loving since Marci's death and they deserved a father, no matter how late he was in becoming one! He hoped they had survived this ordeal with as few emotional wounds as possible. He knew that between Marci and the Turners his wounds were deep and would hobble him for some time to come. Whatever he could do to lessen the pain for Molly and Bill Jr. was a responsibility and love he was only now beginning to understand. With that understanding came the ability to incubate the children with the warmth and caring their Mother had left behind.

In this downtime before the "Allen" bus left for school he thought a quick update with Edith was in order. He climbed the steps to the attic and dialed death central!

"Hello, Bill."

"Hello, Edith."

"I thought maybe you were done talking to me?"

"Never, Edith. You're more a part of this family now than you've ever been."

Humbled she replied, "That's a nice thing for you to say Bill."

"You got me on a good day Edith."

She chuckled her reply, "Regardless, I appreciate it. Now what's happening?"

"As if you didn't know."

"I know Marci is all over me because she knows you're moving against Jeff Blake. She wants you to stop. She says you've done enough and she's afraid of what this anger and revenge is doing to you."

"You can tell her I've never felt better, and when I'm done with Dr. Blake, I'll feel absolutely perfect."

"I'll tell her, but she won't be pleased. I, on the other hand, applaud what you've done and what I think you're about to do."

"It's my turn to thank you Edith. I appreciate your support."

"You know me Bill; I'm an eye for an eye person. Or, should I say, entity? This attitude may never let me out of this place, but you've got to defend what's yours."

"Here, here, Edith."

"By the way, I could have told you about Jeff Blake. You didn't have to go to Findley."

"I know Edith, but I needed an excuse to see him so I could apologize for being such a horse's ass."

"I've enjoyed the opportunity to help. When you figure things out on your own and bypass my inputs I feel left out."

"Edith, I couldn't have done any of this without you. I'm sorry you're not here to have dinner and drinks with."

The silence that followed was Edith's way of showing the warmth she was feeling at this moment.

Finally, she said, "It almost sounds like you're about to throw me away?"

"No, Edith, I'll talk to you as long as we're permitted. Even if it's only about the weather."

"That's wonderful, but what can I do for you now?"

"How's Marci?"

"She's good. She misses you, and the kids, and wants you to know how much she loves you."

"I'll ditto that."

Before Bill could continue he had to swallow hard. The lump in his throat made it difficult to speak. He changed the subject to divert his emotions, "Have you found out where Frank and Pam are yet?"

"Yes, I have. Apparently, there's a lower, or depending on your perspective, worse place than where I am. It's reserved for entities that have committed crimes against man and humanity."

"I suppose there's a piece of space waiting there for me?"

"I can't believe that Bill."

"Whatever, I just hope they receive proper recognition for their transgressions?"

"Based on what I'm told, they'll be receiving more than they want for considerably longer than they would like."

"Good. I hated to think of them somewhere near you."

"I was just happy to hear that there was a place, or places, that were below me."

"What about Gil?"

"He's with Marci."

"Is that good?"

"Gil was a good man. They deserve to be in the same place."

"You know what Edith? I think you're a pretty good person too, and I'll bet you'll be with them before you know it."

"Thank you, Bill. I have a very select fan club; I suspect you're probably the founder and only member?"

"No Edith, the founder is somewhere near you. And don't say I'm the only member, because I have two children that love and miss their Grandmother."

More silence.

This conversation had arrived at a very uncomfortable place for both of them. They were attempting to deal with issues of life, death, and the tenderness of loving. Neither had much practice in this arena and their amateur standing was blatantly obvious.

Bill broke the silence, "I'd better go Edith. I've got some errands to run before I pick up the children at school."

Some excuses are weaker than others. This was one of them, but allowed and accepted due to the circumstances. Edith needed an out too.

"I understand Bill. Talk to you soon."

Disconnect followed.

~~~~~~~~~~~~~~~~~~~~~~~~~~~~~~

The following day, Bill answered the house phone, "Hello."

"Hello, Bill, it's Donna."
~~~~~~~~~~~~~~~~~~~~~~~~~~~~~~

His senses heightened as he replied, "Yes Donna, is everything all right?"

Crying sounds were his answer.

"What is it Donna?"

She blubbered something at him. It was unintelligible.

"Donna, I can't understand what you're saying. You'll have to calm down."

Crying slowly declined to sniffles as she attempted to gather herself. After thirty seconds she said, "Bill, I don't know what do?"

"What is it?"

"Have the police been to see you about Frank and Pam Turner."

"Of course, why?"

"Well, they've been here twice, and each time they stayed for close to half an hour. Jeff got more sullen with each visit. Then, day before yesterday, he came home late from the office drunk, and obviously shaken."

That would have been my little gift to him.

"When I tried to find out what the problem was he pushed me away and locked himself in his home office. Yesterday morning he had me call his business office and instruct his staff to cancel all his appointments. He doesn't come out of his office, accept for meals, and he hasn't spoken ten words to me in a day and a half."

"What can I do Donna?"

"He's been like this before. Usually in a couple of days he's fine, but I don't want the kids to see him. Would you mind watching my children for a couple of days?"

"Are you kidding? After all you've done for me. Of course."

"Thank you. If it's okay, I'll drop them off after school."

"That's fine. Is there anything in particular they eat or anything else I need to know?"

"No. Treat them as you would yours."

"What should I tell them if they ask about you and Jeff?"

"I was hoping you would take them, so I told them that Jeff and I were going away for a couple of days and they would be staying with you. I apologize for that presumption before I spoke to you, but I needed to say something."

"It's no problem Donna. I'm glad to do what I can."

"Thanks, Bill. I'll make this up to you."

"That's not necessary Donna. I just want you to get this sorted out."

"I'll see you later Bill."

"Until then."

Here it was! The opening Bill had been waiting for. Dr. Blake was about to suffer an assisted suicide. Euthanasia could be a very good thing, and Bill was about to prove it.

~~~~~~~~~~~~~~~~~~~~~~~~~~~~~

The following night Bill prepared to leave the house. He had laced the children's dinner with a mild sedative. Given the sleep habits of most kids they would probably sleep through a tornado anyway, but never trust to chance when the help of drugs would tilt the scales in your favor. There could be no witnesses to him leaving home. Besides, if asked, all the kids would say he was here with them.
~~~~~~~~~~~~~~~~~~~~~~~~~~~~~

With his duffle bag packed, and retribution on his mind, he drove to the Blake's.

~~~~~~~~~~~~~~~~~~~~~~~~~~~~

Two hours later Bill eased his car into the garage. Inside the house, he carefully discarded his clothing and all other items of incrimination. Everything was separated and then placed in several different trash bags. After he dropped the kids at school in the morning he would deposit these bags in different dumpsters around town. Different waste removal companies were likely to use different land fills. Try tying someone to a crime, or any event, without major pieces of evidence. He smiled with pride, he couldn't be linked to this, but even if someone tried it would be futile, his plan had been flawless.

~~~~~~~~~~~~~~~~~~~~~~~~~~~~

The house phone was ringing. Bill wasn't sure for how long. He rubbed the sleep from his eyes and glanced at the clock, "5:08 AM."

Who the hell is calling me at this hour?

Fumbling for the phone, he knocked his glass of water off the nightstand. Fortunately the glass didn't break, but the miscue caused him to announce, "Damn it. Pay attention Bill. At least it was only water."

He read the caller ID. It was Donna's number.

He cleared his throat before answering, "Hello."

"Bill, there's been a terrible accident."

Yes, I know. Fuck you too, Dr. Blake!

"What is it, Donna?"

"Apparently, Jeff shot and killed himself."

With the appropriate amount of surprise he responded, "What?"

"I said Jeff killed himself."

"When?"

"Sometime last night. The police believe it happened about one in the morning."

"Oh my God Donna, is there anything I can do?"

"If you would get the kids packed up. Don't tell them anything other than I called and I'm coming by to get them."

"There must be something I can do?"

"Maybe later. Right now, I have to get them home with me. I can't have them hearing this from classmates or seeing it on television before I've had a chance to talk to them."

"Of course. When will you be here?"

"In twenty minutes."

"I'll have them ready."

"Thanks, Bill."

Twenty minutes later Donna rang the doorbell. Bill opened the door and Donna rushed into his arms. After a hug she pulled back and said, "Are they ready?"

"Yes, Donna."

She walked past him to the foot of the steps and in a businesslike tone issued, "Mom's here kids. Let's go home."

They plodded down the stairs holding their suitcases. They were shaking off their sleep and still arranging their clothes as they moved toward the front door. As they passed Bill they mumbled in unison, "Thank you for everything Mr. Allen."

"Your welcome. Come back anytime."

As Donna herded them out the door she said, "Thanks, Bill. I'll call you later when I get some of this sorted out."

Softly he replied, "I'm here for you Donna."

In the immediate aftermath, he wondered what chemical, what hormone, what instinct allowed mothers to become practical, expeditious, and almost military under certain circumstances. With respect to their children, they all seemed to call on whatever reserves were necessary to command a situation. A calm, resolute direction was required and that was exactly what Donna had displayed.

Before Marci's death he would have been unable to recognize these strengths in other people, and least of all women. Between Marci and Edith he had evolved into someone capable of seeing beyond himself, someone able to feel the width and breadth of others. Of course, he had also become a killer, but that contradiction would need resolving at a quieter time. Acknowledging this dichotomy would have to suffice for now!

CHAPTER TWENTY

Bill was seated before his computer finishing a project for work when the doorbell rang. He stood up from his desk and looked out his office window. Sitting in his driveway was an unmarked sedan, a familiar unmarked sedan. As he exited his office the bell chimed again. He opened the door to Captain Romano.

He smiled and addressed her, "Captain Romano. I'd like to say this is a pleasant surprise, but when the police come calling it remains to be seen how pleasant it will be."

She returned his smile and asked, "May I come in Mr. Allen?"

"Of course, Captain."

He showed her in and directed her to an easy chair, "Please sit down Captain. Make yourself comfortable. May I get you anything?"

"I would like a glass of water if it's not too much trouble?"

"Not at all. I'll be right back."

While he was gone she studied the room and its furnishings. The way people decorated offered clues to their personality and character.

Bill returned and noticed her scanning the room. He grinned and said, "I'm afraid the room won't tell you much about me. With few exceptions this house was my wife's. Whatever you learn will be about her, not me."

As he handed her the glass of water she grinned back and said, "Thank you, Mr. Allen." After a quick swallow she continued, "You seem well versed in police work?"

"Chalk it up to too many mystery stories and an overactive imagination."

"Whatever it is, you are very observant."

"Thank you, Captain. That means a lot coming from a professional such as yourself."

They measured each other and then Bill said, "I'm sure you didn't come here for a glass of water or to tell me how observant I am. So, what brings you Captain?"

"Do you know anything about this Dr. Blake incident?"

"Only what I read in the newspaper and saw on television."

"That's all?"

"No, Captain, there is more. I had a brief conversation with Donna Blake right after his death."

"What does right after mean?"

"Well, I was keeping their children for them. They were to be going out of town. Donna Blake called me at 5:08 AM of the morning it happened and described the circumstances briefly. She came right over and got their children. I haven't spoken to her since."

"It's interesting that you would remember the exact time that she called you."

"She woke me from a sound sleep. I looked at my bedside clock and remember wondering who would be calling me at such an hour?"

"What exactly did she say to you?"

"I think it was something to the affect that Jeff had shot and killed himself. And she needed to get the kids home before they saw it on the news or heard it from some classmates. She was very concerned about them. She said she would be picking them up in twenty minutes, could I please have them ready."

"Was that all?"

"As far as I recall."

"Did she say anymore when she got here?"

"No. Just that when she got things sorted out she would call me."

"And you say you haven't talked to her since that morning?"

"That's correct."

"How do you know her Mr. Allen?"

"My wife and she were very close. She's been a Godsend to my children and me since my wife's death. When my wife was alive we used to go out occasionally with the Blakes."

"That's it?"

Bill flared, "No it's not. She's a good person and I'm concerned for her welfare. Is there any reason to believe that Jeff Blake's death was anything other than a suicide?"

"There's no evidence that points in any other direction."

"Then, may I ask why you're here asking all these questions about Donna Blake and our relationship."

"None, other than to confirm what we've already heard from others about her."

"Well, have I confirmed what others have said about her?"

"You have."

"Then, is there something else I can do for you?"

"You can satisfy my curiosity about a few things."

"And what might those few things be Captain?"

The Captain straightened in her chair before saying, "Ever since we originally spoke about Guilford Watson people have been dying around you. Now, that's either a complex matrix of coincidences or something else. Everyone that has ever worked with me knows how much trouble I have accepting coincidence. I believe things happen for a reason. One coincidence I can accept. More than one and I begin questioning the odds that must be overcome to allow these events to occur. Herein lies the rub. You are the most common thread in all these deaths."

She stopped, obviously waiting for a response.

Bill obliged, sort of, "What's your point Captain?"

Frustrated by his complacency she continued, "I want to know where you fit into this chain of events?"

"What chain of events are you referring to?"

"There's Guilford Watson and his wife Edith Watson Turner, who I only recently discovered, had died. There's your wife, Frank and Pam Turner, and now, Jeffrey Blake."

Bill laughed as he replied, "Are you trying to say that I'm responsible for all of those deaths?"

"Of course not. You were no more than a child when Guilford Watson died. Edith Watson Turner died of natural causes, or, that's what someone wanted us to believe. Regardless, you had nothing to do with her death. And your wife died in the hospital. Records show you weren't there when she passed. Even if you had the opportunity you had no motive to murder your wife or your mother-in-law. There was no inheritance coming to you from Edith Watson Turner. What there was came to your wife but she died before she could collect it. It reverted to her half sisters. I'm sure you disliked Edith Watson Turner, but who doesn't dislike their mother-in-law. If everybody that disliked their mother-in-law murdered them we'd have to build prisons for that alone."

Bill nodded his assent and then stopped her with a raised hand, "May I jump in here?"

"It could get deep, be careful."

"I can swim Captain. You made a passing comment about Edith and extenuating circumstances surrounding her death. What exactly was that about?"

Her eyes went cold and her tone became stern, "Mr. Allen, in my effort to get at the truth I'm going to say a lot of things that shouldn't be repeated. We'll all be better off if they are not. For that reason, I will deny saying a word that might compromise you or me. We need to be very clear on that . . . are we?"

"Captain, I'm not a big fan of the police, but if you keep talking like that I could become one." He finished the last word with a broad smile.

At first she was reticent to break her official expression, but as Bill continued smiling, her facade cracked slowly in favor of a smirk, "I'll take that as a yes."

There are moments that change the course of relationships . . . this was such a moment.

"When you asked me about Guilford Watson I told you that I was a rookie cop when he died and I deferred to my partner in that investigation. That was true. It was also true there was no overwhelming evidence that his death was anything more than a hunting accident. As you know, I was of the mind then that there was enough doubt to warrant a detailed look at Frank Turner. Based on evidence that has been collected about the Turners, and specifically Frank Turner, in investigating their deaths I am now convinced that he murdered Guilford Watson. If I tie my beliefs to your inquiry into the death of Guilford Watson, I'm willing to bet my badge that you suspected that too."

She looked at him for a response.

He obliged, "You'd keep your badge Captain."

"Next, based on that belief and the facts that have been uncovered about the Turners; I went back and reopened the Edith Watson Turner file. Based on the inconsistencies in her autopsy and the accumulated negative material we have collected about the Turners character, sexual proclivities, and business dealings I am convinced that Frank Turner and/or his daughters had something to do with your mother-in-law's death."

"Can you prove any of this?"

"No."

"You say there were inconsistencies in Edith's autopsy?"

"Yes."

"Can you explain?"

"I'm not supposed to, but since this is all off the record. The county coroner, because of the nature of her death, ordered an autopsy. He became ill and a coroner in training performed the procedure. It was botched from beginning to end. Before the county coroner could redo the autopsy the Turners obtained a court order for the body and had it cremated. Under the guise of her final wishes her ashes were spread on the ocean. What evidence there might have been was conveniently disposed of."

"Very interesting, Captain."

"Oh, I'm not done."

"Why doesn't that surprise me?"

"During our search of the Turner home and their belongings we came across some rather damning information regarding Dr. Jeffrey Blake and his association with them. That information would lead even the most liberal investigator to conclude that he was far less than an upstanding citizen. If I stretch this package, as I'm prone to do, you might even say that under the wrong conditions, he could be a dangerous man to have around."

"I had the impression he committed suicide?"

"The police investigating the matter believe he did. If you're Captain Romano however, you're obliged to wonder what, exactly, took place?"

"Can you prove it wasn't a suicide?"

"The answer again, is no."

"This is a fascinating array of conjecture, but with all due respect Captain, what good is it?"

"A most valid point Mr. Allen, but remember, when I started I mentioned my curiosity and my quest for the truth."

"How could I forget?"

"If you'll indulge me for a while longer I'll get to the point of this exercise."

"I can't wait."

"I'm now going to make a hypothetical leap. Let's suppose, for the sake of argument that someone else was able to piece this puzzle together and arrive at the same conclusions that I have."

"All right, Captain, I'll play."

"If they were smart enough to solve this intricate web of deception then I believe they would be smart enough to murder Frank and Pam Turner and pin it on Pat Turner. And having accomplished that slight of hand they could then murder Jeffrey Blake and make it look like a suicide."

"Makes sense to me Captain. I do have two questions however?"

"And they are?"

"Don't we need motive and opportunity?"

"You are so right Mr. Allen. You would have made an excellent detective."

Shadows of Sherlock Holmes passed rapidly across his vision as he looked at her.

Romano in turn eyed him intently as she continued, "Opportunity is a given. Motive is more iffy. If we assume these crimes weren't random, but were planned and executed by the same person, or persons, then the motive must fit both crimes. We've already eliminated money - next to go are robbery, sex, drugs, and passion. The only motive I'm left with is revenge or retribution. If we look for a person or persons, that are connected to all the parties involved, and match that to the only viable motive, then I believe our hypothetical murderer is you Mr. Allen."

She waited for Bill's telltale response - a flinch, fidgeting in his seat, sweating, or any outward sign of discomfort.

Instead he grinned and said, "I guess you got me."

Startled, she launched her reply, "What?"

"If I follow your line of logic then you're right, no one but me could have done it. That assumes, of course, that there have indeed been three murders."

She scanned him cautiously.

He continued, "Thankfully it's only a hypothesis, because I can see a few flaws."

"For instance?"

"I don't have the skills needed to accomplish these murders. In case you haven't noticed, I'm a computer geek. It would also require considerable planning and execution to eliminate myself as a viable suspect while placing the suspicion somewhere else. Lastly, and you would know the answer to this better than I, is there any evidence pointing in my direction?"

She shook her head slowly from side to side.

"I'm glad Captain. You're a very capable and determined investigator. I wouldn't want you after me."

"Let's assume you did kill the Turners and Jeffrey Blake. It would be difficult, at best, to prove it based on the accumulated evidence. Oh, let's not be mistaken, I could prove it. There is no perfect crime. No matter how minute, there is always a loose end somewhere. I simply need the time and the inclination to find it. I'm the boss, so I can certainly make the time. It's the inclination that's lacking."

Surprise marked his expression as he spoke, "You don't impress me as the type of person to let a crime go unanswered."

"Mr. Allen, I've been a cop a long time. There's crime, and then there's crime. Sometimes justice is hard to come by. Based on what I know about the Turners and Dr. Blake, they all got exactly what they deserved. And, if the evidence holds, which I believe it will, Pat Turner will get the rest of her natural life to think about it. This assumes that you are the person that could, and would, exact these punishments . . . but that can't possibly be, because we all know, the bad guys never get away."

She paused before finishing. When she did, she cemented his ass to the chair, "But, you know what . . . they didn't this time either."

Bill measured her, but this time it was from several new angles, "You surprise me Captain."

"I shouldn't. Underneath, I suspect we're very much alike. Given the same set of circumstances I might very well have done the same . . . hypothetically."

"If you'll pardon the poor analogy Captain, as cops go, you are cut from a different piece of cloth."

"I'll take that as a compliment."

"As you should."

"One last thing."

"What is it, Captain?"

"If someone did, in fact, commit these crimes I would advise them to never so much as get a ticket for jaywalking. I wouldn't rest until I put them away."

Bill began to chuckle.

She asked, "What's so funny?"

"I almost wish I had committed these crimes."

"Why's that?"

He winked as he answered, "Just to see if you could catch me."

She winked back as she countered, "Be careful what you ask for Mr. Allen?"

There was a long respectful pause before Bill said, "May I assume you're done with me Captain?"

"Unless there's some evidential revelation Mr. Allen, I am."

"I guess I better hope there isn't?"

"I know I do, Mr. Allen."

They rose together and faced each other. Bill offered his hand to her. She took it. They stood, hands clasp in mutual regard.

He spoke softly, "Maureen, if I were fifteen years older, or you were fifteen years younger, I'd be asking you to dinner."

She smiled softly and said, "Bill, if that were the case, I'd be accepting."

He leaned forward, kissed her on the cheek and whispered, "Thank you, Captain Romano."

She whispered back, "You're welcome, Mr. Allen."

CHAPTER TWENTY ONE

The day after his meeting with Captain Romano, Bill picked up his ringing phone, "Hello."

"Hello, Bill, it's Donna."

"Are you okay?"

"As well as I can be under the circumstances."

"How about the kids?"

"They're coping. They'll need some attention, but they're pretty resilient."

"What's going on with the police and Jeff's suicide?" "That's really why I'm calling. The police had Jeff's office closed off with that yellow tape they use to cordon off crime scenes. I had been told not to enter the office without their permission. It was rather strange considering he killed himself. Anyway, not more than forty minutes ago a Sergeant Washington showed up with a uniformed policeman, removed all the yellow tape, replaced all the furniture that had been moved by the investigators, borrowed my vacuum cleaner and vacuumed the carpet. When they were finished, he apologized for any inconvenience they had caused me, offered the departments regrets on my loss, and told me they were going to declare Jeff's death a suicide. Before he left he shook my hand and explained that I shouldn't be hearing from them again, but if anyone bothered me to call a Captain Romano's office. I don't know what's supposed to happen in these types of situations, but it all seemed a little strange."

Bill smiled as he thought, *Thank you, Maureen.*

He replied to her casually, "I'm sure it was all normal police procedure."

"But cleaning up the office and giving me the name of someone to call if I had any trouble?"

"Probably a public relations thing to improve the police force's image."

"Well it worked, I won't speak ill of them."

"I suppose you're glad to have this closed and put behind you."

He realized that didn't come out exactly as he wanted and quickly continued, "I mean from a police standpoint. It will surely take some time to put Jeff's death and the circumstances of his death behind you." There was silence on the line. After several moments Bill asked, "Donna, are you there?"

More silence. Then, after several heartbeats she said in a distant voice, "Yes Bill, I suppose it will take some time. The kids and I -"

She stopped.

He could hear her heavy breathing through the receiver. After several more moments he plunged in again, "Donna, are you sure you're all right?"

More weighted silence. After more heart beats she finally beseeched him, "Bill, are you my friend?"

This question was always loaded and most of the motives behind it lead to very uncomfortable places. He paused to contemplate the path through the underbrush and then said with hesitation, "Well, yes Donna, I suppose I am."

"You don't sound too sure?"

"I've never actually thought about our relationship in those terms. You and Marci were so close, I always felt like a tag along – but since she died you've been wonderful to the children and me. Without you're help, I'm not sure we would have made it. So yes, I'm honored to be your friend."

"Thank you Bill, that means a great deal. Marci was my only real friend, and when she died I lost the only person I could talk to."

"You had Jeff."

"Not really. Men think they communicate. I suppose in their world what they say passes for communication, but few men can truly communicate, particularly with women."

When the truth buckles your knees, it certainly gets your attention. His next thought wrapped itself around his heart and squeezed . . . very hard. *I'm so sorry Marci, I should've done better.*

He tried to deflect the pain and said to Donna, "That's that Mars, Venus thing, right?"

She chuckled, "Right Bill, that Mars, Venus thing."

"Come on Donna; be fair, I'm trying."

"I know Bill I'm just kidding with you."

"All right then, we've established I'm your friend. Now what?"

"I need someone to talk to, would you like to be that person?"

"I'd like that, but only if you'll talk to me when I need someone to talk to?"

"You've got a deal. And, thank you Bill, I appreciate you being there, particularly now."

"Oh yes, there's one other thing."

"What?"

"I never was very good in school with the planets. I'll do my best, but I'm not sure if I'm supposed to be Mars or Venus"

She laughed as she answered, "We'll work around it."

"Fair enough."

"Good. Now, why don't you and the kids come over for dinner? I need some friendly faces around right now."

"Oh, I've got to be a friendly face too? I thought it was just friends. I guess I can do friendly face. It'll be a stretch, but that's what friends are for. However, why don't you and yours come here?"

"Okay. We can do that. What time?"

"How about 6:30?"

"See you then. Can I bring anything?"

"If I knew what we were having you probably could, but since I don't, just bring your team."

"See you then."

~~~~~~~~~~~~~~~~~~~~~~~~~~~~~

Dinner was over. The dishes were clanging in the dishwasher as Bill and Donna sat opposite each other at the kitchen table. All the kids were up in Molly's room playing computer games. They could occasionally be heard squealing as one or another met some terrible fate at the hands of the software maker.

The large cup of coffee, that each caressed, helped bring a piece of sanity to an otherwise adrenaline charged day.
~~~~~~~~~~~~~~~~~~~~~~~~~~~~~

Donna stared at Bill over the rim of her cup and eventually said, "That was a very good dinner, thank you."

"My Mother, God rest her soul, deserves the credit. That recipe was hers - quick, easy to make, and pretty darn good."

They each raised their coffee cups in a toast to Bill's Mother.

Donna studied him for a few seconds and then said, "May I tell you something?"

"Anything, remember we're friends."

"Touché."

"That didn't come out right. You know what I mean."

"I understand. You may not want to hear this?"

"Tell me. If I don't want to hear it I'll forget it."

"I'm serious Bill."

"I simply meant, if it's something that needs to remain confidential, I will forget it."

"Are you sure?"

"Of course."

She lowered her eyes and spoke, "I'm glad Jeff killed himself."

She had been right, he didn't need to hear this, but once committed you had to follow along, even if it meant trudging through quicksand.

He offered the appropriate amount of surprise . . . at least, he thought it was the appropriate amount, "What?"

"I'm glad Jeff killed himself. I know it's a terrible thing to say, but I mean it."

Shocked, but pleased that she had no involvement in the Turner Circus he probed, "But why?"

"Please don't repeat what I'm about to tell you?"

"No, never."

"When we were first married he was a wonderful husband. Then when the kids came along he became an equally wonderful father. Something happened five or six years ago. He began drinking and then somewhere along the way he ventured into drugs. He began chasing other women and eventually our home became a place for him to eat and sleep. He ignored the kids and me. The job of keeping our family together fell entirely on my shoulders. I asked him for a divorce many times but he always refused and promised to change. Then two years ago he met the Turners and became involved with them. They were evil people Bill. I'm glad they're dead too. Anyway, as his involvement with them grew he became more and more abusive."

"How?"

"He would explode and beat me for no reason. When I threatened to go to the authorities he told me if I did he would kill the kids."

Bill smirked internally as he thought, *where have I heard that before. Jeff had the best teachers in the business . . . the Turners!*

"Our life had become hell. I used to watch the stories on television about abused and battered women and wonder why they put up with it. I now understand. I hated myself for allowing him to treat us that way, but my fear for the kids' safety outweighed any other consideration."

Donna scooted her chair back several inches from the table, took a deep breath, and said, "That's it. That's why I'm glad he's gone. The kids and I can begin to live again."

"Donna, we had no idea. I'm so sorry. You should have told us, we could have done something."

"Marci suspected, but I always denied it. What were you going to do against someone like that? You're a good man Bill and you couldn't stand against him."

Well, I guess my recent behavior shoots that theory all to hell. Not to mention, this gives me three more reasons for doing what I did.

"I don't know Donna, I would have done something."

"Thankfully, we won't ever have to know, he solved the problem for us."

"Okay, what now?"

"The good news is that he left me very well off. I'm just going to take some time and decide what will be best for me and the kids."

"I'm here if you need any help with anything."

"I appreciate that. It's very comforting to know that you're here for us. I'm going to lean on you from time to time, I hope you won't mind?"

"What are planets and friends for?"

They both laughed. They continued a while with small talk. After fifteen minutes Donna rose and said, "I'd better get home. I'm sending the kids back to school tomorrow. It's time for them and their Mother to start their new lives"

Bill rose to help her collect the children and see her out. As he came toward her she stopped him, placed her hands on his shoulders, stretched up, kissed him on the cheek and whispered, "Thank you Bill. Thank you for everything."

He was caught off guard, he fumbled his reply, "You're more than welcome ... anytime."

Her lips brushed his ear as her warm breath formed the words, "I'll hold you to that."

As he stood in the front door and watched Donna and the kids drive off down the street he drifted back to the scene of he and Donna minutes before in the kitchen. As he visualized her closing remarks and her lips against his ear, he shivered. She was a beautiful woman. The tenderness and warmth of that moment caused a twitch in his penis. He covered his guilty feelings with an outward excuse, "Well hell, at least it proves I'm starting to live again too."

CHAPTER TWENTY TWO

Life was returning to normal, or as normal as it would ever be without Marci. Bill and the children had settled back into their daily routines. He went to work. They went to school. He cooked and did laundry. Laundry was pretty straight forward, but cooking was a learning experience. At first, even he was complaining about the quality and lack of variety in his culinary selections. With lots of crashed experiments and considerable on-line training he had become almost accomplished in the kitchen. At least now when he served dinner, Molly and Bill Jr. had mercifully stopped making the finger down the throat signs at each other. Cleaning, on the other hand, had become a subcontracting issue. He had tried keeping the house presentable. It became very clear, very quickly, however that even with the children's assistance, they would soon be living in a domestic landfill. Three days after that realization a two day a week housekeeper had been retained.

With this more routine and stable home environment he, and the world around him, had reached a truce. His drinking had been reduced to social and his emotional status had gone from typhoon to the occasional thunderstorm. With each passing day his life, without her, was becoming more tolerable. He would never stop missing her, but that chronic pain in his heart was being replaced by their daily conversations concerning all the issues any family faces. With her invisible support, he felt more connected, more in charge, and better able to cope with the world and its moving landscape. He felt guilty that their dialogue was one-sided, but the "Marci" sounding board somehow made his decisions more pragmatic, more logical, and even more load bearing.

"What am I going to do about that C Bill Jr. got in math?"

Silence.

As though responding to her recommendations he would continue, "I tried that already, he doesn't seem to care."

Silence.

"What do you think about dangling summer baseball camp in front of him?"

Silence.

"Oh, I agree. For that prize we need at least an A. Then it's settled, I'll discuss that with him after dinner tonight."

"Okay, now, what about this bra issue and Molly."

Silence.

"I know she doesn't need a bra yet, but she started asking me questions about bras the other day. Before I turn around she'll need one. And the question of her period . . . well, I'd rather have a root canal than that particular conversation. What in the hell am I going to do?"

Silence.

"Right, ask Donna. Why didn't I think of that?"

Silence.

"I know. That's why you're here."

Pause, and then, "I'm thinking of changing jobs."

Silence.

"No we don't need more money, particularly after my slight of hand with the Turners' bank accounts."

Silence.

"Yes, I do like my job, but I don't think I'm being appreciated anymore."

Silence.

"I suppose you're right, I can just ask for a raise. If they don't give it to me then I'll look for something else."

Silence.

"What would I do without your rock solid advice?"

Silence.

"I know I can't hear you, but it helps to think I can."

Silence.

Then, hobbled by his loneliness he would always send his offering, "I miss you so much. I'll never stop loving you."

After this admission there was nothing left to him but sorrow and self-pity. He muffled his sobbing so as not to alarm the children....

~~~~~~~~~~~~~~~~~~~~~~~~~~~~~

It was a Saturday and the children were at Donna's for the afternoon. He was to join them for dinner. He had three hours before the dinner bell rang and an urge to get current with Edith. He moseyed up to the attic and took his seat of honor. He sat his drink on the floor, reached for the receiver and tapped Edith's speed dial number.

Two rings later she answered sarcastically, "Hello, Bill. What brings you to my world?"

Apologetically he said, "I know it's been a while Edith. There's a lot happening here."
~~~~~~~~~~~~~~~~~~~~~~~~~~~~~

As soon as the excuse was out of his mouth he realized the mistake. She could, if she chose to, see anything he was doing. How painful would she make this?

"I can see everything you do Bill . . . remember? Or do I have to relate in graphic detail what you were doing to yourself in the bathroom the other night?"

Surrendering, he replied, "No Edith, that won't be necessary. It was wrong to say and you have rightfully corrected my slip."

"Thank you, Bill. Now, other than not needing my input anymore, is there a particular reason you have chosen not to speak to your dead mother-in-law?"

He had hoped a quick admission and apology would limit the beating . . . it hadn't! Possibly a frontal approach could slow the assault, "Edith, I'm sorry I haven't called. Whatever you have to say, can we get it over with?"

"How long has it been since you called?"

"I don't know Edith, six weeks?"

"Try two months."

"All right Edith, two months."

He paused briefly and then said, "Can we get on with it?"

She continued her onslaught, "It's not the time Bill, time means nothing here, it's the principle. It's the fact that . . ."

As Edith rambled on Bill laid the phone on the ground facing him. He rose slowly, turned his back to her voice, bent forward and dropped his trousers in the classic "moon" position. While he turned to face the receiver he readjusted his clothing. He reseated himself and pulled the phone to his ear.

There was a steady hum on the line. For a moment he was afraid she had hung up on him. Just as he was about to disconnect she said, "Real cute, Bill. That was infantile, even for you."

"No more infantile than you continuing to scold me after I have apologized profusely. I know that was a childish thing to do, but you've made your point. I would like to talk about some other things."

She relented, and then salvaged a more receptive mood, "You're right. I've made my point. Just one last thing and then we can move on?"

"Okay, what is it?"

"You've got a nice ass Bill."

She waited for his response. When it came it was the truce they both needed. He began laughing. Through the laughter he managed, "Only you Edith. You're a lot of things, but never dull or predictable."

She laughed with him. They enjoyed the moment. As their laughter subsided she said, "What now?"

"I'd like to talk about Donna?"

"Of course you would. What about Donna?"

"Why didn't you tell me about the abuse?"

"You didn't ask?"

"We talked about Jeff; there must have been a way for you to give notice?"

"You know the rules Bill."

"But still?"

"If I was going to break the rules I would have done it with information about Marci and me. That was a lot more important than Donna's abuse at the hands of Jeff."

He pondered, then spoke, "I suppose, but Donna and her children were in danger. Maybe something could have been done sooner."

She skewered him, "Well, aren't you something. I guess Marci and I are dog droppings? We're dead, she's not."

"That's not fair Edith. It's true that you and Marci were already dead. Your retribution could have waited. Donna is alive, and she and the children needed to be protected."

"Stop trying to crawl out of this Bill. You're just feeling guilty because you're starting to like her."

His reply was jagged and full of too much defense, "That's not true Edith. I love Marci, and I always will. So stop with the innuendos."

She chuckled, "I fear he doth protest too much. Did I say you didn't love Marci? I struck a nerve, didn't I?"

He back peddled, "No, but you're not being fair to Donna, or any of us."

"Why don't you cut the bullshit Bill? I saw that little scene in your kitchen - that little kiss on the cheek combined with her whispered invitation. I also saw both of your reactions."

"Both of my reactions?"

"Your emotional reaction and your physical reaction."

"I was taken off guard. The one was surprise and the other was just a reflex."

"You were lucky you weren't taken . . . period! She could've had your gonads in the palm of her hand, and there was nothing you would have done to stop her. Reflex my ass that was a response to a very pleasant stimulus. Sell this crap to the tourists, I know better."

He almost begged his response, "I love Marci Edith . . . I do."

"I know that Bill, and for that matter, so does she. I don't care what you do. Besides, Marci adores Donna; she doesn't have a problem with you and her together."

"She doesn't?"

"Of course not. She loves you. She wants to see you happy. If that means being with Donna, or anyone else, it's fine with her as long as you're happy."

"But I thought -"

"That's your problem Bill, stop thinking. I've told you before; we're driven differently here than you are there. We want your world full of peace and contentment. We love you Bill, we want you happy."

He choked out his reply, "You said we, Edith."

"I know Bill. Scary isn't it. When I said 'we' it scared the hell out of me too – but, watching you grow, watching you become a confident protector of this family, and watching you accept the softer side of yourself has made me, in spite of myself, respect and love you. Yes, Bill, I said it. Now, if you say something stupid I'm going to break this connection." He inhaled sharply, and then said, "I don't know what to say, so I can't very well say something stupid."

He paused before continuing, then softly and resolutely spoke, "I'll need time for this to register, but for now, I'm honored and privileged to have the two of you watching over me."

"That'll do for now."

The quiet that lay between them was full of warmth and tenderness. This poignant respite was finally broken by Edith, "Bill, it's time for you to move on."

Bill gathered himself and replied, "Move on?"

"Yes, Bill. Marci and I have discussed it. She and I feel exactly the same. Life is for the living. You need to make a new life for you, Bill Jr. and Molly. You must do whatever it takes to do that."

"But, I don't want to stop talking to you, or Marci, through you."

"You're going to have to. It's not healthy, talking to a dead person. Your attention needs to be directed at you and the children. Marci and I know that and you need to know it too. Besides, I'm not certain how much longer this line will be open."

"No, Edith. I don't want this to end."

"It may soon be out of our hands."

"How do you know that?"

"I don't for sure, but I can feel something different about to happen."

"Can't you hide, or disguise what we're doing?"

"I will talk to you as long as I can."

"I don't want to lose you Edith. Worse, I don't want you punished for talking to me. Let them punish me."

"It doesn't work that way Bill. I must shoulder whatever happens. That includes communicating with you and manipulating you to seek my revenge."

"I'm the one that killed, not you."

"That's true, but the vengeance was mine. I very discreetly pointed the way."

"I beg to differ Edith."

"Whatever, we're jumping the gun. Nothing has happened yet and hopefully it won't. So let's not press our luck. Say goodbye, Bill."

"But Edith -"

As though slapping the wrist of an ill behaved child she stopped him with, "Bill."

"All right. Goodbye, Edith."

The line went blank.

CHAPTER TWENTY THREE

The months had stacked up since the Turners' demise and Jeff Blake's "suicide". They backed into each other so rapidly that Bill was pressed to accept their existence. Jeff's death had been officially declared a suicide and stamped "Case Closed". Pat had been officially charged and then quickly indicted for the murders of her father and sister. Because the crime had been so heinous, and the facts surrounding the case so sordid, there had been a public outcry for a speedy trial. Pat's lawyers had pulled every legal trick in the book to delay and confuse the march to judgment. In the end however, their skills were no match for the politics of an election year, and the pressure of the electorate won the day. In response to the pre-election polls, the judicial system established a state record and brought her to trial in five and a half months.

The evidence was so overwhelming that only some catastrophic seismic event could possibly have saved her. It had become a television sideshow, and an editorial prize perfectly designed to boost publication sales. Each day the public was bombarded by the real and the fabricated analysis of varied and assorted "experts". Did she or didn't she, with the pros and cons of each position discussed ad nauseam. Unfortunately, the defense side of the arguments started in a deep hole. It's difficult to refute dead people in a room locked from the inside, when the only remaining person is smeared with their blood and her fingerprints are all over the implements of torture. Add to that an abundance of drugs in the systems of all parties and, enough in the deceased to kill. Well ... the mountain against grew rapidly. The defense created a small opening with the programmable locked door, but every expert for both sides concluded under intense examination that there was no evidence of software tampering or malfunction. The final nail was the fact that the day before the alleged murders large sums of money were transferred from the accounts of Frank and Pam Turner into the account of Pat Turner. She had, of course, cried foul. It was difficult to buy into her pleas of innocence however when it was revealed that she had a university degree in Computer Sciences. There were numerous other incidentals that pointed in her direction. One such, were the e-mails that Frank had sent to his friends stating that she had been acting strangely. In and of itself, it was refutable, but combined with other circumstantial details and placed on top of everything else . . . well, that mountain began to take on avalanche proportions.

Her attorneys put on a good show. After all, their reputations and their fees demanded it. In an effort to misdirect and confuse the jury they introduced every complex legal maneuver known to contemporary trial law. Their ability to complicate and divert issues was only matched by their incessant use of "objections" to control and dictate the pace of testimony and its meaning. In an effort to be fair, the judge stretched the limits of accepted courtroom protocol and behavior, but when the defense attorneys exceeded these already stretched limits, the judge was forced to intervene. The meeting in chambers was brief, but when the trial resumed the jury and the viewing public were treated to a much less flamboyant and aggressive performance. This led all the "experts" to speculate that the defense team had tread dangerously close to a contempt citation. When the dust had settled and the smoke had cleared, Pat's lawyers had confounded all the pundits, by prolonging a rather straightforward prosecution for seven weeks. The few arguments the defense did win were hardly enough to turn the tide. The television news shows hardly had time to examine the pros and cons before the jury returned their verdict. Four hours after receiving their final instructions they had returned to their seats.

Pat rose to faced the twelve good men and women that decided her fate.

The judge faced the panel and said to a standing foreman, "Madam foreman, have you reached a verdict?"

"We have your honor."

"How say you?"

The verdict was down and dirty. In a clear and resonating voice the madam foreman announced "Guilty" on the first charge of murder in the first degree, then quickly repeated "Guilty" on the second charge of murder in the first degree.

Pat slumped. Her attorneys held her up as she began to cry.

The judge outlined the remaining details of the proceeding. She waived sentencing until a date two weeks in the future.

The expected appeals were requested and granted pending appropriate filings with the court.

Two weeks later the Honorable Jane Houseman announced the verdict to the world. Along with a brief statement admonishing Pat for the brutal and heinous acts against her Father and Sister Judge Houseman sentenced her to two concurrent life terms without the possibility of parole.

In the two months since Pat's trial Bill had been to see her several times. Always upbeat and supportive, he had continually stated, "I'm sure you'll get a new trial once the appeal is granted."

"I hope you're right Bill, but my attorneys aren't very optimistic."

"You just need to keep you're spirits up and have faith that it'll turn out in your favor."

Bill had carefully set the stage for today's visit with Pat. It was time to place the figurative axe right between her eyes! As he drove to the jail he hummed that Sousa March with vigor. If all went as planned this would be the last time he would ever hum that particular composition. At day's end he would be retiring any vestige of these times and his involvement in them. That would include Mr. Sousa and his March.

He sat in a cubicle, arms resting on the counter in front of him, and staring through the shielded glass. He was awaiting Pat's arrival. He closed his eyes and replayed the script he had written for the upcoming conversation. Rehearsal complete, he opened his eyes to find her seated on the other side of the clear barrier.

"Damn, Pat, you startled me. Why didn't you say something?"

"You looked so peaceful I didn't want to disturb you."

Peaceful, he thought, *what an interesting choice of words. It won't be peaceful much longer!*

He offered a covering excuse, "I was just thinking about a picnic Marci and I took the children on when they were still small.

Pat responded with an empathetic, "That's nice."

"Enough of that. How are you doing?"

"About the same."

"No word on your appeal?"

"Not yet."

"Do you need anything?"

Dejectedly she answered, "No."

"You're sure there's nothing I can get you?"

"No, I've everything I need for this place."

"Bill Jr. and Molly said to say hello to their Aunt Pat."

She brightened and replied, "Please send them my regards. How are they?"

"At their age, how bad can they be? They complain about school and they always want the latest computer game."

Pat smiled as she remembered a softer time and then said, "I wish I could see them sometime?"

"They're not old enough yet to be visiting here."

"I know Bill, I was just wishing."

Pat paused. Her expression saddened before she continued, "May we talk about something else Bill? The children bring up too many things I'd prefer to forget."

"Of course Pat. This is your time; we can talk about anything you'd like."

Bill paused before continuing, "Have you or the attorneys had any luck in determining who might have done this to you?"

"No."

"There must be someone of interest?"

"Father was a tough businessman. Over the years he certainly made some enemies. The lawyers have poured through the police reports looking for someone with motive and no alibi. They found a number of persons with a motive, but all had airtight alibis. They were also hoping the investigators missed someone, but that doesn't seem to be the case. In an effort to preclude the alternative crime theory being offered at trial the police treated everyone as a suspect, even you."

"Even me?"

"Yes. Because of your family ties to us they looked at you carefully before eliminating you as a person of interest."

His response expressed the appropriate amount of surprised concern, "My gosh, I had no idea."

"Relax Bill, they dismissed you almost immediately."

"Well, at least that's good to know."

Pat chuckled as she said, "You're safe Bill. No one believes you have the disposition or the where with all to carry out such an act."

He displayed a deflated expression as he said, "That doesn't say much for me."

She backpedaled slightly, "I didn't mean it that way Bill. I only meant that whoever did it had to be very resourceful and very angry. Not that you can't be both, but your talents lie in other areas."

"Well, I suppose, but I've always believed that given the right circumstances anyone is capable of killing."

Half way through his statement Bill's eyes narrowed and focused on her.

Pat's head moved back slightly from the intensity of his look. She inhaled sharply as she offered, "The way you said that almost scared me."

"I'm sorry Pat, I don't know where that came from. I guess the thought of murder just upsets me."

"I understand Bill, but that's a side of you I've never seen before."

"And I'll make sure you don't see it again. How's that?"

"Well, okay."

"May I ask you another question about this situation?"

"Sure."

"Do you or your lawyers have any ideas about why you were left to take the blame for this?"

"Not really. I mean, I've wondered, 'Why me?' but I haven't come up with anything that makes any sense. Why, do you have any ideas?

He was invitingly noncommittal as he replied,"I suppose not. Besides, I shouldn't be speculating if you or your team doesn't have any ideas."

She pleaded with him,"Come on Bill, if you have an idea, please tell me. I need all the help I can get."

"Well, it seems to me that you were chosen because you're the youngest."

"The youngest? I don't understand?"

"The consensus of the press and the experts is that this was a crime of passion and money. But, if you didn't do it, then those motives don't fit. With passion and money eliminated, I would be inclined to believe that it becomes a crime of revenge. If it were revenge, aside from needing a stand-in, it seems to me the intent of the real killer was to make one of the family suffer for as long as possible. Since you're the youngest, by the accident of birth, you got the job."

"I don't know if you're right, but that makes more sense than anything we've been able to come with."

"I'm just speculating."

"At least you're thinking. I think everyone else has given up."

"Don't talk like that. I'm sure you're legal team is doing everything they can."

"The other issue that has me buffaloed is why all three of us? I understand that Father may have had enemies. He could be rather unpleasant, even vengeful, if he didn't get his way in business. He wasn't as bad in his personal life but he could certainly be difficult, but why Pam and me? We never hurt anyone. I understand the need for a fall guy, but to come after both of us doesn't seem fair. Who could possibly want to hurt us?"

Gee Pat, you and Pam were such angels. How could anyone be so inconsiderate?

Bill's face moved to a large grin as he answered, "Well, let me see."

As the word "see" fell from his mouth he gave Pat a very pronounced wink!

Her mouth fell open and she gasped, "What are you saying Bill?"

With feigned ignorance he bounced back, "Who, me? Nothing."

"Why the grin and the wink if you're saying nothing?"

"I think you're confused Pat."

She eyed him skeptically. Then as the tumblers began to fall into place she asked, "Are you saying that you did this?"

He continued grinning as he replied, "Oh, no, couldn't have been me. The person who did this would have been 'very resourceful and very angry'. Isn't that what you said?"

"Yes, but-"

"Well that obviously rules me out. I'm not very resourceful and what do I have to be very angry about?"

He stopped for effect, then moved forward, "It would probably take someone like the person, or persons, responsible for killing Guilford Watson, your Mother, and Marci."

Her eyes widened as she responded, "Are you saying they were murdered?"

As though confused by her statement he said, "I'm still just speculating."

She looked around before replying, "How did you know?"

"Know what?"

With surprise and anger sharing the same question she said, "You know what I mean?"

With a misunderstood tone he replied, "Oh no, Pat, I didn't mean to imply that the three of them had been murdered. I simply meant, if they had been, it would take a hypothetical person, or persons, as resourceful and angry as that to kill Frank and Pam and pin it on you."

Another stop for effect, and then, "Thank heaven we ruled me out. Of course, we all know that I can't walk and chew gum at the same time."

He paused long enough for his eyes to narrow, before forcefully burying the axe, "Don't we!"

She stared at him with disbelief.

He punctuated her disbelief with a closing grin and another wink!

Her face began to redden. When the red got to the tips of her ears she began slamming the phone receiver against the Plexiglas window and screaming, "You son of a bitch, you did it! You did it! You did it! It was -"

Her own rage strangled her yelling in the middle of her tirade.

At that moment two very large guards arrived and lifted her off the ground. Held under each arm and six inches off the ground she was told to stop shouting. Between the directive to cease and her hatred for Bill she could no longer speak. Instead she glowered at him. The fire in her eyes was so intense it threatened to consume the four of them.

With concern meant to impress the guards, he spoke loudly into the mouthpiece, "What's wrong, Pat? Can I do something?"

One of the officers retrieved Pat's phone and said, "I'm sorry sir, but you'll have to leave now."

"Of course, officer. Thank you."

Bill hung up his receiver. He then leaned very close to the pane of glass between them, gave a wave goodbye and mouthed the words very slowly and distinctly, "I'll come back another day Pat. Some day when you're not so agitated."

Her response was to break a hand free and pound on the glass and begin screaming, "You did it! You did it!"

Bill raised his hands, palms up, and out to his sides. He shook his head back and forth as if to say, "I can't hear you."

Pat continued screaming hysterically as he rose, turned with a concealed smile, and left.

~~~~~~~~~~~~~~~~~~~~~~~~~~~~

In the days to come, Bill would try many times to see her. She, of course, refused repeatedly. All was as planned. His concern for her condition and welfare was for public consumption only. After all, it wasn't his fault that she had mysteriously cut off contact!

Pat, on the other hand, became morose and withdrawn. She sank into a deep depression. So deep, that eventually her attorneys gave up trying to communicate with her. She tried twice to commit suicide. After the second attempt failed she was placed under close psychiatric care and administered heavy daily doses of anti-depressants. She would live out her life in a vegetative state, mumbling to herself and her wadded up blanket.
~~~~~~~~~~~~~~~~~~~~~~~~~~~~

CHAPTER TWENTY FOUR

It had been ten days since his final visit with Pat. It had been a few days more since his last conversation with Edith.

He plopped his butt on the attic floor and hit the speed dial. The first ring wasn't complete when, "Hello, Bill."

"Hello, Edith."

"I saw that little tête-à-tête you had with Pat."

"How'd you like it?"

"You're a very mean man Bill."

"When I have to be."

They chuckled together.

"She's not doing well with your revelation."

"Good. I didn't want her to. I want the three of them and Jeff to suffer the way they've made all of us suffer."

"You can trust me, they will."

"How's Marci, Edith?"

"She's fine. Concerned about you though."

"Why? I've never been better."

"She's worried what all this killing is doing to you."

"What about you, Edith?"

"I'm not the subject of this inquiry."

"I'd still like to know what you think?"

"I'm still stuck here where I started because of what I think. You know I'm a "pound of flesh" lady. They got what they deserve."

"Thank you Edith. I appreciate that."

"Don't thank me, all your balancing the scales may cost you dearly."

"There's nothing I can do about that now."

"True, but that's what has Marci concerned."

"Right, wrong, or indifferent, you tell her I'm the man I should have been when she was here. That doesn't balance the scales, but it's a small compensation."

"We both love you. We're happy you're a better person, but we don't want you overshooting the mark."

"You can both rest assured that I'm turning out to be a pretty decent individual."

"That's good enough for me. Now, let's move to another subject that she and I are anxious about."

"What is this, reshape Bill day?"

"Stop it Bill. We both want to help you."

"I know Edith, but have I given the impression lately that I can't take care of myself?"

"No, but everyone can use a little help from time to time. So shut up and listen."

"Aye, aye sir."

"Cut the crap Bill."

"All right, what is it?"

"It's been long enough; we think it's time for you to move on with your life."

"Didn't we have this conversation already?"

"We did, but now that all the loose ends are tied up it needs to be revisited."

"First, I'm not sure it's any of your business. Second, maybe I'm not ready to move on yet."

"Marci wants you to have a family again – and, in your case, that takes a woman. You and the children need a woman in your life."

"What's that, 'your case', about?"

"If all this murder and mayhem had somehow changed your sexual orientation then we'd want something else for you and the children. That's what love is about Bill."

Irritation laced his reply, "I'm glad we've decided that I still belong with women. I can't wait for what's next?"

She graciously added, "We believe you should be with Donna."

Irritation was replaced with sarcasm, "Oh, please Edith; please tell me why?"

"Donna has fallen in love with you. All the children get along and the two of you will be great parents."

"Does anyone care what I think?"

"Bill, men don't always know what's best for them."

"But women do?"

"In this instance, yes. I suspect, as you learn more about her you'll come to appreciate just how perfect she is for you."

"And just what am I going to learn about her that makes you think that?

"You know I can't divulge that information."

His patience was threadbare as he countered, "Here we go again with it'll change the future."

"Bill, we all have constraints. By now, you should be fully aware of mine."

He exploded, "Jesus Christ, Edith, what have I done to deserve this?"

She replied in kind, "You threw your fucking phone against the wall and you got me. I didn't ask for this. Now stop being such a baby and try listening."

Her outburst trumped his. He calmed and said, "I'm sorry Edith. I know you and Marci are trying to help, but it feels very much like interference."

"I understand, but there may be forces at work beyond all of us that require our compliance. I don't know. We're simply asking you to give it a chance. If it's right, or wrong, you'll know and we'll support your decision."

"It's tough enough trying to stand against one dead person, what chance do I have against two? I'll stay open to the idea. That's the best I can do for now."

"That's fair. Thank you, Bill."

"Anything else Edith?"

"No."

"I know you'll be watching, so I'll talk to you later."

"Good luck."

~~~~~~~~~~~~~~~~~~~~~~~~~~~~~~

Two months had passed since Edith had issued her love life directive. His relationship with Donna had cemented faster and stronger than he was willing to admit. His resistance, a definite backlash to Edith and Marci's prodding, had slowly eroded. Donna's beauty, intelligence, and charm had worn down his defenses. She was not the same person he had known before Jeff's death. Before, she was cordial, attractive, and concerned, but always in a proper, almost protective way. Now, she was engaging, warm, and sharing. Without Jeff's repression she had gone from a gray, withdrawn moth, to a colorful outgoing butterfly!

Donna had raised the issue of marriage. It was always in passing, and always lighthearted, almost joking. He had let these hints and innuendos fall humorously by the way, but their impression was growing from within. He wasn't in love with her yet, but given time and her continued presence, he knew he would be. There was one issue preventing him from taking the final step to a new life for him and the children. It was this issue that constricted his movement forward . . . .

~~~~~~~~~~~~~~~~~~~~~~~~~~~~~~

He stared at the Messenger XD 500. Was he ready to take the word of a dead person as the final authority? Sure, he'd listened to her, he'd even felt directed by her, but was he ready to commit his life based on her opinion? He needed someone, in her case, something, to talk to. He had talked to himself long enough. Chasing your own tail only got you frustrated and dizzy.

In the middle of the argument with himself the phone rang.

He answered, "Hello, Edith."

"I couldn't take it any longer. Were you going to pick up the phone, or not?"

"I was."

"What's the problem?"

"I'm struggling with something and I need your input."

She started to chide him, but stopped. This was a big step for Bill. To admit that he wanted her opinion was new ground for the both of them.

She moved lightly, "What is it?"

"It's my relationship with Donna."

"Really? It looks from here as though the two of you are getting along fine."

"We are, but I'm struggling with my feelings."

"Meaning?"

"I think I'm falling in love with her."

"That's a good thing."

The resounding silence that followed her reply spoke volumes to Edith. After several more moments she spoke, "Well, it is, isn't it?"

"I suppose."

"Let's see if Mother Edith can sort this out. You think you're falling in love with Donna, but you're still in love with Marci . . . correct?"

"Yes."

"What's your point Bill?"

"I feel like I'm betraying Marci."

"Why?"

"We never had the life together that she deserved. It took dying to make me understand how deficient as a husband and a lover I really was. Now, if I have those things with Donna, I feel as though I'm betraying Marci, and her memory."

Her reply was calm, compassionate, and caring, "You're turning into a pretty neat person Bill."

"Excuse me?"

"What you're feeling means you're becoming a warm, caring, loving person. That's what you're supposed to be. That makes Marci and me very happy, proud even. Marci loves you. She wants you, Donna and the children to have a life together. We knew this was coming and we've discussed it. She told me to tell you that she doesn't feel betrayed or forgotten, she feels fulfilled. Your love for her has allowed you to now love someone else. That's a special gift to her. She also knows that you'll always love her. She'll always love you and the children – and, when you're all united again you'll be able to share it. She wants you to move on; move on with her love and her blessing."

"She said that?"

"You can be very exasperating Bill. You know I have to tell the truth. Now, go forth and live. We'll be waiting here when you're done."

He started to speak, but the line went dead. He redialed several times, but obviously Edith had said all she cared to say. His comments would have to wait until their next conversation.

~~~~~~~~~~~~~~~~~~~~~~~~~~~~~

They sat across the table from each other. It was an off night and the restaurant they had chosen was only half full. They had chosen it because of the menu and the wine list, but mostly because it offered them a quiet, comfortable atmosphere to talk.

The waiter had just placed their drinks before them. As he stood beside the table he asked, "Would you care to order now?"

Bill answered, "We'd like some time to talk. I'll wave when we're ready."

"That will be fine sir. In the meantime, if you'd wish another drink just nod."

"Thank you, I will."

Waiter gone, they were now left with that awkward silence that precedes any serious negotiation. They each took a sip from their drink to help fill the gap.

Bill reached across the table and took her hand in his. He looked into her eyes and said, "I have a lot to say, but before I do there's something I have to tell you."

"Anything, Bill."

"I've grown very fond of you. I -"

"That's it?"

"That's what?"
~~~~~~~~~~~~~~~~~~~~~~~~~~~~~

"You're very fond of me, nothing more?"

"I've had two other women in my life that interrupted me. I didn't appreciate it when they did it, and I don't appreciate it now."

His scowl caused her to retreat, "I'm sorry, that wasn't very polite."

"If I may continue?"

Her nod was his answer.

"As I was saying, I've grown very fond of you. I think I'm falling in love with you, but there's something you need to know before we discuss any next steps."

Her smile indicated her acceptance and willingness to proceed.

"I'm still in love with Marci. I will always love her. I don't think it's fair for us to move forward without you knowing that."

Her smile broadened as she replied casually, "That's it?"

Somewhat surprised he answered, "Well, yes."

"I knew that."

"You did?"

"Of course. Why shouldn't you love her? You had two beautiful children together. I've seen what she meant to you. If you didn't love her I wouldn't want anything to do with you. It would mean you have no staying power. I had a life with someone that had no staying power. I love you. For now, that's enough. You'll love me too, I'll see to it."

She leaned across the table and gave him a kiss. She teased him by just letting the tip of her tongue brush his lips. She sat back.

Bill started to speak, but her raised hand stopped him.

"As long as we're doing true confessions, you need to know the type of woman you're getting involved with."

"I think I do."

"Maybe, maybe not."

He eyed her questioningly and said, "You've got the floor."

She exhaled slowly before saying, "Remember the night of Jeff's death?"

Bill drifted back to that evening. He'd driven to the Blake's resident anticipating the extermination of Dr. Blake. He had been mentally and physically prepared to extract the full measure of retribution. As he neared the house he had been surprised to find the flashing lights of several police cars and a fire rescue vehicle. He pulled to the curb and waited. When a body-bagged corpse was placed in the ambulance, and driven off, he realized that his second option had occurred. That being, the fear of discovery, driven by the Turners death and Bill's anonymously mailed disk, had compelled him to take his own life. This was later confirmed by the announcement on television and the accompanying articles in the newspapers. When the accompanying suicide note was released Bill had subconsciously stamped the case closed and moved on with a smile.

He returned to the moment, and said, "Yes, very well. I was surprised that he would do that."

Donna inched forward in her seat and calmly said, "He didn't do that."

Bill blinked, and then questioned, "I'm sorry?"

"Jeff didn't kill himself, I killed him."

Confession was right, but this was overdoing it. He took a gulp of Scotch and asked, "Did you just say what I thought you said?"

She moved her head very deliberately up and down.

His mind was reeling as he stared at her.

She eyed him before saying, "Well? Don't you have something to say?"

As an impish grin crossed his face, he reached forward and raised his glass toward the ceiling and announced, "Edith, when you said she was perfect for me . . . well, I never could have guessed."

Donna straightened and said, "What are you talking about?"

He leaned across the table and kissed her. She resisted at first, but he took control when he said, "I love you. Will you marry me?"

She pulled back, stared at him curiously, and then said, "What?"

He smiled confidently and mouthed the words, "Will you marry me?"

"That's all you've got to say?"

"I thought that was quite a bit?"

"It is, but -"

"Okay, I thought there was a suicide note?"

She smiled back and responded with, "That was easy. I've been paying the bills for years and signing his name to the checks. His handwriting was second nature to me – and his name, well, I could write that better than he could. What else?"

He scanned her face and pressed, "You seemed to want me to ask a question, so I did."

Somewhat perturbed she pressed, "It doesn't bother you that I'm a murderer?"

He smiled and tossed out, "It would bother me if you got caught, but you're obviously very good at it."

His flip attitude about this very serious subject had cracked her patience. She reached to slap him – he caught her hand mid-flight and said, "I'm going to ask you one question. If you give the right answer we will never speak of this again."

"All right. What's the question?"

"Why did you do it?"

She eyed him skeptically, and then answered, "Because I was afraid of what he might do to the kids."

"That's it?"

"Well, me too, but basically the kids."

He waved to the waiter. While the waiter worked his way toward their table he said, "Are you going to marry me, or not?"

She beamed and replied, "I guess I gave the right answer?"

"It was good enough for me."

"In that case, yes."

"Yes?"

"Yes, I'll marry you."

"Good. Now, can we order, I'm starving."

Bill was famished. He'd need a very large dinner. It required a lot of energy to plan a life. Particularly a new life with a murderer!

CHAPTER TWENTY FIVE

Legs crossed, Bill gathered himself and his Scotch before the Messenger XD 500. The Scotch was a celebration of the complete package his life was becoming. He also wanted to thank Edith and Marci for their care and guidance. Finally, he was going to needle Edith about omitting Donna's dip into the killing pool. He owed her one for setting him up. He took a sip from his glass and reached forward to activate the phone. As the line rang through, he pondered his journey. For the first time in his life he was truly at peace with himself and the world around him. He had grown, in no small part, to the prodding and pushing of some very special "people". He chuckled as he thought, *People, dead, and alive.* He wasn't discounting his own contributions, but without three wonderful women behind him it might have taken years, or it may never have happened at all.

On the tenth ring he began to wonder if Edith was going to answer. On the twelfth a voice said, "Hello."

The tonal quality was different, but not enough to warrant concern. He responded, Edith?"

"I'm sorry, she's not here."

His breathing became ragged. He wasn't ready for this!

"May I speak to her please?"

"She's not here anymore."

"Is there any way to get in touch with her?"

"Not that I know of."

"May I ask who you are?"

"I'm with repair."

"Repair?"

"Yes. I'm here to take this line out of service."

Not now Edith. We've come so far.

"Is there anyone else I can speak to?"

"I wouldn't know how to put you in touch with anyone else."

"Why not?"

"I told you, I'm with repair. That's all I do. I'm not trained to forward calls, I just repair malfunctioning lines."

It couldn't end like this. There had to be more.

"But, I'm very concerned about her. I need to explain to someone that she was not responsible for this connection. I was."

"Yes sir, that's all been sorted out."

"But, I don't want anything to happen to her because of me."

"I'm not in charge of discipline, but I believe she is comfortably settled."

"How do I know that?"

There was affront in the tone of the return, "Because I told you so. We, at repair, pride ourselves on our work and our integrity. If you have nothing else I have other stops to make."

Bill was frantic, he couldn't think fast enough under this gun. He blurted out, "Well, did she leave me a message?"

"Sir, I don't do messages."

"Please."

"All right, give me a moment and I'll look."

"Thank you."

The silence that followed seemed endless. Finally, "Sir, is your name Bill?"

He replied anxiously, "Why, yes, yes it is."

"There is a message for you. It says that she is fine. She is joining friends and they are anxiously awaiting your arrival."

"That's it?"

"Yes, sir."

"What friends?"

"Please sir, I've already extended the rules."

"All right, but I'm still concerned about her being punished?"

"Sir, I'm not permitted to divulge that information."

"If you could just tell me? It would mean so much?"

"Well, if it will ease your pain, and end this conversation, I suppose I can offer some information. It certainly won't affect the continuum. Repair is here to make adjustments. On my work order I'll just call this an inter-worldly adjustment. That should satisfy my superiors."

"Thank you, thank you so much."

"Wait while I check the notes."

More silence, and then, "She is to receive no reprimand for the use of this line."

"Because it was my fault?"

"No, because we were not aware that this line existed, she had never been informed that she couldn't use it. That was an error of omission at the highest levels and therefore she wasn't blamed for its use."

"That's great. Can you tell me if she's in a better place?"

"Sir this must stop, I have other work to do."

"I know. If you'll help me with this one last thing I will be eternally grateful."

"Sir, with all due respect, your eternal gratitude doesn't do a thing for me. Having said that however, if it will terminate this conversation I will relate what I have here in the notes."

"Oh, yes, absolutely."

"She was given credit for truly loving two people. It doesn't say which two. She was also given credit for admitting she had manipulated someone in your world; and that her manipulation was driven by revenge. Her genuine guilt seems to have been the final component in allowing her to move on. She is now in a better place."

"Is she with her daughter Marci?"

"Sir, this conversation is over."

"But, I-"

The line went blank - blank, as in, a chilling silence . . . blank - blank, as in, completely devoid of sound . . . blank – and, blank, as in, time took a deep breath . . . blank!

~~~~~~

Bill sat, unmoving for nearly an hour, appraising the events and the many months that had brought him to this place on the continuum. After all that had happened, it was disturbing at best, to have it end so suddenly . . . so completely, and with such finality. He was constricted by the enormous loss on one hand and the enormous personal gain on the other. For the first time in his life he understood the real meaning of ambivalence. As he savored his last sip of Scotch this accumulated ambivalence encircled his psyche and he began to cry. With tears rolling slowly down his cheeks, he lifted the Messenger XD 500 from the floor and studied the speed dial pad. He rose, moved to an old bookcase stored against one attic wall, and placed it reverently on its own shelf. That would do for the time being. He owed this instrument a debt that was incalculable in human terms. The best he could do would be to return later, dust and wrap its exterior, and each and every day of his remaining life, thank the forces that had brought him and this cosmic link together.

He walked the two flights of stairs down to the main level of the house. He poured himself a triple Scotch on the rocks and moved to the living room. He had one final page to turn before closing the book on his old life and opening the book on his new life. He moved to the center of the room and lifted his glass toward the ceiling. As he raised his glass, those pesky tears again rolled down his cheeks, and he said softly, "Here's to you, Edith and Marci. What's a life worth? You gave me so much and I returned so little. I will always love you."

With that he broke down and sobbed. For five minutes he mourned them, and the old Bill Allen. When he was done, he wiped the residue from his eyes with his sleeve and smiled.

It was time to celebrate the new Bill Allen.

He raised his glass again and spoke, "Till we meet again."

The house phone chimed. He walked to it and lifted the receiver. He was met with a dial tone. He replaced it and started to move away. It rang again. He waited a moment to be certain that it wasn't a ring back.
~~~~~~

He lifted the receiver and was again met with a dial tone. This time however, the dial tone went to "dead" silence. He smiled broadly and looked toward the ceiling as he spoke, "Thank you, ladies."

Without the adrenaline that had sustained him for months he crashed. He flopped into his favorite easy chair and nodded off.

A familiar head rose above the sofa back and said, "Well Bill, I guess I got you through this mess. You could at least say, 'Thank you', but I rarely receive the recognition I deserve. Why should I expect any more from you?"

After a pause Mr. Murphy continued to wallow in self-pity, "I'll tell you why I expect more from you. We've been through a lot and I think I deserve more than disregard."

Bill opened one eye and said, "Murphy, when are you to going to stop feeling sorry for yourself?"

Murphy swallowed hard and said, "You can hear me?"

"You're damn right I can hear you – and frankly, I'm getting a little tired of you're incessant chatter. I'm also getting tired of you taking credit for everything that I do."

"How long have you been able to hear me?"

"Since your very first wisecrack."

"You're not supposed to be able to hear me."

Bill chuckled, "If I can deal with the dead, hearing you is a cakewalk."

"Why didn't you talk to me before?"

"How could I get in a word with your incessant prattle?"

That tore it. Murphy didn't have to stand for this, "You hold on. All I was trying to do was help – and this is the gratitude I get?"

"You're idea of help is sometimes counterproductive, but you're right, you've been there all along and I appreciate the support."

"Murphy softened and said, "Thank you, Bill. I try."

Bill looked impatiently at the mist that housed Murphy and said, "I don't want to interrupt this love fest, but are we done?"

Murphy thought for a moment, then spoke, "I guess we are."

Bill said with finality, "I want to get this straight, once and for all . . . are we done?"

As Mr. Murphy slowly sank from sight he concluded sadly, "Yes Bill, we're done . . . ."

WE'RE ALL DONE!

Murphy's head had hardly disappeared when it bounced back up - and, with that impish grin, that was his alone, and a wink, he finished, **"At least, until the next time you need me."**

www.ingramcontent.com/pod-product-compliance
Lightning Source LLC
Chambersburg PA
CBHW020612310726
48979CB00008B/1451/J
* 9 7 8 0 5 9 5 4 9 6 0 8 2 *